Prowl

Gordan Runyan

DEO VOLENTE
PUBLISHING

Gordan Runyan, *Prowl*
© 2000 by Gordan Runyan
Published by Deo Volente Publishing
P.O. Box 4847
Los Alamos, NM 87544

Printed in the United States of America

ISBN: 0-9658804-5-1

For Joyce,

Worthy Wife

Part One

"The wicked walk on every side..."
- the 12th Psalm

Prolog

Liegert's life drains away like dirty bath water.

The killer enjoys the comparison. You're dirty, you take a bath. When the water drains it carries off all the filth. You're left naked and clean, ready to move on to something new.

So the watcher waits, eager to be rid of Liegert's defilement. He wants this finished, so that he may leave feeling cleansed. He is motionless except for slow breaths through his nostrils. With the ventilation system shut down, for inport ops, the smell of hydraulic oil is stronger than normal. But he likes it that way.

This is his space, after all, and he is in control here. Shaft Alley is the aftermost place on the whole submarine, the pointed portion of the boat's tear-drop profile. Here, the bulkheads taper in and converge around the sub's yard-thick main shaft. The shaft itself, now still, divides Port from Starboard.

The space is crammed full of industrial equipment and storage lockers. There is not much room to maneuver, it smells bad, and there is nowhere to sit.

No one comes here unless they have to, especially at this time of night. *Time.* The waiting man glances at his watch. The Shutdown Electrical Operator isn't due for several minutes. Liegert hangs by his neck. The rope is thin and tar-coated, tied to a metal support bracket for one of the fluorescent lights. The watching man almost frowns. Liegert "hangs." Such a passive-sounding word to describe such an animated flurry of motion. Legs thrash, kick, and jerk as if searching for support. There is none, and the killer is tempted to smile.

The light jerks with Liegert's frenzy, so the shadows in Shaft Alley join the struggle in one, unified dance. A flailing heel knocks an orange handle out of place. The watcher's hand reaches out and returns the hydraulic system valve to its proper position.

The hanging man strains against the duct tape wrapped around his wrists. No escape. *Stop fighting, Liegert. You cannot change what has been ordained from eternity past.* The watcher allows his lips to curl into the slightest smile. *It will be worse for the others.*

Twisting and rotating at the end of the rope, Liegert's body turns until they are face to face. The watcher tries to read his expression. It is difficult, due to the involuntary contortions, of course, but panic is there. Unmistakable, and delicious.

Something changes, something small but perceptible. The killer's smile melts to nothing. His stomach sinks, and, later, the memory will make him mad all over again. Liegert is looking down at him.

The panic of a moment ago is gone. It isn't panic now, but pity.

The watcher wills himself calm. "Just die," he says. The words are half-whispered, half-hissed.

The rope cuts into Liegert's neck without warning or fanfare, and his civilian shirt turns blackish red down to the middle of his chest. The thrashing stops, yielding to the inevitable.

He checks the time again. 0257. He knows that EM3 Reynolds is the SEO, and that Reynolds is punctual to a fault. *Still, if the young man is early on his rounds at all, he thinks, he might interrupt things, and we would all hate that.* He decides to get out of there, A.S.A.P.

He cuts the tape from Liegert's wrists and leaves the suicide note on the hydraulic sump five feet away. As he starts up a ladder into Engineroom Upper Level, he looks back. The corpse is still, surrounded by the consistent hum of one vent fan in slow speed, and the intermittent operation of the hydraulic pumps. *All continues as it should,* he muses.

He whispers to a lifeless Shaft Alley, "I offered you mercy, Liegert. Now behold the awful price of blasphemy. The others will join you soon."

Chapter One

The USS Omaha (SSN-692) sat motionless, tied up at the US Navy base at Guam next to a submarine tender. Omaha was shutdown, most of her multi-million dollar equipment turned off and cooled down. Only a third of her crew was onboard and only six of them were awake.

At 0259, Electrician's Mate Third Class (EM3) Dan Reynolds made his way, clipboard in hand, to the aft end of Engineroom Lower Level. He checked the #2 Auxiliary Seawater Pump by touching the motor switchbox with the back of his hand. Normal temperature, no ozone smell of electrical components overheating, no unusual vibrations, no electric tingle or shock. He yawned.

His duty section had run a fire drill just as he was laying down in an attempt to snag two hours of sleep prior to watch. "Sleep?"

He said the word out loud, to no one, in his best approximation of a voice of authority, or Eastern Bloc dictator, maybe. "First tings first! Ve vill drill before ve sleep! Ve must prepare for all contingencies!" He smirked and then answered himself in his own, exhausted voice. "I signed up for the Navy, not the Boy Scouts."

Reynolds grabbed a rung on the starboard ladder to Shaft Alley, yawning some more as he ascended.

There was, of course, the irritating high pitch of a single

air conditioning unit running in Slow. That was normal. Then there was the stench of human waste. At least, that's what he thought it was. One could never tell in Shaft Alley. Shutdown, the trickle of seawater pooling under the main shaft got pretty rank, especially if it was hot. And Guam was always hot.

Then he saw the dead man. Still gently swaying, face bulging and purple. Several seconds passed while Reynolds tried to determine whether he'd fallen victim to an extravagant practical joke. The worst thing about getting caught by some prank was the fact that the tale would become legend, told for years even after he transferred off the boat. Reynolds's name would become an unfortunate fixture in Omaha mythology, the Eternal Idiot.

So he looked more closely. It really was Liegert, he decided. But how was he making his eyes bug out like that? And all that blood... He dropped his clipboard and bolted back down to the Main Seawater bay.

Shaking, his hands fumbled with the fire-engine red Collision Alarm switch; finally he got the switch to turn. The steady siren vibrated even the deckplates.

Reynolds snatched up the nearby sound-powered (2JV) phone. He tried to keep his voice even, knew he'd be unsuccessful, tried to remember to speak slowly, knew the Shutdown Reactor Operator would have the monitor on, so he wouldn't have to wait for his call to be acknowledged.

"Maneuvering, Shutdown Electrical Operator. Medical emergency in Shaft Alley!" he said.

Reynolds heard the phone being juggled on the other end.

"Say again, SEO?" came the voice of ET2 Matt Cousins.

"Medical emergency in Shaft Alley! Just call it away!"

Reynolds slammed the 2JV back into its holder and raced up the ladder again. He vaulted into Shaft Alley and heard Cousins on the shipwide 1MC announcing system, alerting the sub to the casualty.

In seconds, he heard the pounding of steel-toed shoes hurtling down the ladder from Engineroom Upper Level. It was the Shutdown Roving Watch, Machinist's Mate Second Class Jason Lorde. He saw the dead man right away and blasted out a short obscenity. They converged on the hanging body. Lorde, a burly mechanic, an ape really, poster-child for Evolution theory, threw his arms around the body's waist and lifted.

Reynolds felt frozen until Lorde jolted him. "Get my knife! From my belt!"

They managed to cut the man down. By the time they laid Leigert's body on the metal deck, Lorde's blue dungaree shirt was wet with blood, along with his forearms and the left side of his face. Senior Chief Markiss arrived in the cramped space a minute later, his khaki shirt untucked, his black boots with laces untied, hair mussed from how he'd been sleeping on it. He cursed, too, using the same expletive as Lorde.

One by one, members of Omaha's crew crowded into the space. The mechanical hum of Shaft Alley's automatic equipment was overcome by their clamor.

For several minutes, grown men, all trained to handle a nuclear submarine, possibly the deadliest instrument of war ever imagined, yelled at each other out of near-hysterical helplessness. Some of them were close to tears.

Reynolds felt his legs shaking. The chaos around him built, feeding off the collective panic. He noticed that one of them was not screaming, not crying. One of them looked at ease. Serene, even. *That's strange*, Reynolds thought.

A minor detail--soon forgotten.

****

A diesel engine rumbled in the distance. It roused one of two men on the fishing boat. He could tell it was a large diesel, even from far off. He shook his snoring buddy's shoulder.

They were anchored thirteen miles off the coast of South Korea, avoiding territorial waters by precisely one mile. They scrambled about in the moonlight. The intensity of the engine noise increased. One of them fumbled with a pair of "binoculars," an American-made nightvision scope.

Almost as soon as he raised it to his eyes, he lowered it again. He blinked a few times and looked like he wanted to ask a question. He peered through it again. He brought it down, then yelled to his partner in unaccented English. "It's her! She's out early! Send the message!"

The steady rumble was like an approaching train. It caused him to add, "Quickly!"

The other Korean scurried into the hold of the boat and threw a smelly fish net across the space, revealing a sonar screen and several keyboards. He began to type in commands and codes. The other raised the scope once more, and said, "What's she doing so close to the twelve mile boundary?"

The typing man said, "Radio coms initiated."

He was answered by a repetitive beep coming from the computer behind him. He sat back from the screen he'd been viewing and his fingers froze over the keyboard. He swiveled in his chair, but without enthusiasm.

The monitor was filled with glowing green lines on a black background. There, heading toward the center of the screen from one side, was a blinking dot. It moved fast, and each blink brought a beep from the computer.

His mouth dropped open. *A torpedo? We're being fired on? This couldn't be happening.* He thought about alerting his partner to the development, then realized nothing could be done. He had only enough time to grin in lunatic amusement at the idea that his last conscious thought was going to be something like, "Why bother?"

His musing ended in a brilliant fireball. It began below the waterline of the fishing boat and quickly erupted into the night sky, scattering very tiny pieces of the small craft and her occupants over an area a quarter mile wide. The fireball came from a warhead designed to sink military cruisers and destroyers. Like swatting a fly with a baseball bat.

As abruptly as it had appeared, it disappeared. The brilliant light burned out and the thunderclap fell silent. Debris rained down for several seconds, unevenly, making smaller or larger individual splashes. A few chunks of wood and cloth continued to burn in the stillness, floating on the once again gentle current. They went out minutes later. And so there was only blackness and the heavy smell of gasoline.

The vessel that had fired the torpedo secured its diesel, lowered its snorkel mast, and descended into an apathetic sea. Onboard, her Captain straightened himself and walked away from the periscope. Standing in the dim glow of the Control room instruments, he was oblivious to the cheers of the crewmen around him.

The Captain's gaze extended far past the narrow confines of the boat. His vision encompassed both past and future, and saw them intimately connected by a demand for revenge.

****

An ocean away, some interrupted radio traffic was received by a listening station at Pearl Harbor, Hawaii. A printer then spat out a piece of paper. After a paragraph full of codes and verification data, it read, "Quiet Tiger is loose".

* * * *

The Omaha was tied alongside the submarine tender, USS DIXON (AS-37). Side-by-side, it wasn't difficult to tell where the Navy's priorities had been for the last several decades. Omaha, a Los Angeles (688) Class fast-attack sub, sported a new paint job on the upper fraction of the boat that was visible above the surface. The flat, midnight black served to enhance the sub's naturally menacing appearance.

The American version of a lioness in the cat-and-mouse world of Cold War sea power, the 688's were more silent than most of the "mice" and at least as fast. They were the hunters, designed with a singular purpose--to find Soviet ballistic missile subs. And kill them.

Omaha, like all her sisters, had a huge nuclear engineroom. She could push the most advanced sonar technology, plus a devastating assortment of weapons, through the water at speeds and depths that rightly made her a terror in the minds of Communist Bloc military analysts around the world. The Cold War had been the glory days of the 688 Class.

The Soviets were reduced to playing an obsessed game of "catch up" once Los Angeles came on the scene, a game they never finished (despite the best efforts of an American traitor named Walker). The Americans built the 688's in a somewhat modular fashion, an innovation that kept them top-of-the-line. Until the L.A.'s, if you wanted to build a sub with the latest sonar system, for example, you nearly had to create a brand new class of sub to fit it. The 688's were different. If you came up with new sonar, you could simply hoist out the old system and plug the new one in. The USSR pursued a standard that kept changing and improving.

Granted, the Evil Empire, as Reagan called the Soviet Union, got a few lucky breaks along the way. Most notably, there was the aforementioned Johnny Walker spy case. It wasn't long after Walker that the Soviet Akula class appeared, which shocked the whole Naval intelligence community by taking a giant leap, several really, in closing the gap with the L.A.'s.

It was too little, too late. Sorry, Gorbachev.

By that time, Congress had cleared the way for the SSN-21. Like Reagan's Star Wars project, the 21's real value had been in the hypothetically outrageous advantage it would give the Americans. The SSN-21, or, according to the hype, the nuclear attack sub which would see the United States through to naval dominance in the whole of the 21st Century, didn't appear in time to affect the Cold War with her actual presence. The 688's finished the Cold War as the recognized, reigning fast-attack champs.

Then there was Dixon. The Submarine Tender looked old and tired, with several spots on her hull crying out for a new coat of battleship gray to cover the rust.

As a warship, Dixon made a good pier for Omaha to

tie up on. Rather rounded and bulky, by design she was supposed to sit practically welded to a dock somewhere, providing a consolidation point for the myriad services the submarine fleet demanded. So she did, until a member of Congress noted that her lack of at-sea time was probably hurting the careers of her 35% female crew. Off to sea went Dixon.

Her last two Commanding Officers had started a practice of taping a bumper-sticker to the six-by-four foot photograph of Dixon which hung in the wardroom. The first one had said, "Don't laugh: it's paid for". The current one said, "My other car is a Porsche".

A gangplank extended from the pier, up thirty feet and over to an opening in the third deck of the Dixon. Two dungaree-clad women stood watch behind that opening's double doors.

Eight hours after the death on Omaha, Machinist's Mate First Class (MM1) Mark Reed walked up to them from within Dixon and saluted. The older of the women, also a First Class Petty Officer, returned his salute. He noted her grin and saw that she looked up and down his six-foot frame, obviously approving. While he was flattered, he was also irritated. Lack of professionalism...he shook his head. *Is this a fighting unit, or The Dating Game?*

"Request permission to go ashore," he said, performing the ritual flawlessly.

"Permission granted," she replied, still grinning. "And, sorry to hear you're leaving. The scenery won't be as nice without you."

Mark shook his head again, and walked out on the gangplank. The women giggled behind him. He stopped after several steps and saluted the flag flying from Dixon's main mast.

He continued down the plank and was met by a Second Class Petty Officer heading the other way. This one's dungaree shirt was badly faded and the "crow" insignia on his sleeve was all but invisible. He stopped and smiled at Reed.

Mark closed his eyes for a moment and tried to breathe deeply.

"Is it true?" the young man asked.

Mark answered, "Fraid so."

The other man laughed and slapped Reed's shoulder. "Afraid so, my foot, man! Omaha needed to find 'A.J. Squared-Away,' and they darn sure did!"

The second class laughed. Mark joined him in spite of himself.

"Hey, Jamison," Mark said finally, "No hard feelings…? I mean I know I rode you pretty good for the past year or so, and…"

Jamison shook his head. "Look at me, man. I'm still the same. I have survived the reign of terror of Mark Reed!"

They both laughed.

Jamison grabbed Mark's starched dungaree shirt between his fingers. "You just take this stuff a lot more seriously than I do. That's okay. Besides, I figure I gave you enough trouble in return to make up for it…"

Mark nodded, not smiling any more.

They were silent for a moment, and then Jamison changed the subject. "Y'know, I thought I heard that when there's a suicide or something like that on a sub, they weld it to the pier for a few weeks, and then, like, all the chaplains and psychologists come in and rake everybody over the coals…"

Mark nodded.

"So how come Omaha's shoving off right away and taking you with them?"

Mark shrugged and said, "Well, I hear her skipper is some real hot-runner. Looking for his birds."

Mark fingered his shirt collar, indicating the silver eagle pins worn by Navy captains. Jamison nodded.

Mark said, "So the CO, Parnette's his name, I guess he gets on the phone to Squadron and says, 'Hey, the best thing for my boat right now is to get right back at it,' and they agreed. They said Omaha could go on their spec-op early. They needed a guy to replace their Leading ELT, and so here

I am. I'd already been approved to transfer to the Indy once we got back to Pearl. And, since Indy and Omaha are in the same Squadron…"

Jamison nodded knowingly. "In other words, this Parnette guy's got pictures of Squadron 7 naked with a Waipahu hooker…"

Mark snickered. "You're not going to change no matter who's in charge, Jamison."

With that, they parted and MM1 Reed left the ship to perform a most unpleasant duty.

****

Mark sat in a burgundy phone booth, rubbing a pewter keychain trinket between his thumb and forefinger. The booth was located in a place called "Andy's Hut," a Navy operated establishment that sat about a mile off the submarine base pier. Andy's was a combination bar and dance floor/short-order-grill/laundromat/bus stop and long-distance phone center. "Andre's Chateau by the Sea," some called it.

The phone began to ring on the other end. Mark slipped his phone card into his pants pocket. A female answered, with an Asian accent thick enough to make her almost unintelligible.

"Plaza Hotel, Honolulu. May I help you?"

For an instant, Mark entertained the thought of leaving a message for his wife, J.L., at the front desk. *Yes, um, could you inform my wife that her husband called to say he'd be a little late…say, three months or so? Thanks.* Or maybe if he simply hung up, and went off on a two-and-a-half month cruise without telling J.L., she'd manage to hear the voice of God telling her it was okay to go ahead and get the divorce, putting them both out of their misery.

Instead, he said, "Yes, could you connect me to Room 412, please?"

"Yes, sir. One moment, please."

The day the Dixon left San Diego, J.L. had driven down

to the pier at the Sub Base at Point Loma to see them off and say goodbye to him. Mark had gone up to the fantail, not too close to the edge.

He had seen her there at the back of the crowd on the pier. Male and female sailors in dress uniforms milled around, tearily hugging little children and spouses. J.L. was more stunning than the day they met, there was no doubt in his mind, and yet it failed to stir him at all.

She had dressed in an attractive blue and white striped blouse and white straight-legged slacks. Her shoulder-length curly hair blazed, like a miniature sun on top of her head. She was wearing dark sunglasses and he could see she was holding a single red rose.

Mark had waited to go down and see her until he figured he had only a matter of minutes before the crew would be called on board.

"Sorry," he had said, mentioning something about being saddled with some last minute paperwork.

J.L. took off her sunglasses and smiled at him. She blinked her eyes a lot. They were red and puffy. Must've stopped crying only moments ago. When he got close he could smell the perfume on her, not overpowering but obvious. It was one he liked, but she had confessed months ago that it irritated her. He knew she was wearing it for him. She held out the rose to him and he took it.

"Mark, I'm really sorry," she said, and he saw her eyes watering.

Not now, he'd thought. "Okay. It's all right."

He had probably not been very convincing. He looked at his watch.

She dropped her gaze for a moment, then said, "Maybe, I was thinking. Maybe we could talk to somebody when you get back..."

"About what?"

"About us. How come we have so much trouble."

He knew why they had trouble. J.L. was trouble.

He rolled his eyes and exhaled strongly. "J.L., I'm not

going to go talk to somebody I don't know about how my rotten childhood has made me incapable of having a normal relationship, so they can point out all my unresolved issues. My need to purge..."

J.L. was looking down at the flower and slowly shaking her head. "Maybe I'm the problem, Mark. Maybe I need to talk about it."

That was a brilliant deduction. "Can't you do that while I'm gone?"

He had been saved by the blare of a loudspeaker summoning all Dixon personnel to board the ship. Mark and J.L. were the only people on the pier to say goodbye without a kiss or a hug or a touch. Barely even eye contact.

Now, the phone was ringing again. A sense of dread settled over him.

"Hello," came J.L.'s groggy voice. Mark remembered that the time difference put his wife in the middle of the night.

"Hi, it's me," he said, "Sorry I had to call at such a bad time."

J.L. still sounded drowsy. "It's okay."

"Um, I called because I've got some good news and some bad news."

J.L. took a while to answer. She sounded more awake when she said, "Good news first."

"My transfer to a sub has been moved way up!"

"What do you mean? I thought you were going to the Indianapolis once you got back?"

"Well, I can't really say very much over the phone, but circumstances on a sub over here have put them in need of a guy with my qualifications. They've offered me a chance to transfer there now and take over a division. Plus, I'm thinking that if I do this, it will probably mean another Navy Achievement Medal and a Sea Service Ribbon..."

Mark paused. J.L. was silent. He knew she was going to freak out when they got to the bad news. She always did. She would freak out even more if she had known that this was really the latest in a long series of events that Mark had deliberately chosen.

That was the key. She tended to blame bad scheduling and big inconveniences on the Navy in general. If she had only known that, more often than not, when faced with a choice between doing something good for his marriage, and doing something good for his career, Mark had come to a simple conclusion: J.L. was completely unable to help him make Chief; and so could be decided against with some justification. If she knew that, he thought, then she would really lose it.

Mark continued. "I'm not gonna make Chief without those things..."

"Well," said J.L., "I guess that's good, then. What sub is it?"

Mark sighed. "It's named after the city where your oldest brother lives..."

"O--Oh, really."

J.L. asked if Mark's transfer would mean that they would have to move again. Mark tried to make the news that Omaha was based in Pearl Harbor, eliminating the need for another move, sound like better news than it was. They talked about how her search for housing was working out. She was getting tired of living in a hotel room, even the Plaza, even at the Navy's expense.

Then she asked about the bad news. Mark took a deep breath. The stuff would hit the fan now. He could already hear the whining and crying, and he steeled himself against it.

"It's going to delay me coming home for a while--"

"How long?"

"Well, I think about seventy-five days or so--"

"Seventy-five days! Mark! I..."

She stopped. *Just gathering steam.* When she started again, the pitch in her voice had gone down.

"All right, I guess," she said, "The Lord's really opened up a unique door for you, huh?"

Mark cringed and squeezed his eyes shut. It was too much to ask that J.L. would've dropped all her new religious jargon over the last month and a half. Still, this was an unexpected response, considering he'd planned on having to hold the phone at arm's length by now.

"Yeah, well, maybe so, J.L. He's got a pretty gruesome way of doing business if it's His work, " he said, recalling what he'd heard of the incident on Omaha.

"It is His work, Mark," J.L. said without hesitation. "All things work together for good--"

"O.K., O.K. Whatever you say," Mark said, squirming on the booth's wooden stool. "So...what's it like in Hawaii?"

J.L. was adjusting to life on Oahu, she said. They made enough small talk for Mark to think he could get away with ending the phone call.

He was about to, in fact, when J.L. changed her subject. "Well...I wondered if I should tell you or not, but...I think, I'm pretty sure I'm pregnant..."

He'd have traded a swift kick in the guts for that news. He didn't know what to say, couldn't make himself say anything. Then, feeling stupid as soon as he said it, he stammered, "How do you know?"

"I haven't seen a doctor, yet...but I'm pretty sure...I think it's from right before your ship left...."

Mark was unable to speak. They'd had a huge fight, then made up. It had seemed, yet again, like they might really patch things up. That optimism had lasted about a day.

"Listen, Mark," J.L. said. Her voice was firm, more certain somehow. "I know this comes at a horrible time considering...how things are with...us, and all that. But I really just know it will all work out--"

"All things work together for God, right?" he said, making the sarcasm as obvious as possible.

"For good. All things work for good."

"What's the difference?"

"Well, I guess, God is good, but goodness isn't God, maybe. And, God doesn't just want things to work out for

Him--He wants good for you, too."

"All right, all right!" he said, "That's enough. J.L., I'm gonna have to get going. You gonna be all right with all of this?"

"Guess I have to be, huh?"

"Yeah, sorry."

"Yeah, me too. Mark, I love you."

"I know. Me too. Gotta go. Bye"

Mark hung up, and took a "cleansing breath." He relaxed the death-grip he had developed on the key-chain. The joints in his fingers ached. He looked at the little horse in the palm of his hand.

It had been a gift from his grandmother many years ago. When new, it had been a stylized carousel horse, complete with ornately carved bridle and saddle and wide eyes, to go with the wide-open mouth. The carousel rod, extending from above its back and through it, to below its hooves, had had a spiral design carved into it then. Now it was worn smooth, a vaguely horse-like figure with a stick through its torso.

Looking at it did him good. It always had. It was a sissy-thing, sure. What salt-air-hardened sailor consoles himself with a carousel horse? But, regardless, it took him away, to a place he had never been. He knew instinctively that it was a better place. A place with no J.L.'s. And especially no pregnant, born-again fanatical J.L.'s.

He allowed that brief moment of escape, then straightened himself and tried to clear his head. He couldn't afford distractions. Omaha could be the key to realizing his goals. It was an opportunity for him to shine, and he wasn't going to blow it.

He strode through a deserted room furnished with video games and a pool table. A television mounted high in the corner of the room talked to no one. A middle aged female news anchor read the following report as Mark left Andy's:

"President Clinton expressed alarm in his weekly radio

address over the continued anti-Japanese rhetoric coming from North Korea's new hard-line government. Again, the North Korean remarks centered on the upcoming anniversary of Japanese occupation of Korea early in this century, in which Korean women were forced to provide sex for Japanese soldiers. Clinton said he was very disappointed with the latest statement and hoped North Korea would see that it is in their best interest to continue to work, and act, like a member of the world community. Republican leaders in congress were quick to recommend stronger action be taken against what they called a 'rogue Communist government whose foolishness threatens an entire region'..."

Mark walked purposefully back to the pier. The farther he got from the phone, the more free he felt. He knew he had less than two hours to get moved onto Omaha, and then she'd be heading out.

Chapter Two

The 1MC shipwide announcing system blared, "Station the Maneuvering Watch!"

About a dozen muscular types in dungarees and bright orange life-vests had assembled topside on Omaha by that time. Mark lugged his hundred pound pea-green "sea bag", full of his personal items, on his back across the thirty-foot horizontal gangplank from the pier. He was met by a petty officer in dress whites, whom he saluted.

"You the new Lead ELT?" the man asked, returning the salute lethargically.

"Yeah. MM1 Reed."

"Welcome aboard. You're late. Skipper was about to leave you here."

The petty officer yelled over to a man in a life-vest, who also wore a headset sound-powered phone, "Phone-talker! To Control: Liegert's replacement is on board!"

The phone-talker nodded and spoke into the mouthpiece. *Great*, Mark thought, *My first action on Omaha is to nearly miss ship's movement.*

"I was told I had two more hours," Mark said, more to himself than anyone else. The watchstander wasn't listening to him, too busy dismantling his small desk in order to take it below. Mark took the occasion of the pause to set down his sea-bag. It thudded on Omaha's black hull.

The phone-talker in the life vest shouted to Mark.

"Hey, MM1, Maneuvering's gonna send someone up to escort you down."

Mark nodded back.

On the pier, he watched a couple of sailors pumping some hand-wenches at the head of the gangplank. With each clickety-clickety of the wenches, the end of the plank on Omaha raised up only slightly. Mark took a deep breath and shook his head. *Literally seconds away from missing this stinking sub... seconds away from never, ever making Chief...*

He heard the sub's 1MC blare, "Prepare for main engine test."

There was one open hatch, located about twenty feet aft of the sub's sail. After a minute or so, a skinny, dark-haired kid scrambled up without a life-vest. He walked quickly to Mark, his right hand was extended. The stencil above his shirt pocket said, "Reynolds".

"Hi," he said, shaking Mark's hand. "I'm Dan. We better get you below before the XO has both our hides."

Reynolds reached for the sea-bag, but Mark waved him off. "I got it."

It wasn't that he was sensitive about his stuff, or too proud to accept help. He was a little worried that the bag might have outweighed his guy. Mark slung the bag back over his shoulder and followed Reynolds to the hatch.

The smell wafting up from below was not new to him. He'd had occasion, in his duties with Dixon's Radiological Controls division, to go below on many subs. But the odor caught him off guard each time nevertheless. It was a not-so-delicate stench that mixed boiled-down, day-old coffee with melting plastic. Oh, and the slightest hint of dead fish. He hoped it would not be long before acclimation made it unnoticeable.

Reynolds started down. Mark thought the space around the shiny, steel ladder looked impossibly small. "Hey, Reynolds," he said, "what in the world is that disgusting smell?"

The sailor stopped in mid-climb and sniffed the air, as

if he had not noticed anything. He said, "Oh, that! Yeah, that's pretty bad, huh? That's the amines in AMR . They use them in atmosphere control."

Mark shook his head and started climbing. It was not an easy process. The hatch had been built for one adult at a time, and not one adult plus a bag that was as big as a high school freshman. It was slow going, and he felt frustration rising in him.

He was only a few steps down when the 1MC startled him. "The following is a test of ship's alarms from Control: General."

Immediately, a very loud, minute-long series of short "bongs" of the General Alarm sounded.

The 1MC: "Weapons Emergency."

This was even louder, and nearly painful because of the few seconds of high-pitched wailing.

"Propulsion Plant Casualty." An annoying pulse of alternating pitch.

"Test Complete. The following is a test of ship's collision alarms. Disregard all alarms."

As Mark grunted his way to the bottom of the twenty-foot ladder, the 1MC called out a series of spaces onboard, which then answered by sounding their collision alarm sirens for a second or two. Most names were of spaces Mark had yet to see: the Torpedo Room, Control, Diesel and such. He had visited most of the engineering spaces in his radiological work already: Engineroom Forward, Engineroom Lower Level, and Maneuvering.

1MC: "Test of collision alarms complete. Regard all further alarms."

Reynolds was waiting for him at the bottom. "Just shove your sea-bag up against the bulkhead, there, until the Maneuvering Watch is secured. Then, somebody from the Ship's Office'll deal with you."

Mark did as he was told.

Reynolds motioned toward the forward end of the boat. Mark turned and looked. In less than five feet, the narrow passage he and Reynolds occupied opened into Crew's Mess, a space about twelve feet across containing five tables. Close to two dozen blue-shirted sailors were crammed in there.

The 1MC again: "The Officer of the Deck has shifted his watch to the Bridge."

A very large man, a Senior Chief Petty Officer in khakis, stood at the forward end of Crew's Mess. He had two adult human heads worth of skin and fat crammed into one face. The expanse of his grin made it worse. He seemed unnecessarily excited, almost giddy. He rubbed his chubby hands in front of him as he talked, and the sailors around him laughed.

"This is where I leave you," said Reynolds.

"Okay. Thanks."

Reynolds nodded. "Welcome aboard."

Mark nodded back. Reynolds headed aft, away from Crew's Mess, and disappeared through a hatch. Mark walked to the back edge of the crowd to hear what was being said.

"Submarines are made for sailors," the Senior Chief declared, grinning gleefully, "and sailors were meant for sea!"

Several of the men just shook their heads. Mark found himself wondering how long it had been since some of these guys had slept. Several pair of their eyes were puffy and red. None of them seemed quite as eager for the trip as the Senior Chief. One man closed an eye and snarled out of the corner of his mouth, "Har de har, there, Popeye!" Several others laughed.

As the men continued to talk, a pair of khaki-clad legs descended a short ladder into the forward end of Crew's Mess from what Mark would later learn was the Navigation and Radio space. The Senior Chief looked up, saw who it was, and announced, "Attention on Deck!"

All of the crewmen in the mess stood up and the Mess fell silent. The Commanding Officer of the USS Omaha walked into the space, smiling--not unlike the Senior Chief. "As you were," he said, and the crew sat down.

The CO was a man of medium build. Early fifties, Mark guessed. Except for his notable, square jaw and marble-blue eyes, none of his features were remarkable. He carried with him an air of confidence and command.

Commander Parnette immediately fixed his gaze on Mark Reed. Mark knew he was undergoing his first inspection as a submariner.

The CO smiled at him and said, "You must be my new ELT." His voice was what Mark had expected, a strong baritone.

"Yes, sir. MM1 Reed."

The CO nodded. He turned to the Senior Chief and said, "Cob, can you get my new Leading ELT a rack to sleep in?"

"A rack?" the Senior Chief asked, "I figured he wouldn't be sleeping till way after Spec-Op, what with all the qualifications he's gotta do and all..."

"Look, Senior!" broke in one of the enlisted men, "He's a skimmer puke!"

The man was pointing at Mark's chest. Mark was suddenly self-conscious about the Surface Warfare Insignia he wore. The grinning Senior Chief said to Mark, "Yeah, we'll take care of that soon enough. We'll get you some silver dolphins to put there instead. Then you'll be a real man."

Most of the crew laughed at that. Mark forced himself to smile.

The CO said, "Petty Officer Reed, were you aware that there are only two kinds of ships at sea?"

Mark shook his head. He could sense the crew anticipating how the CO would answer his own question.

"There are submarines," said the commander, "And there are targets."

Crew's Mess erupted in laughter.

The CO cleared his throat and stopped smiling. Mark guessed it was time for business. He was thankful that the crew's opportunity to give him grief seemed to be over.

He also wondered at the bantering of Parnette with

his men. This was unlike anything he'd seen at other commands. The CO is supposed to be aloof, above it all. Or so he'd thought. But then he looked around Crew's Mess and how tightly packed it was with sailors. It was possible that the cramped quarters made a sharp distinction between officer and enlisted difficult to achieve.

"Men, from this moment until the end of our Spec-Op, you have all been temporarily granted upgraded security clearance. This mission is classified Umbrae Delta. That classification code itself is Top Secret. If you ever tell anyone, the Navy will hunt you down and kill your family." A few men chuckled. The CO went on.

"As soon as we secure the Maneuvering Watch, we'll submerge and do a hydrostatic test of the Diesel at depth. Once that QA package is closed out, we'll be hitting it pretty hard for a while, a lot of ahead flank, maybe get this boat up to forty knots or so...whaddaya think, Cob?"

The Senior Chief smiled quickly and hitched up his belt. "Y'know, Cap'n, the engineers have been complaining for some time and sayin' Omaha'll do forty-three easy..."

One of the men at the table smirked and shook his head.

The CO smiled and said, "We're heading for a deep spot about fourteen miles off the coast of South Korea. Of course, if you know your geography, that means it's also just a few more miles to North Korea,

"Basically, here's the situation. You'll all remember a few years ago there was a big deal made about North Korea trying to build nuclear weapons. Well, our macho leaders said, 'Hey, you better cut that out!' North Korea said, 'We don't want to,' and then we said, 'Well...all right, then.'"

A few of the men laughed.

The CO continued, "Now, the thing is, it's almost easier to build a nuclear weapon than it is to design a system that will reliably get that warhead away from you and over to the guy you're shooting at.

"Our latest intelligence is that North Korea may now

have both," said the CO. He scanned the room, looking directly into the eyes of his men.

"In 1996, North Korea sent a bunch of commandos into South Korea, commandos transported by an old diesel boat. So, it's apparent that they see submarines as tools in their covert operations. Now, we believe they are at it again. This time, we think that they've bought some technology from China, possibly India...battery technology."

The CO's eyes fixed on Mark. Reed's stomach tightened. "Petty Officer Reed, this is your first sub. Can you tell me why there are so many more nuclear subs than diesel-battery boats?"

"I think so, sir. It's the difference between a Mustang and a golf cart. A golf cart's range is measured in holes, not miles. You constantly have to go recharge its batteries. And then, even when it's charged, the Mustang's still gonna leave it in the dust."

The CO smiled and held up one finger. "But, which one is louder? We sub sailors are concerned about how much noise we make."

"The Mustang."

"Right!" said the Captain. "Now, we don't have a combustion engine making noise; no one can hear the uranium in our reactor splitting apart...but we do have a 900 psi steam plant, we do have dozens of pumps running to support that plant; we've got several steam turbines turning at 4200 rpm. We've got noisemakers that we have to silence. About all a diesel boat has running when it's on the battery is enough electric current to turn the screw, not even that if they just stop and get quiet. What if you invented a battery that would allow you to submerge for maybe a month at a time? What if you had a battery that could put enough turns on the screw to push a boat around at thirty-five, thirty-nine knots?"

No one had an answer. So he provided one. "Well, gentlemen, if you invent that battery, you've just effectively erased forty years worth of technological advantage that a nuke sub now enjoys."

After some seconds of silence, he went on. "The United States is not going to invent that kind of battery. It's not where the research money has been. In fact, our own battery technology is basically the same as it was during World War II. But, we have reason to believe that both China and India have been working on one, and that North Korea has paid a lot of money to get one in a submarine.

"That submarine is code-named Quiet Tiger. She launched for sea trials early this morning. Our spy boat, slash fishing troller, like the one the Russians have off Pearl, reported seeing her, then we lost contact. Our mission is simply to get there and watch her, see what she can do....any questions?"

There were no questions. The CO looked at his wristwatch and said, "By the way, here's the official shtick you're supposed to repeat if it should become necessary. We will be respecting the international twelve mile boundaries at all times. If something should go wrong and we are apprehended and taken into custody, our mission is to determine and map thermal gradients and underwater currents."

Mark was taken a little aback. He'd never gotten talks like this on Dixon.

****

After Mark's phone call, J.L. Reed slept fitfully. She'd never liked the idea of Mark transferring to a submarine. His being at sea on a normal ship was bad enough. Truth be known, she'd never liked the ocean...period.

She probably had the movie "Jaws" to thank for that. She'd seen it on T.V. one night as a girl. Her father had been called out on some emergency around two in the morning. J.L. was the only one in the family not to sleep through his leaving. She'd turned the sound way down on the T.V. and congratulated herself on getting to watch some late-night HBO unattended. "Jaws" was the first R-rated movie she'd seen. She sat there, simultaneously mesmerized and terrified the entire time. When it was over, she'd grabbed Mr. Bear and retreated into bed with her mom for the rest of the night. Then, like now, she'd slept fitfully.

The one time she had drifted off deeply since Mark's call, she had dreamed. She couldn't remember much of it, other than the sense of being stalked. She hadn't been running or chased, but she felt that she was being watched, and measured somehow. Maybe that explained her strange recollection of "Jaws", with its monster shark that remained unseen until it was too late for escape, and the haunting two-note musical phrase that warned of its approach.

Ah, but who's fooled by that? she thought. If Jaws had anything to do with her "creeped-out" feeling, it was that the shark represented something terrible coming after her, faster than she could ever swim and completely inescapable. The shark's name was "Divorce," and she could sense him getting closer. A feeding-frenzy was about to begin, with J.L. Reed playing the role of chum. She was dog-paddling in the middle of her own vast ocean while Mark played sailor at the other end of the world.

When she thought of Mark again, she was overcome by regret and dread. She regretted the past, and dreaded the future. Her eyes began to tear up. Unconsciously, she blinked them back. No observer would've been able to tell how close she was to crying. It was a neat little deception she'd perfected at a very early age. As an adult, she performed it without effort or notice.

Mark was gone. His last impression of her was surely of a blubbering lunatic. Beating him upside the head with her newfound faith was just the icing on a very bad cake...

J.L. felt nauseated. Whether by anxiety or morning sickness, she didn't know--or care. It made little difference. The sprint to the toilet bowl in the dark was just as long either way.

When J.L. emerged from the bathroom, morning light was beginning to invade her hotel room, and she was happy for it. She went to the window and opened the curtains to facilitate the invasion, turning off the air conditioner at the same time. The only thing particularly Hawaiian about her view was the mountain, Diamondhead, on the eastern horizon, dramatically darkened by the fiery sunrise. Nimitz Highway, in the bottom left corner of her window, was crowded with cars heading west to Pearl Harbor and Hickham Air Force Base, most of them with headlights still on.

J.L. could see a small piece of the roof of the nearby church she had visited soon after arriving on the island. The preacher was an older, black man. When he spoke it was not in the cadence and rhythm she had come to expect from black preachers by watching television. He'd seemed assured of the fact that what he said was of sufficient weight that it didn't need his screaming to make it important. That was her impression, at least. His message had moved her deeply.

The sermon was from a passage in the Old Testament book of Jeremiah, about the faithfulness of God. The preacher, called Brother Robbie, was teaching on God's intended symbolism in sunrises and sunsets.

Her eyes were now drawn to the deep red and purple ribbons of cloud, draped loosely across the sky like party streamers.

Brother Robbie had said that, for God's people, the rising and setting of the sun were meant to be like mile markers on a highway, each one reminding them that they walked a path of God's love and care. "The day the sun doesn't rise," he'd said, "on that day you can doubt God's love for you."

She thought about what she'd said to Mark a couple of months ago. A wave of embarrassment came with the memory.

She had been so emotional, a little electric bundle of enthusiasm and naiveté. All that had motivated her was a desire to share the wonder and awe of her own recent conversion to faith in Jesus Christ. Surely her husband, Mark, the most intelligent, rational man she knew, would see the sense it all made, the clarity of the Truth of it all. His reaction had been rather less energetic than J.L. had hoped.

She focussed on the sunrise again. Another day,

another chance, maybe. Of course, now it would be another three months. She turned and sat down at the room's single small table and turned on the light. The novel she'd stayed up reading was still open. *Terrible way to treat a book*, she thought. *Really hard on the binding*...Then she smiled. It's a little late to worry about this book's binding!

It was a copy of *The House of Seven Gables* by Nathaniel Hawthorne, and she'd picked it up for exactly fifty cents at an estate sale a few days before flying to Pearl. It felt almost brittle. She had to take care to keep the pages from falling out whenever she handled it. But the best thing about its condition was the smell. No doubt about it. She had heard once that great books don't ever get musty; they simply acquire the faint smell of forgotten wisdom. That's what this book was--forgotten wisdom.

She thought about the different times in which it was written. They were straightforward, at least. Hawthorne wasn't out to deceive anyone by preaching subtly. He stated upfront that his purpose was to simply illustrate a single, great truth. In *The House of Seven Gables*, that truth was that the sins of one generation are visited upon those that follow.

Still a great truth... J.L. was mentally yanked back to the real world by that thought, and how easily it could be applied to her own life. The sense of dread came creeping back.

J.L. put Hawthorne away, gingerly, and reached for the other book on the table. She spent the next twenty minutes reading her Bible. When she was finished, she began to pray. She couldn't help but feel guilty when she thought of Mark, the shambles she had made of their marriage, and, of course, the baby growing inside her. She brought all of these things up in her prayer.

The sins of one generation... It all centered on her father. It always had, of course. He was the one from whom all the sin flowed. As miserable as his neglect and scorn had made her own life, she knew that some of his ugliest traits lived on in her. The willingness to belittle his own family, the temper, the insensitivity; they were his sins and now they were hers.

He had never physically abandoned her, and yet, he might as well have. Although he had been present during her childhood, J.L. had felt fatherless. And now, here she was, with a husband a couple thousand miles away, having just extended his time separated from her by nearly eleven weeks.

Tears threatened again. But she would not cry. She would not give her father the satisfaction of seeing that he had, indeed, caused wrenching pain with his words. She would not give him... She stopped, almost embarrassed at the realization that she was alone with God. The little trick of stopping the tears was useless here.

God could see, she knew. Whether the tears actually rolled down her face, He knew about the pain. There was no one else who could know. She was deceiving herself, and *only* herself, if she thought she could hide anything here, from Him.

There were other anxieties as well, centering around the fact that she was going to have to complete the move from San Diego to Hawaii by herself. The Navy was paying to put her up in the hotel for now, but would a spot in one of the military housing areas open up for them before her allotted house-hunting time ran out?

She was tempted to be intimidated by the fact that she knew no one on the entire island except for Rita, the friend she'd made at church. She'd met others, of course, like some Navy personnel, and Brother Robbie and his wife, JoAnna. Though Robbie and JoAnna seemed nice enough, they'd merely shaken hands. Only Rita was really a friend.

As she prayed, she developed a strange conviction, the origin of which she could not determine. But, from some-where, she knew God was real and present with her. There was no promise that her prayers would be answered in the manner she desired. There was, however, the solid confidence that whatever did happen, God would continue to be present with her.

J.L. got up to go shower and prepare for her day. It wasn't until she was in the bathroom with the light on that she realized that her nausea had subsided. Another thing struck her as odd when she looked in the mirror. Her eyes were a little puffy, and there, plain as day, were the tracks of tears going all the way to her jawline. Not only had she not blinked them back; she hadn't noticed them.

Two feelings immediately warred within her. There was the habitual disgust she felt for having shed tears at all, in direct violation of two decades of self-discipline. And there was the peaceful, calm feeling that the tears had washed away a lot of junk that really needed to go. She was surprised at how refreshing that was, and decided to go ahead and enjoy it... but with caution.

****

Reginald Nelson began his affiliation with the North Korean submarine navy in a manner that seemed appropriate to the whole of his life. That is, characterized by chaos.

First, Reginald lost his job with a leading firm working on computer security software and encryption. Bummer. But, hey, he was a smart guy, still young and edgy at twenty-two. He'd find something else. Something better.

A couple of weeks turned into a month. Nobody was beating his door down to give him a job. A month became two, then three.

He knew that the pittance he was getting in the unemployment check was not going to be able to continue supporting him in the lifestyle to which he'd become accustomed. (Beer and cigarettes had gotten terribly expensive over the course of the eight years he'd enjoyed them both.)

Four months later his girlfriend, Sherry, broke up with him. Seems she grew into the opinion that Reggie was a loser. And a bum; he still owed her money. She kicked him when he was down. That's what it amounted to. He couldn't blame her, really. He'd have done the same. You gotta go with the flow. And if that flow is going nowhere, you gotta find you a new flow.

Did he hate Sherry now? No. Hate is a strong word, signifying a strong emotion. Reggie had never had any strong emotions for Sherry. He didn't hate her, but he probably would keep his eyes open for opportunities to get back at her.

At about five months out of work, Mr. Lee's men did, in fact, beat his door down to give him a job. The three Koreans in black suits said no more about the source of the job offer than that. They were from Mr. Lee.

Reggie was hanging around his apartment, drinking beer and watching some basketball. They hadn't knocked.

The door blew open, as if suddenly subjected to something close to hurricane-force winds, and two monsters in suits (*wait a minute...I thought Asians were all small!*) charged through it and grabbed him by both arms. He hadn't made it past saying, "Wha...?"

One of them swatted the can out of his hand. It crashed into the TV screen, but didn't break it. The beer was all white foam running down the glass, leaving a rainbow colored trail.

"Do not talk. Do not scream. Do not make a sound. You will listen," said the third guy, who had come in last. He was more gaunt by far than the two who held Reggie to face him.

Reggie had always had a problem with authority figures. He said, "I don't know who in the..."

And suddenly there was a gun barrel about one inch away from his left eyeball, which made him think he should stop talking.

When he shut his mouth, the thinner man smiled. Some guys look scarier when they're smiling, Reggie thought. This guy was one of those.

The man lowered the gun and replaced it in the shoulder holster under his suit jacket.

"We are here to offer you a job."

Reggie had laughed. "What, are you guys from the government? Is this, like, Welfare Reform or something? You all Republicans or something? Huh?"

Reggie had turned to look at each man, to see if anyone had understood his joke. Apparently, they lacked senses of humor. The third man's eyes bored into him.

Reggie said, barely above a whisper now, "Okay...okay...I'll be...I'll be quiet. Your turn, buddy."

It was then that the third Korean spelled out the plan, and the part they wanted Reggie to play. Their plan boggled his mind, challenged his imagination, and the role they had reserved for him stroked his ego. He possessed two things they needed badly. One: his name had, until recently, been among the top five among software designing rising stars, especially in the area of electronic security. Two: he happened to be fluent in Japanese.

"If you cooperate, you will be paid $50,000 up front, then $75,000 more when the operation is completed successfully."

"Well, what if I don't think..." he started.

The gun barrel was at his eyeball again, even closer. The man was smiling as he said, "We are not barbarians, Mr. Nelson. But you have now heard our plan. We would have to take some rather extreme measures to ensure that you communicated it to no one. You know how these things go."

Reggie thought that a silent, obedient nod was the smart thing to do, but spoke anyway. "No threatening to chop off my fingers with a hedge-trimmer?"

The man smiled and lowered his gun again. "We were thinking we'd do that to that girlfriend of yours. What's her name? Sherry isn't it?"

"I've got a counter offer for you," Reggie said, noting that their "intel" on him was a little behind on current events. The Korean stopped smiling. "I'll do this job for you. You pay me the hundred and twenty-five thousand. And, as a bonus, you go ahead and whack Sherry's fingers anyhow."

All three Koreans busted up at that one.

Within a week, Reggie was working for them, writing a computer program. It wasn't easy. Oh, granted, it was easier for him than it would've been for anyone in the world, save one or two guys he knew. No, on second thought, just one. Still, it had been a challenge; the Japanese were serious about their computer security.

But he figured he was even more serious about not getting on the wrong side of Mr. Lee's men. The two Oddjob clones were bad enough, but it was the skinny guy that gave him the creeps. Reggie had been working for two days when he decided that they were going to kill him anyway. It made sense. They were not joking around.

Their "plan" was huge and they were serious about "extreme measures" to keep it under wraps. He would write their program, show them how to use it. They would say thank you. They would shoot him, or shove his head in a food processor, or something. He was like the guys who designed the pyramids. He would work long enough to get the job done, then they would bury him.

That was starting to bother him when he realized something. Not one of them was even close to computer savvy. They were computer stupid. And so he made up a lie. That was the easiest part of the whole deal.

(The Japanese system is unique. It's darn near artificial intel!) They bought it.

"I can write the program that gets the ball rolling," he'd said, trying to look like he was breaking bad news. "But there's no one in the world that can write one to keep it rolling. The Japanese system has got a sort of constant reconfiguration. It's going to require nearly constant attention. And, a much faster processor than what you say you're working with."

He had convinced them that he was needed throughout the entire operation, close to it, but in a neutral country, with his personal, customized laptop. They had agreed, although obviously suspicious.

Reggie held that laptop firmly now. It was, he knew, the only reason he was still alive.

The pilot's voice had jolted him out of a nice, alcohol-induced nap on the long flight. "Ladies and gentleman. We are landing in Seoul, South Korea. The weather is sunny, about 80 degrees. For those continuing to Hong Kong, please return to the aircraft in one hour. Enjoy your stay and thank you for flying with us."

That would be me. Continuing to Hong Kong. He smiled to himself. Won't the flight crew be delighted!

The attendants always wrinkled their noses when they walked by. Rather than offend him, he liked it that way. They were from a different world than he was. In their world, all women have super-tiny waists and makeup applied with precision. In his world, all the cool people looked like stage-hands for grunge bands, like "The Lice Muffins" and the "Bottom Feeders."

Reggie satisfied himself with the notion that he had several more hours in flight to bother them with his smell. He had better hair than they did, too, long and curly, like mud-colored ivy commandeering a wall.

He sighed and caressed his laptop. Once this was all over he would need to figure out a way to disappear. He knew the Far East was a big place. He would survive. And thrive. He would go with the flow. Preferably, it would be flowing away from Japan and the Koreas.

****

A stocky guy with red hair and mustache, carrying a black bag, squeezed through the blue-shirted crowd in Crew's Mess to get to Mark. When he spoke, it was the sound of a deep Southern accent filtered through sandpaper.

"Hi, Reed," he said. "I'm the Doc."

He was a First Class Petty Officer, a corpsman, no doubt. The 688's didn't rate taking a real doctor with them. He opened his bag and said, "I've got to get a blood sample from you, Reed. Sorry. Got to get it fast and send it back with the tug for analysis. Did you know you're six months over-due for an HIV test?"

Mark shook his head. The Doc motioned for Reed to follow him. The gruff man half-yelled at a couple of guys at one of the tables to move so they could sit down. The guys half-yelled back, but they moved. Mark sat down across from the Doc.

Mark held out his left arm. As the blood was being drawn, he asked, "What happens if it's positive?"

The Doc looked up at him, eyes wide, and said, "You have reason to think it's gonna be?"

Mark laughed and shook his head, no. "No, no. Just curious. How's that handled?"

The Doc went back to watching the syringe fill with blood. "Well, if we're out at sea, we'll be notified as part of the normal radio message traffic. It's kept pretty confidential. Classified, even. I'd go and inform whoever came up posi-tive. Then, pretty much, he'd be gone. They'd transfer him off at the next opportunity without saying a word."

Mark nodded. The Doc was finished. He shook Mark's hand, welcomed him aboard, and squirmed his way out of Crew's Mess.

After an eternity of constantly trying to make good first impressions with his new shipmates (Belmont, Drom, Byars, Ratcliff, Dain, Scholz, Corvin, Burger, Ely, Clemmons, Petresin, on and on) Mark heard the 1MC announce, "Secure the Maneuvering Watch. Station underway watch section three. Rig ship for dive."

The crowd of blue shirted sailors scurried off much more quickly than they had shuffled in. Mark was left alone with a coffee cup that wasn't his. The sub rocked port and starboard. His lips started to tingle. He tried not to watch the coffee flow to one side then back to the other. Getting seasick within minutes of almost missing ship's movement on a new command wouldn't quite make the impression he desired.

Several silent minutes later, he heard a hatch slam shut.

Footsteps of a heavy, steel-toed stride approached from aft. Then there appeared a barrel-chested Second Class Petty Officer with a head full of brown hair that pushed the boundaries of military regs and a huge smile, all teeth. He saw Mark and thrust out his right hand to greet him. It was MM2(SS) Lawrence, an ELT Mark had worked with on a large transfer of radioactive material from Omaha to Dixon just last week. Mark was glad to see a face he recognized.

"Petty Officer Reed!" Lawrence said, "All we've had is rumors about who was gonna be our Leading ELT. Man, I'm glad they got you!"

"Thanks, Lawrence. Glad to be here."

Lawrence grimaced and said, "Dang! It's Paul, call me Paul. I'm the SNOB. I've earned the right to be addressed by my first name like God intended!"

"Shortest Nuke On Board? Getting out pretty soon?"

"You betcha. I get out of this man's Navy in eighty-two--no, wait, eighty-one days!" Paul's eyes sparkled. His massive chest inflated as if he'd just announced the birth of a son.

A seaman, a kid who looked all of fifteen, ran into Crew's Mess from forward and said, "Hey, are you MM1 Reed?"

Paul answered for him. "You're darn right! The only real sailor from the Dixon. We had to take him with us! What do you want with him, Elgin?"

The seaman had a nervous aura about him. "Th...the Captain wants to see you in his stateroom--right now!"

Mark said to Paul, "Sheesh, I didn't think I was here long enough to get in trouble already."

Paul laughed. Mark noted that he had never seen someone actually throw back his head to laugh in as pronounced a manner as Paul did. "Hey, it don't take much around here, buddy!"

The seaman led Mark forward from Crew's Mess, down a narrow passageway. They passed a ladder down to what Mark knew was the Auxiliary Machinery Room, or "Diesel".

At the end of the passage, they turned starboard and went up a ladder.

The seaman looked back over his shoulder and said, "This is a command passageway up here. No...no enlisted allowed — normally, anyhow. But, until we dive it's best to stay away from Control, so it's O.K. for now."

They entered another shorter hallway and headed aft. They passed a door on the right that said "XO's Stateroom". The end of the passageway formed the forward entrance to the Control room. Just before that, though, on the right was the CO's Stateroom. That door was open.

Commander Parnette sat at a desk next to a single rack that was made up impeccably. There was also a heavy-set man in his forties, with sheet-white hair and mustache, and the gold oak leaf collar devices of a Lieutenant Commander, standing opposite the Captain. The black name-tag, the first name-tag Mark had seen, on his khaki shirt read, "Lt. CDR Adam Shelby, Executive Officer". Neither man noticed Mark and the seaman at the door.

Parnette raised a hand to the XO as if to say, "Enough." Then he said, "I really don't give a rat's behind what the reason was, Adam. I don't care. It was sloppy, that's all."

Something clicked in Mark's head now. The command structure was going to function on a good-cop, bad-cop sort of wavelength. This would allow Parnette to be the beloved CO, the father figure for all the men. Then, he'd send out this Shelby, however reluctantly the latter might go, to be his enforcer. Mark made a mental note to keep that in mind when he spoke to the XO, or received direction from him. It would most likely be coming from Parnette himself.

Commander Shelby shifted his weight from one foot to the other. He opened his mouth to say something, but his Captain cut him off. "For Pete's sake, XO! We're heading off on a career cruise, here! You and I might as well retire right now if this is how it's gonna go...."

Mark realized that the longer they stood in the open doorway, the worse it would be for them once the officers noticed them. So, he reached up and knocked twice on the doorframe, clearing his throat.

"Cap'n, sir. MM1 Reed. I was told you wanted to see me, sir," Mark said.

Deciding to cut his losses, the seaman bowed out and retreated. The CO turned to the XO and nodded. Shelby left the stateroom, ushered out by a terse order from Parnette. He said, "If your department heads can't handle those instructions, you bring them with you to explain to me why that is."

"Yes, sir," said the XO in a resigned manner as he passed Mark.

With a quickness that made Mark uneasy, the CO's voice and expression changed to one of cheery hospitality. The good cop was back. "Come on in, Petty Officer Reed, and, by the way, welcome to Omaha."

Reed went in. The Captain motioned him to a seat on a small blue vinyl stool by his desk. Parnette stood up, unlatched his stateroom door and shut it. Mark noticed his own service record lying open to the performance evaluation section on the Captain's desk. As he had suspected, this was to be his "Welcome Aboard" speech. He was looking forward to it. First impressions represented great opportunities. He would excel.

****

Standing at the aft end of *Omaha's* Control space, the man watched MM1 Reed enter the CO's stateroom, watched the door close them in. He heard his own blood begin pounding in his ears. His eyes remained fixed on the blue and yellow arrowhead design that hung on the door.

He wondered if they were talking about him.

His eyes were immovable and unblinking. As long as the CO's door was in his sight, they couldn't pull anything over on him. Enlisted sailors in the Control space had already changed into their "underway uniforms", blue polyester coveralls ("poopie-suits") and civilian tennis shoes. They went about their business around him, sometimes walking between him and the CO's door, which irritated him. But he held it together.

The Navigator stood on the low-raised dais in front of the twin periscope wells, reading a clipboard, facing the helmsman, planesman, and chief-of-the-watch. *Idiots. And worse. They're ignorant. They don't know the judgment of Almighty God hangs over their heads like Damocles' Sword. And they don't know that I am the minister of His wrath.* He allowed himself a half-grin.

Reed was troubling to him. *What part does he play here? A demonic one, no doubt.*

What are they talking about in there? He shouted the question inside his head. Beads of sweat formed on his temples.

Then he forced himself to relax. It couldn't possibly matter. What he would make crooked, no one would be able to straighten.

****

J.L. emerged from the lobby of the Plaza at five minutes till noon. Of all the things there were for a Texas girl to get used to in Hawaii, the style of dress was about the easiest. She stepped out of the air conditioning into the sunshine and saltwater air wearing a pink tanktop, black sweatpants, tennis shoes and a garish neon yellow visor.

She was looking forward to spending the day with Rita. Thoughts of her new friend still caused some amazement for her. J.L. was the twenty-two year old daughter of a Jewish physicist from Amarillo, Texas. Rita was a thirty-six year old black woman who had been raised by her grandmother in Riverside, California. Defying convention, they clicked.

They had met at church just two Sundays ago. J.L., a shy visitor, planned on sitting in the back row somewhere. Rita had met her at the door, grabbing her by the arm. "Come on and sit with me up front," she had said, more a command than an invitation. After church, when Rita had invited/ commanded J.L. to join her for lunch, they found out they had more in common than their love for Jesus.

Rita turned out to be a civilian employee at Pearl Harbor's Subase, which would be Mark's new place of business once he arrived. Rita's job seemed to fit her to a tee. She worked as a Morale, Welfare and Recreation liaison. J.L. had asked what that meant. "I work my tail off planning parties!" had been the immediate response.

J.L. smiled at the thought of spending an afternoon walking the malls with her. The Plaza's automatic doors closed behind her, and she looked out over the lower level of Nimitz Highway, the eastbound lanes heading into Honolulu and Waikiki. The cars ran from left to right shaded by the upper level, each one eerily orange-colored because of the many overhead lights.

Right at 12:00, the agreed-upon meeting time, Rita drove her white Honda into the Plaza's loading/unloading zone. The women smiled at each other through the windshield as she came to a stop. J.L. climbed in and buckled her seatbelt. They drove off talking and laughing.

****

One block away, in a nondescript rental car, two men whose demeanors were far less cheerful listened to the women through a small radio receiver sitting on the armrest between their seats. They looked at each other but said nothing. They had not anticipated the stop at the Plaza, but it made no real difference. In fact, it probably made their job easier. As long as the black woman was wasting time with the new blonde, whoever she was, she would not be able to spoil the operation.

As Rita and J.L. got on Nimitz Highway and started toward Waikiki, the gray car followed, but not too closely, and listened.

Chapter Three

"I don't know about you, but I'm in the mood for Mexican food," said Rita as she drove.

J.L. turned toward her with eyes wide, lips parted. Rita looked over at her, noticed her gaze, and put on an overdone look of shock. She said, "Now don't tell me you don't like Mexican food. You've got way too much drawl in your talk to try to tell me you don't like Mexican food. And here I was, thinking you were from Texas..."

J.L. smiled and shook her head. "No, no that's not it," she said, "I love Mexican food. It's just that...this is Hawaii! You're the one that was telling me that Hawaii has the best seafood in the world, and here you're wanting to eat Mexican food."

"I've got two words for you: Shark Tacos," said Rita.

J.L. sat slack-jawed.

Rita nodded and raised her right hand from the steering wheel as if swearing an oath and said, "I don't care if your momma used a jalapeno pepper as your pacifier when you were a baby! You have *not* had real Mexican food until you've had shark meat tacos."

J.L. laughed, even though her own stomach wasn't exactly leaping for joy over the prospect of anything much spicier than bean curd.

The road began to crowd with pedestrians on either side. The two women drove past the marina area on their right, starting with the Fisherman's Wharf Restaurant. Each boat on the pier was its own commercial, painted with words advertising "Lee's Whale Watching Tours", "The Big One: Offshore Fishing" and such.

Sometimes it still filled J.L. with a small sense of awe to scan the horizon and see most of it in monochrome. There were only a few places she'd been on Oahu where the ocean was not in view, where she couldn't see the rich blue of the sea mingling and intertwining with the lighter blue of the sky in a perfect sort of peacefulness.

Even as she sat next to Rita, realizing that a casual observer would have been most struck by their obvious differences, she thought of the high plains region of the Texas panhandle she called home and remembered its horizon. No peaceful mixing there. Dark, fertile land, dotted with cattle, stood out almost defiantly from the sky. God's a big fan of variety, she thought with a smile, glancing at Rita.

****

The unremarkable car followed like a loyal puppy, without making quite so much noise as a puppy. Both cars were filled with the same conversation as the voices of the women were transmitted from one to the other.

****

Rita made a left, away from the beach on their right, just a couple of blocks before their final destination for the day, Ala Moana Mall. They pulled into the cramped parking lot of Herve's Hacienda. The decor of the building was about as Spanish as it could be, considering it was located at the heart of Honolulu's tourist area. Its "Spanish tile" roof was more day-glo pink than red, and its near-fluorescent green walls were dotted with black and yellow images of geckos, the small indigenous lizards which had roughly the same social standing in Hawaii as cattle in India.

****

The car following them pulled over to the side of the

road.

****

Rita opened the over-large canvas bag, with seashell print, which she used as a purse. She was about to throw the car keys inside when she saw something in the bag that caught her attention. She pulled out a small rectangle of stiff, pink paper.

"Oh, here's your Sub-Ball ticket, before I forget," she said, handing it to J.L.

J.L. almost winced, but took it anyway. "Rita, I don't know...I don't think I'm really in the mood for a party, especially with Mark gone, and me not knowing anyone..."

"Hey! Don't call Sub-Ball a party! I worked hard on this. Sub-Ball is a gala event: tuxes and tails, dress uniforms, medals, evening gowns, the whole nine yards. Everybody who's anybody in the submarine world will be there. The head man for all the subs in Pearl is Admiral Crabb—can you believe that? Guy's an admiral, name's Crabb. Heck, we've even got two admirals coming from D.C., the Joint Chiefs guy—I'm talking about big-whigs here, J.L.! You go, then if you wish you hadn't, I'll give you your money back."

J.L. grinned and shook her head in resignation. Rita had paid for her ticket.

****

The two men stayed in their car. They waited.

****

Commander Parnette unlatched his stateroom desk and folded it up into the fake wood-grain panel of the bulkhead. He turned his chair to face MM1 Reed. Recalling what he had read in an article about body language several decades ago, Parnette forced himself to keep his arms and legs uncrossed. This was supposed to communicate welcome. He smiled at the young man. The *young* man!

"MM1 Reed," he said.

"Sir."

"What are you doing here?"

Parnette watched his eyes. He hoped his question might put Reed off his guard.

Reed half-grinned. He said, "I assume you mean what am I doing on your boat."

No nervous tone had entered his voice. His smile looked genuine, almost as if he knew he was being put on the spot.

"Well, sir, I'll be very honest with you. I want to make Chief. I think coming to Omaha is the sort of move that will make that happen."

"Why's that?"

"Smaller navy. They keep advancing fewer and fewer MM1's to MMC, three or four a year. It takes more than just great evals... you have to do something that makes the board notice you."

The CO nodded and leaned back in his chair.

"So, Petty Officer Reed, you're planning on using my boat as a career opportunity?"

A round gray speaker in the bulkhead by the door broke into the conversation.. "Cap'n, sir, this is the Navigator. We've completed a 60 degree port turn, passing navigation checkpoint Echo. The ship is rigged for dive."

"Excuse me one moment," the CO said, then reached out with his left arm and hit a white button on the speaker console, "Very well. Who signed the rig?"

"Um...Petty Officer Kresge forward and...MM2 Jones aft, sir."

"Very well. Officer of the Deck, dive the ship."

"Dive the ship, aye, sir."

The same voice from the speaker then said over the 1MC, "Dive, dive!"

An alarm sounded. It was more the sick-duck bawl of a model-T than the diving alarm of the movies. The CO loved the old "ah-wooo-ga!" version so much better...he would have to see about getting that changed.

He looked back at Reed, who seemed to be more anxious than before.

"First dive, huh?"

"Yes, sir."

"What are you expecting?"

Reed smiled. "You mean beyond surfacing again?"

The CO laughed. That's what he was hoping for, some indication of how Reed would handle stress. *One bullet dodged.* He hated having to bring on a brand new guy with no personal observation at all. Reed's service record was amazing. The kid was obviously sharp and dedicated. If he had a sense of humor, maybe he'd make it where MM1 Liegert had not.

"We were talking about how you were planning on using my submarine to advance your own career."

"May I speak frankly, sir?"

"Oh, you haven't already?"

Reed remained unshaken. "I want to make Chief as an ELT. That means I have to be the most stellar ELT the Navy has seen. I think that's good for both of us. You want me to do a good job for you, and I've got personal reasons for wanting to make that happen."

The CO had planned to encourage Reed to take the Laboratory Division and make it his own. Don't be afraid to lead, and all that. He decided he could skip that part.

The side-to-side motion of the sub quit. Just that quickly. With it, all sense of motion of any kind stopped. He'd never tell anyone, but the CO figured no one on the boat was more relieved by the calm nature of the sub's underwater movement than he was. It made him feel at home. He hit the speaker button again.

"Officer of the Deck, make your depth 800 feet. Let me know when we pass 700."

"Make my depth 800 feet, inform you at 700, aye, Cap'n."

A few seconds later, the stateroom angled, the forward end pointing down slightly.

The CO held up a hand. "Listen."

He and Reed sat still. There was a series of muffled

creaks and groans and pops from all around them. The CO got some entertainment watching Reed's eyes widen with each one.

"Hear that?"

Reed nodded, still listening.

"You didn't know the hull of a submarine expands and contracts with the changes in water pressure."

"Um, no, sir. Sounds logical, but I hadn't thought about it, sir."

Reed was going to work out. The CO was relieved.

Rushing things, because 700 feet would come soon, the CO let Reed know he didn't expect him to know everything right away, that he could deal with honest mistakes, but not with lack of effort, or lack of honesty. Yadda-yadda-yadda. Standard ration. The CO also let him know he had some good people to work with, especially MM2 Lorde, and that he ought to take advantage of their *Omaha* experience.

"Yes, sir," Reed said.

The CO took a deep breath. He wasn't sure how much he needed to say to Reed about the suicide of last night. "Petty Officer Reed, I've looked at your record. I've talked to your leading Chief from Dixon. I have no doubt that under normal circumstances you'd hit the ground running here and do a great job."

Reed's face dropped a little for the first time. The young man was bright enough to hear a "but" coming.

"But, I wouldn't be dealing honestly with you if I acted like things are normal. MM1 Liegert was not well liked, from what I understand. I'm sure you'll hear a bucket full of rumors about him before anything else. His suicide note mentioned the fact that he'd had an affair and that he was sure his wife was going to find out. Didn't know how to deal with that. Figured he had destroyed his marriage, didn't want to deal with it."

Reed's lips formed the word, "Oh..."

"Anyway, on top of having to take over a division full of men you've never met, on a boat you have no experience with, I need to ask you to watch your people."

"Sir?"

The CO nodded. "A couple of years back, *Indianapolis* had a Topside Watch put a bullet in his head during a mid-watch. They had three more attempted suicides in two months after that. I don't know. I guess suicide's kind of like flu. If you're too close to it, there's a danger you'll catch it."

The CO threw his hands in the air. He mumbled something about psychobabble and mumbo-jumbo.

Reed nodded now. "So you want to know if my guys start dropping hints about hurting themselves."

"Right. You've heard about this before."

"Leadership training. Threatening each other is normal, but threatening yourself is something different."

The CO smiled, rose and extended his hand. Reed stood and shook it.

"Go to work, Petty Officer Reed, and welcome aboard."

"Yes, sir. Thank you, sir."

****

The streets and trolley tracks began to fill with the evening rush hour traffic in Yokosuka, Japan. At first glance, and several more after that, the whole road and track system looked like something Picaso might come up with on a really bad day.

There was no such thing as a right angle. Roads ran parallel, then veered into one another and crossed at acute angles, only to angle again to avoid a cluster of buildings or a circular track-switching station. Roads came out of nowhere and curved sharply to go to some other nowhere...Chaos Theory applied to infrastructure.

No signs, no traffic lights. Yellow trolley cars and light green transit buses hurtled headlong, and compact cars, bumper to bumper at insane speeds, somehow managed to stay out of their way.

A computer inside a Civil Defense office building

popped to life. This was automatic, in response to a signal sent from Line 87, the Japanese counterpart to the American system known as SOSUS. The Line had a nickname that meant "worthy wife" or "Shogun's wife". The image was of a quiet, traditional Japanese woman who, even while sleeping, listens attentively to her husband and is ready to wake up and answer his requests.

The Line was a net of passive sonar listening posts anchored to the ocean floor some twenty miles off the Japanese coastline, encircling the island nation, a multi-billion dollar Cold War expenditure. The Japanese government had denied making that expenditure until the mid 90's, even to the face of President George Bush over sushi and rice wine.

The admission to the existence of "Worthy Wife" did not come until Russian President Boris Yeltsin had laughed himself delirious in a meeting with a top Clinton aide at the U.S. Embassy in Moscow, gasping for air between great bellows and howls over American incompetence in the intelligence business. Yeltsin had commanded the American envoy be given the complete KGB file on Worthy Wife, to the obvious dismay of the Russian lackeys and advisors.

On that day, the Japanese government agreed to share Line 87 information with the U.S. Navy as a routine part of their cooperative naval operations in the Pacific.

The Civil Defense employee, a thirty year old native of Tokyo, put down his magazine and his Coke, a can slightly taller and thinner than those meant for Western consumption. He rotated in his chair to face the computer. The screen's background turned yellow, then red images began to appear, shimmering like a desert horizon. The image became the outline of a submarine moving from left to right. Bright green crosshairs then appeared across the sub's length and height, followed by a flurry of Japanese letters.

Next to the words, "Sound Signature Verification in Progress", there was a percentile figure that raced toward 100. It stopped at 97.75%. Then came the words, "Signature Match Confirmed. Target ID: *USS Omaha* (SSN-692), US Navy,

Squadron 7 under COMSUBPAC, Pearl Harbor, Hawaii."

More crosshairs appeared. This time, they centered on a blinking white rectangle located about midships. Japanese characters next to the square read, "Uranium fuel reactor vessel. Xenon control rods. Standard S1W/688 configuration. No special weapons detected."

A rather loud ink-jet printer, an anachronism at Civil Defense, began its "mosquito-on-a-megaphone" cascade of whining and clicking, copying the computer's information. It would become an "eyes only" file.

The real-time image of *Omaha* dissolved and was replaced by a tactical map of Japan and her immediate neighbors. A single red light in the lower left corner blinked, indicating the sub's present location. A red line extended from the light toward South Korea, highlighting the computer's "dead reckoning" of the boat's predicted positions in 6, 12 and 24 hours, a simple projection using *Omaha's* current vector.

The map was soon replaced by a detailed profile of the submarine's sound signature, a graph that resembled a jagged mountain range. Each peak was labeled by the computer, providing best-guess as to which of her many pieces of equipment was making noise. A ventilation fan just forward of the Reactor Compartment was vibrating at 62.3 Hz. A pump bearing in the lower level engineroom was scraping. A pressure regulating valve, either seawater or steam, was cycling high then low, unable to stabilize at a setpoint, a mechanical malady the Americans called "hunting". (Its location, at the aft end in the upper level, pointed to the 10,000 gallon per day distilling plant as culprit.)

This graph also dissolved, replaced by a short personal profile on one James D. Parnette, Commander, under the heading, "Commanding Officer." The Civil Defense employee smiled and sat up straight, seeing that he shared his *alma mater* with the CO...Georgia Tech.

Hours later, he would be tasked with making note of this whole event in the daily Line 87 report, to be delivered to the US Navy liaison along with the weather report. His report would say that Worthy Wife had detected a "submerged contact", "probably American", "possibly 688 Class".

Omaha didn't look to provide much entertainment. The employee returned to his can of Coke and the *Sports Illustrated* article that *Omaha* had interrupted.

****

As the Worthy Wife information continued to print out in Yokosuka, it also came up on a smartly customized laptop computer. The laptop was owned by a "small businessman" staying in a room at the Empress Hotel in Hong Kong. Reggie Nelson grinned the entire time the *Omaha* data danced before him. Then, later, he made some phone calls.

****

Herve's Hacienda didn't really smell that bad. The heavy grill aroma hadn't made J.L. sick...yet. Other than the Whaler's Room at the Plaza, and a Golden Corral near Rita's church, this was the only restaurant J.L. had been to on Oahu. The entire front section was open-air, under a canopy. The menu was interesting, taken up with local fresh fish, usually blackened and smothered in red or green chili. Most interesting were the Mahi Mahi enchiladas and Rita's smothered shark meat tacos. J.L. asked the Asian waitress if she could get a couple of flour tortillas and a side of "unsmothered" refried beans.

Rita took a sip of her soda, in a tall glass complete with a little green umbrella. Then she said, "J.L."

"Huh?"

"No, I mean *J.L.*! Is that J.L. as in just the letters, J and L? Or is that *Jael* like the Jael in the book of Judges?"

J.L. smiled and used her straw to stir her iced tea. "Both. My initials really are J.L., but, I told you I'm half Jewish. They named me Jael Leah. My grandfather once told me that the proper pronunciation of my name is *Yaw-ale*, but who the heck wants to be called that?"

Rita crinkled her nose and shuddered. "Yaw-ale?"

"Everyone else in my family always said it like the letters J and L. Somewhere along the line my teachers and friends got confused about whether they were calling me by my name or my initials. It's so unusual, it was easier to tell people they were my initials, I guess. I normally sign my initials, though, if that's what you mean."

Rita smiled and picked up her glass again, saying, "I'm glad to hear you really have a name. I was hoping you weren't like that Dr. Hunneycutt on M.A.S.H. B.J.! That's all. Just a B and a J. Guy didn't even have any names!"

J.L. nodded and laughed. "No, no. I do have names. I didn't grow up quite that poor!"

Rita laughed. "It's a pretty good name, too. Jael. She's only in there once, but it's hard to forget her."

"Really? What about her?" J.L. asked.

Rita leaned forward. "Jael! You know Jael! You've gotta know her, you're named after her."

J.L. sipped her tea and shook her head.

"I thought you said your family was Jewish!"

"We were, on Dad's side, anyway. We ate Passover, we lit the Menorah. But, honestly, I don't remember going to synagogue even once. I was seven years old before my brothers and I realized that the Menorah wasn't part of Christmas. My dad was very, very proud to be Jewish, but I think it was more like a racial thing for him, you know?"

Rita's eyebrows were raised high. J.L. nodded and went on. "For my father, being Jewish meant that you are supposed to be smarter than everyone else. And he was good at letting you know just how smart he was, and how dumb you were by comparison."

"Sounds like a lot of pressure."

"How so?"

"Well, it seems like then he'd sure as heck want his children to be these brilliant little Jewish kids."

J.L. smirked. "You'd think that, wouldn't you? And I guess it was true for my two older brothers. No son of his was going to do anything but excel!"

Rita frowned. "It wasn't the same for you?"

J.L. took another sip of tea and shook her head. She realized she had not really ever shared this stuff with anyone else. Not even Mark. But Rita seemed genuine in her interest. "No. I don't know what the difference was, really. I came along a little later. By that time, I guess my parents' relationship had kinda deteriorated, y'know? I don't know if maybe my dad saw me as a little carbon copy of my mom or what, but for whatever reason, he never took the same interest in my education. None of the private schools for me. I don't think he even really cared about my grades."

Rita's tongue clicked off the roof of her mouth and her voice was tainted with some mild anger when she said, "No offense, but that sounds chauvinist to me. Like his daughter didn't deserve as good as his sons..."

J.L. smiled. "No, it's all right. You're probably right."

Rita's own smile returned and she said, "Well, anyway, you might want to look up Jael in the Bible. She's in the book of Judges, in the early chapters, I think. And when you find it, you should make a copy and send one to your Dad. Israel was trying to get a hold of this bad guy, and they couldn't. They beat his army, but he got away. He shows up at Jael's doorstep and she agrees to hide him. When he's sleeping, she drives this big old nail through his temples."

J.L.'s eyes said, "Oh, really?" Rita nodded.

A small but insistent beeping noise caught their attention, and they both looked around. Then Rita opened up her huge purse. The beeping got louder. "Oh, darn," she said, as she started pawing through the bag.

"What is it," J.L. asked.

"Oh, it's this stinking pager. Can you believe those officers at Squadron want to page me on Aloha Friday? Probably had a volleyball go flat and can't figure out what to do..."

She dug up the pager and read the number on its display. Her expression dropped a little bit, and when she spoke again she was more serious. Rita looked around, searching for something.

"Who wants you?" asked J.L..

"Oh--no one. It's no one really--probably not very important, but--" Rita stopped scanning their surroundings and focused on a building across the street.

The building had a sign that read, "Aloha Nerd Surf Shop. Computer supplies. Internet. World Wide Web". Rita stood and gathered up her bag and said, "Y'know what? I need to run over to this place for a minute, okay? Can you wait here just a little while?"

Before J.L. could answer, she was gone. J.L. watched her jog across the street, her big, red Hawaiian print shirt billowing behind her Levi's.

****

The large, Asian men in black suits, seated in the gray rental car, sat up straight when Rita ran across the street directly in front of them. One of them had a cellular phone in his breast pocket. It rang, and he answered it.

****

The pimply kid with the stringy blonde hair at the Nerd Surf Shop took a ten dollar bill from Rita and led her to a terminal in a corner that was already switched on and connected to the Internet. He tried to help her, but she shooed him away like an irritating fly.

Rita quickly gained access to the information she sought. As she read, butterflies churned in her stomach, and she could feel her fingers quivering. She began to pray silently.

She looked up from the screen, through the storefront glass, and over to Herve's where J.L. sat. Rita thought, maybe she should just get the girl a taxi back to the Plaza.

She shook her head, angry with herself. She couldn't do that. It was already too late, and J.L. was defenseless. To leave her might just be to kill her.

She tore the cellophane from a brand new 3.5" disc and shoved it, probably too roughly, into the machine in front of her. She made a copy of what she'd just read, and then deleted it from the computer. She tried to pray some more but was simply too agitated.

****

J.L. had eaten one and a half flour tortillas, and picked at the beans enough to know she didn't want them, when she saw Rita emerge from the computer store. She was walking briskly, clutching her bag around the middle, rather than by the straps. Her face was sullen.

Rita approached their table and threw a twenty dollar bill between the dishes. J.L. noticed that sweat was forming on Rita's smooth forehead.

"What's the matter?"

"Nothing. We have to go, now. C'mon."

J.L. motioned to Rita's untouched Shark Tacos. "You sure? You want to take those with you--"

Rita bent over at the waist and grabbed J.L.'s upper arm with her free hand. J.L. was startled, then saw the humorless look in Rita's large, brown eyes. J.L. got up quickly. Maybe she really should get to know Rita a little better before she continued to share intimate details of her life with her...

Rita hissed at her, as if trying to whisper, and not quite succeeding. "J.L., you are going to have to trust me on this. If we don't leave now, we could be in some serious trouble."

****

Inside the small, gray rental car, the man in the passenger seat finished the cellular call with the same man who had been so persuasive in getting Reggie Nelson to cooperate with them.

Rita refused to let go of J.L.'s arm. She was almost dragging her out of the restaurant. J.L. had to run to keep up. She was mortified by the realization that she was being led by the arm (*Hey, Rita's got one heck of a grip!*) in public, like a child who had misbehaved.

"Rita, what in the world?"
****

The driver of the rental car saw the women leaving Herve's patio and started the engine
****

"Rita! Stop it!"

But Rita kept dragging her. J.L. decided enough was enough and she yanked her arm away as they hit the sidewalk. The sudden motion brought a stinging sensation, as Rita's fingernails scraped the underside of her bare arm.

J.L. stopped. Rita whirled. She looked furious. J.L. exaggerated her own frown.

"Rita, stop it! I don't know what in the world you think--"

"*We've got to go!*"

The unexpected power, even rage, in Rita's voice caught J.L. off guard. Rita's whole face now glistened as the sun flashed off beads of sweat. J.L. thought she saw tears welling up in her eyes.

****

The man in the passenger's seat chambered a round in each of two Chinese machine-pistols. He placed one in his own lap and one in the driver's.

****

J.L. stopped asking questions. They hurried to Rita's car.

"Buckle your seatbelt," said Rita, calmer now, almost business-like. She started the car, looking intently in the rear view mirror. They left the parking lot and headed back the way they had come, passing a gray car with two occupants who avoided eye contact with them. Rita turned right on the main road that would take them back to Nimitz Highway.

"Can I ask what's going on now?" said J.L., trying to speak as evenly as possible.

Rita stared straight ahead, lips pursed. J.L. watched her nostrils flare in and out. She was breathing fast.

Rita looked in the rear view mirror, then at J.L.. "I was paged by someone who had just sent me an e-mail. They aren't supposed to send stuff that way, so I have to guess he was under some kind of pressure."

"Stuff?"

"I'm sure it's not a big deal. I'm probably getting worked up over nothing. I just need to take the disc I made of it to Squadron real fast, then...we can shop or whatever..."

J.L. snorted, tried to laugh. "Sheesh. You guys are awful serious about your parties."

Rita had to stop because of some bumper-to-bumper traffic. She checked the rear view mirror again. Closing her eyes, she blew out a breath. She looked at J.L.. Whatever tears had been forming were gone now.

"Look. I really need you to do what I tell you, okay? We need to go to Pearl Harbor for just a moment. Admiral Crabb has to get this immediately. I almost called a cab to take you back to the Plaza...but I don't know if they think you're working with me, or what..."

"What? Who's they?" J.L. asked, now genuinely frowning. "Will you tell me what in the heck is going on?"

"No. Not if I don't absolutely have to."

The traffic started moving again. Rita checked the rear view mirror. She didn't look away for a long time. As she accelerated, her fingers opened and closed around the steering wheel.

When they reached Nimitz Highway, the traffic opened up to five lanes. They were on its upper level now, fully exposed to the sun. J.L. had decided not to ask anymore questions. Instead she prayed silently. *God, I don't know what's going on, and Rita's kind of scaring me. Help.*

Rita was now spending more time watching the rear

view mirror than the road ahead. She sped up and they began to pass the cars on all sides of them, weaving in and out of the traffic. The alternating tug of gravity and centrifugal force as they changed lanes at high speeds made J.L.'s stomach feel queasy.

The sensation was faintly familiar. For a moment, J.L. was transported back in time three years. The smell of rain, mixed with an underlying hint of blood came up from her subconscious. She was back in the passenger's seat of Mark's old, pea-green Plymouth, the Tank, he'd called it. It had taken three tries to start, had almost flooded out. If it had, she probably would've died right there in the front seat.

Mark had threaded between cars, spraying water everywhere. J.L. wanted to close her eyes because keeping them open was too terrible. The windshield wipers might as well have not been there at all. Everything was blurry darkness. Mark was hunched over the steering wheel, his profile illuminated by the blue dashboard light.

"What's the name of the hospital exit?" he had yelled.

She had been too weak to answer. He'd looked over at her, longer than he should have. She had watched his eyes widen as he looked at her lap. She looked there as well. The insides of her naked thighs were black in the dim light. Her white bathing suit was black below the waist. The black now came up to the middle of her stomach. At the edges of the blackness, the poor light was enough to see that what looked black was really very red.

She had lost consciousness concerned, crazily, about two things. One, she knew something was wrong, horribly wrong, with the baby. And, two, she hoped Mark would not get too mad about the blood on the seat of his car.

J.L. turned to look to the driver's seat. She was a little surprised to see Rita sitting there, taking only momentary glances ahead of them, paying most of her attention to the mirror. "J.L.," she said. "We're being followed."

****

When their radio receiver relayed Rita's last statement, the driver abandoned all pretense, and floored the accelerator.

The passenger opened up his cellular phone, extending the antennae. He hit "redial", then "send". When he heard the phone ring on the other end, he pressed 1, 2, 3, then 0.

Suddenly, over the traffic, in the direction of Pearl Harbor, a black pillar of smoke rose into the air. The top of the pillar became a ball of rolling orange, white and black. A second later, their car jolted as if it had hit a pot-hole. Several cars around them swerved momentarily.

Then there was a noise like thunder.

****

The smoke, the shockwave, and the massive explosion had come from a package sitting in the floorboard of a red compact car. The car was in the parking lot of the Naval medical and dental clinic located half a block down the street from the entrance to Pearl Harbor's Subase. The place was Navy property, though not within the gates of the base, and, thus, unprotected as a newborn.

The phone had rung twice, detonating the bomb, a shoebox full of plastic explosive. Spraying glass showered the area for hundreds of feet. Pieces of smoking, twisted metal landed in and across the street. Clouds of dust rose slowly into the sky.

The parking lot had been almost empty. Since it was Aloha Friday, when most businesses let their employees go home at noon, only the emergency room was open. But the three cars that were there had the glass blown out of their windows. A blue sport pickup had been flipped on its side. The large plate glass that formed the front of the building was gone as well, replaced by swirling clouds of dirt and smoke, and muted cries from within the emergency room.

Down the street, at the gate to the Subase, stood a booth on the median between the lanes on the road. The Third Class

Petty Officer on watch there, in dress whites, picked himself up off of his knees. His ears hurt. Bad. He put his hands to his ears, then brought them down and looked at them. *No blood. Sure did hurt, though.*

The phone in the booth rang. He barely heard it through the ringing in his ears. The windows were gone, and he crunched over the glass on the concrete to get to it.

"Charlie Gate," he said into the phone.

"What in blazes happened over there?" came the voice of the security chief.

"I don't know, looks like something blew up over at Medical. We may have wounded here."

A stream of profanity came from the other end. He held the phone away. The yelling didn't feel too good on his ear.

The security chief said, "Close the gate! No one gets in, no one leaves. Until you hear different, we're at Defcon Delta, you got that? "

"Yeah."

He felt dizzy. He wiped his nose on his sleeve. It left a thick, bloody trail.

He said, "Hey, I may need a relief here. I don't know if I'm injured or what."

More expletives. "Roadblocks are on their way. We're sending some .12 gauges, too. Get one of those guys to relieve you."

It was easy to stop the flow of traffic through the gate. The bomb had taken care of most of that. A handful of cars in the street beside the medical clinic were stopped in the road, most of them angled crooked in their lanes, windows missing, people inside moving slowly.

Sirens approached.

Chapter Four

Rita took the exit off Nimitz Highway at 35 mph over the recommended speed. J.L. clutched her door handle to keep from sliding into her lap.

"Rita," she said through clenched teeth, expecting their car to turn over at any moment, "Is this a drug thing or what?"

Rita only smirked and shook her head.

They went a few blocks in the direction of the Subase gate. It became obvious that the hanging black clouds and the lighter colored dust from the explosion were hovering around that location. The blaring of sirens and fire engine horns increased as well. J.L. watched understanding creep into Rita's face.

"They've closed it off...the whole base."

"What?"

They pulled up to the last stoplight before the final left turn into Subase. They could see the pulsating red and blue of flashing lights, reflecting off of the full green trees lining the road to the gate.

"They set off a bomb. The whole base--every military base on the whole *island*--it's all going to lock down tight, like they're under attack..."

"A bomb! Who?"

Rita looked into her rear view mirror. She glanced up at

the red light in front of them. A square, green sign read, "Pearl Harbor Submarine Base Gate" and pointed left. Below that, the sign said, "Pearl City/Ewa Beach" and pointed straight ahead. The light turned green. Rita stomped on the gas pedal and their car leapt forward. They had been in the left-hand turning lane, but now they sped past the cars that were next to them.

"Where are we going?"

"Away from here."

The engine revved high. Its automatic transmission seemed caught off guard. They were on a highway heading north, or "ewa", which didn't quite mean north, but rather "away from the mountain", Diamondhead. On their left was Subase, hidden behind a high fence. A mile later, they blew past the base's Supply Gate. Its giant chain link doors were shut, and yellow and black roadblocks had been set up behind them.

J.L. looked back. She saw a gray car matching their speed, about ten car lengths behind them.

"Who's following us?"

"I don't know."

"Rita, really, I'm about sick and tired of this. Who are they and what do they want? Are you in trouble or what?"

Rita swerved to dodge a couple of cars. They seemed to be standing still as she passed them.

"Okay, okay...you didn't ask for this," Rita said, sighing, "I think those guys behind us are probably North Koreans, but I suppose they could be Chinese, no, probably North Korea..."

J.L. sat back in her seat. She realized her mouth was hanging open. She could almost hear her father asking if she was trying to catch flies. She closed her mouth.

Rita just kept watching the road.

"Who set off the bomb?" J.L. asked again.

Rita's gaze switched quickly from the road to the rear view mirror, again and again. J.L. looked behind them once more. The gray car had made up half the distance.

They roared past the Arizona Memorial on their left. In the seconds it took to pass it, J.L. could see that sailors in dress white uniforms were herding tourists in outlandish flower print shirts toward the parking lot.

"Okay, Rita. I get the hint that you don't want to tell me about the bomb. But why are those guys following us? You can tell me that much, I think—"

"J.L.!" Rita said. She had taken a moment to turn and glare at her. "Can you do me a real big favor?"

J.L. was a little surprised, but said, "Well...yeah, I suppose I —"

"Good," Rita said sharply, looking back at the road in time to avoid a car. "I need you to shut up."

They met and passed two yellow fire trucks heading to Subase, their sirens piercing and lights blinking. The highway made a slow arching left hand turn ahead of them, following the curve of the harbor, then rose slightly as the terrain turned from lush jungle green to the crowded buildings of Pearl City another couple of miles ahead. J.L. could see that the traffic was getting thicker. Rita was going to be forced to slow down if they stayed on the highway.

Even as that thought entered her mind, their car lurched and their tires squealed. Rita cut right across three lanes of traffic. J.L. could see that she was aiming for an approaching exit. She could also see clearly that Rita was going to overshoot it. And she did. Their car was jostled as they ran over and through a row of two-foot-high shrubs. The jostling came to a sudden stop when they bounced into the exit lane.

J.L. put her hand over her mouth, realizing that she was emitting a shrill, high-pitched tone. She looked back. No cars followed them.

"Hey! You lost them."

Rita shook her head. "They'll be back. Soon as they stop and back up to get up here."

J.L. looked ahead of them. The exit lane opened up to two, then four, then six lanes. Ahead of them stood what looked like toll booths. Beyond them was a huge, mostly empty parking lot surrounding an enormous rust-colored structure. Across the top of the building, in white letters, were the words, "Aloha Stadium: Home of the Rainbow Warriors".

Rita pulled up to the only booth where a person stood; a pot-bellied, gray-haired man in a yellow visor, wearing a yellow tool-belt contraption around his waist. A sign in front of the booth said, "Flea Market Fri. thru Sun. $5 per car. $3 for Exhibitors." Rita rolled down her window and said, "Hey, mister. You got a phone?"

He looked a little offended. "Why, yes, but you can't use it. There's pay phones at the Stadium--"

"No, no! Get on your phone and call 9-1-1!"

He looked more offended. "What for? Now, if you want in to the Flea Market, that'll be five dollars--"

"No! Call 9-1-1 and get the police out here right now!"

J.L. looked back. No gray car yet.

"I'll tell you what, young lady, I've got half a mind to *call* the police and have 'em take you away if you don't give me five dollars--"

Lord, please don't let that car come back.

"Please, you've got to listen to me. I don't have five dollars, and in a couple of seconds you're really going to wish you had a bunch of police out here."

"Oh! What's this? Are you threatening me now?"

"No, sir! I--"

"See here, young lady! I may be an old man but I'll have you know my mettle was tested on the sands of the Philippine islands."

The back windshield of Rita's car exploded. J.L. screamed as she was pelted with glass. A rapid succession of fire-cracker pops filled her ears.

Rita stepped on the gas, pinning J.L. to her seat. The gray car was close behind them now, as J.L. could see through the non-existent back window.

"Keep your head down!" yelled Rita. She intentionally kept the car swerving side to side in the large parking lot. They followed its curving lanes as it wrapped around the stadium.

The flea market then came into view. It stood out in stark contrast to the flat gray of the parking lot. Row upon row of booths were emblazoned with colors and signs, each one seeking to out-do the next, many of them flying sample T-shirts and beach towels like banners.

The gray car started shooting again. J.L. shut her eyes tight. She heard the rounds explode in rapid successions of three. Over and over. More unnerving were the answering sounds of glass breaking and the occasional *plunk-plunk* of metal being pierced, as if by a can opener.

The rounds stopped. She opened her eyes to see that their windshield was now a spider-webbed mess of cracks and fissures. The headrest behind Rita's neck was opened up, off-white stuffing bulging out. Rita's entire left arm was red with blood. She held the steering wheel with that hand. The other was digging in her bag. She brought out a pistol, the size of which amazed J.L. She wondered for a moment how in the world she carried something that big around unnoticed.

"Hold on!" said Rita.

J.L. couldn't think of anything to hold on to. Rita grimaced in pain as she jerked the wheel around with her left arm and nearly stood on the brake. J.L.'s head hit something hard as she was thrown into her door. The tires shrieked and the car spun, then stopped. Now, looking directly out the driver's side window, J.L. saw the gray car coming at them.

Rita raised her weapon and placed the bottom of its handle in her bloody left palm. From the gray car, a snappy burst of three flashes just outside the passenger's window. Rita's gun answered. J.L. saw her trigger finger moving fast and heard the loud bursts, one right on top of the other. She lost count. Five, six, seven...ten, twelve? Empty shells flew like popcorn from the top of Rita's pistol, each one smoking. One came back and landed in J.L.'s lap. It burned. The smell of gunpowder filled her nostrils.

Rita's first, second, and third bullets hit the gray car's windshield and passed through. The glass cracked in a pattern of three crystalline snowflakes, each a foot in diameter, with two-inch holes in the centers. The driver jerked the wheel to the right, a reflexive act.

The fourth bullet impacted in the post between the windshield and the driver's window.

The fifth hit the driver's door as the car turned right, and shattered on a metal mechanism inside it.

The sixth passed through the driver's door, careened almost straight up, scraping the driver's head, barely breaking the skin.

The seventh shattered the back seat left window.

The eighth missed the car completely and slammed in the parking lot three hundred feet away, throwing up a golfer's divot of black tar. The ninth and final round pierced the gas tank. Gasoline dripped out onto the asphalt, flaming.

In all, her gunfire took two seconds.

Rita turned back around, grabbed the steering wheel with her left hand, wincing again, and stepped on the gas. They were at one end of several rows of parked cars separating them from the flea market. J.L. watched the gray car slow down and finally stop, trailing fire behind it. She held her breath, half-hoping the whole thing would explode. It did not.

Rita drove past the rows of parked cars, then by the first row of booths of the market. A grayish cloud started to billow out from beneath the hood of their car, bringing with it a smell of radiator steam mixed with burning rubber.

Shoppers and peddlers had either one of two reactions. Either they stood frozen, watching the shot-up vehicle limp by, or else they sprinted to their own cars. With each passing second, the latter option gained in popularity. Mothers and fathers scooped up children. Rita put her gun in her lap and began digging through her bag again.

When she spoke, it was through clenched teeth. "They'll

be back, just as soon as they hijack another car" she said, "and ours isn't going much farther. I'm going to give you the disc. Hold on to it or hide it or whatever."

J.L. wanted to protest but couldn't speak. They came to the end of the flea market rows. Rita stopped the car and handed the 3.5" disc to J.L.. Rita's thumbprint was left on its label in blood.

Rita turned to her and said, "Get out. Hide yourself. I'm going to lead these guys as far away from here as I can."

"What?"

"Get out!"

J.L. unbuckled her seat belt, opened her door and stumbled out. Almost before she could shut it again, Rita was moving. J.L. watched in amazement. So many bullet holes...The car made a loud metal-to-metal clanking noise as it drove off.

J.L. looked back down the row of booths. Dozens of people stood staring at her. Because she could think of nowhere else to hide the disc, she slipped it under the elastic band of her warm-up pants at her left ankle. Bending over almost made her pass out. When she straightened, her head pounded.

An engine roared in her direction, from back beyond the booths. The spectators turned their heads and looked for the source. Seconds later, a tan Chevy Blazer with a white top, jacked up a little higher than factory issue, appeared and flew past them all, chasing Rita's car.

Pray for Rita.

J.L. told herself that wasn't her thought. *Oh, great, I'm now coaching myself.*

Pray for Rita.

Definitely not her thinking. Her thinking at this moment would be more like one long, uninterrupted scream, not some calm, almost comforting, whisper to pray.

As she stood and watched Rita's car cut across the parking lot, in the direction of the stadium, she realized that she was not shaking. In fact, she felt strangely peaceful. *Peace-*

ful? Yes, as insane as it sounds, that's what I'm feeling.

For a moment, she drifted back to the hotel room that morning. She remembered being overwhelmed with the sense of the presence of her God. Then, it had made her realize how vulnerable and open she was before Him. Now, though, the same sense of His presence gave her strength, and peace. She figured that had to be the result of faith. Well, either that or mental illness.

She shut her eyes and began to pray as Rita's car disappeared behind the stadium, the Blazer very close. She didn't get much said before she was interrupted by rapid, staccato gunshots, followed by a squeal of tires and a loud crash, metal and glass in conflict.

It was a real struggle to keep from running across the parking lot to the stadium. Rita had asked her to hide, wanted her to wait. So she prayed some more and watched. She longed to see her friend's car come limping back...

The Blazer blasted out from behind the stadium and barreled directly at J.L.. She took off. She ran between the rows of booths.

The flea market was now a ghost town. The vendors had, of course, left their precious wares unattended. Something about that was almost funny. Bullets had a way of determining real value.

She looked back. The Chevy was closer than she would have ever guessed. Less than twenty feet, accelerating. She lurched to her right and ran between a booth selling sunglasses and one that was stacked high with coconuts. Then she passed by an awning that covered rack upon rack of T-shirts, and a fresh fruit stand. She heard tires screech behind her, then an enormous crash.

A coconut flew by her right shoulder, spraying milk.

The crashing lasted a couple of seconds, then left only the engine noise, revving up again. She glanced back as she ran. The grill of the Blazer dripped white liquid and had some orange peels sticking out of it. A day-glo green T-shirt was wrapped around the radio antennae, fluttering.

J.L. looked at the booths around her, panicking now. They were all flimsy, meant to stay up only hours at a time. None of them could provide any protection against the multiple-ton truck bearing down on her. Out of the corner of her eye, she spotted a booth featuring some televisions, VCR's and portable stereos. It wasn't great, but it was heavier than T-shirts. She ducked behind it and kept running.

Seconds later, she heard the crash she expected as the Blazer plowed through the electronics. Pieces and parts hurtled in all directions.

I'm going to die. My legs will give out, or my lungs, or something. Anyway, I'll have to stop a long time before that truck will. All things work together for good. That's what the Bible says...maybe it's better this way, really...

She ran by a booth that caught her eye because of the many flashes of reflected sunlight. The booth was filled with knives, spears, Japanese swords, martial arts supplies of every kind, stuff she had never seen except in movies--bad ones. She stopped.

She heard the truck's transmission shift into the passing gear. The passenger started to lean out his window, gun in hand.

On the booth's front counter was a small, black velvet display stand. Arrayed in an arch on the stand were about twenty Chinese throwing stars, six- and eight-pointed, star-shaped blades in various sizes and designs.

The truck's passenger loosed a burst of three rounds. J.L. winced, thought she felt something hum past her right ear.

In one motion, she swept the stand full of stars off the counter, onto the ground between the truck and herself, and she jumped as far as she could to her left, trying to roll on the scorching asphalt.

There was a smashing noise, then the *ping, ping, ping* of a rain of assorted knives and swords hitting the ground. The Blazer tore past her, barely missing her leg as she rolled. She forced herself to get up and start running again.

She looked over her shoulder. The truck's brake lights were on and it was swerving. She heard the repeated thumping of a flattened tire starting to unravel from the rim. Out of control, the Blazer went cleanly through the large open flap of a white tent emblazoned with the words, "Ahmed's Fine Imports: Hand-crafted rugs, tapestries". The truck hit the far end of the tent and drug it a yard or so before coming to a stop. The tent dislodged from its moorings and fluttered down over it.

J.L. turned away and, feeling strengthened, sprinted toward the stadium. When she crossed the hundred-or-so yards, she was winded. She entered the stadium's shadow and allowed herself another look back. The two men, both carrying guns, had made it a third of the way across the open space.

In front of her was a door labeled "Deliveries." Locked. She ran to her right, following the curve of the stadium. A closed ticket window, then an unlabelled door. It was also locked. She could hear footsteps behind her, though she could not see the men because of the building's curvature.

Then she came to an open arch. It was the entrance to a hallway that led toward the center of the stadium. It was dark, and as she ran into it, the slap of her tennis shoes echoed.

No light at the end of this tunnel. Appropriate.

The hard, heavy footsteps of men running behind her seconds later drowned out her own.

J.L. almost ran into the closed double doors at the hallway's end before she saw them. She fumbled for the handles. *Lord, I really need these to be open.* She tried them. They were unyielding.

Breathing hard, she whimpered a little and turned around. She tried to catch her breath. The men had stopped running, as if the game had ended. Funny, she thought, they're not so scary. The thought convinced her she had snapped. She was officially crazy. They looked like walking shadows against the bright sunlight at the hallway's entrance.

They strolled up to within ten feet. "Who do you work for?" asked the one on the right, with a heavy Asian accent. The question was repeated by the hallway's echo.

J.L. smirked and decided to tell the truth. "I haven't found a job yet."

The men's heads turned toward each other, then back to her.

"Where is the disc?" the other yelled.

"What disc?"

The disc! Tell us and you may live!"

"Oh, yeah...right...you've shot at me all this time, but now maybe you'll let me go...c'mon."

Her own voice shocked her. It was steady and defiant. She wondered where it had come from.

The one on the right lowered his gun. He said to the other,"Shoot her in the head and then we'll search her."

As if in slow motion, J.L. watched the other man nod then raise his gun in one hand, to the level of her forehead. The presence of God again seemed to descend on her, bringing with it an unexplainable sense of well-being and peace. It was all right if she died. She would get to see her unborn baby a little sooner than she'd thought, in Heaven, and that was good.

She recalled something she had read a few mornings ago. Its matter-of-fact sort of understated courage had struck her, and she had tried to memorize it. In the last letter of the Apostle Paul, he had written to his young disciple, Timothy, and was probably martyred a short time later. He said, "I know whom I have believed and am convinced that he is able to guard what I have entrusted to him." In that instant, she knew that Paul's words were true for her as well.

A flash of light, and the thunderclap of the gunshot was amplified several times by the walls of the hallway. J.L. blinked her eyes, fully expecting to open them in the awesome, brilliant presence of her Lord, but she was still in the dark hallway, now with ears ringing.

The man in front of her fell down without dramatics.

The other one whirled around, raising his weapon. There was another flash and thunderclap, and his arms flew over his head. He fell backwards and skidded a foot or so toward J.L.

She looked to the hallway's entrance and there, surrounded by its light, was the dark outline of another. Female.

"Rita!"

Rita fell to her knees and dropped her gun. Her shoulders slumped.

The two forms at J.L.'s feet were not moving. She stepped around them, not wanting to touch them at all. Then she ran to Rita.

She dropped to her knees beside her and put her arm around her. Rita slumped into her, nearly knocking her over. She lowered Rita's head gently into her lap. Now, in better light, J.L. could see that Rita's eyes had closed. She was covered in blood.

J.L.'s stomach churned when she realized that Rita had been shot in the neck and twice in the chest. Rita was breathing, but barely.

It came again, the quiet thought, not a voice, but a silent suggestion: *Pray for Rita.*

And she did. Then she cried, not able to believe the events that had led to this.

In three minutes, two police patrol cars arrived. The four officers exited their cars with guns drawn and pointed at J.L. She ignored them, praying and crying. They soon decided she was not a threat. An ambulance came and sped the women away.

Chapter Five

Mark stepped out of the CO's stateroom. The muscles high up in his shoulders relaxed, now that he was done with his private conversation with Commander Parnette. Paul Lawrence was standing there waiting for him, with his thumbs hooked in the pockets of his navy blue poopie suit. He rocked back and forth on his heels, grinning. Mark shut the door behind him.

Paul leaned forward and whispered, "What'd he tell you?"

Mark shrugged. "Ah, I'm sure it was the usual speech."

"Yeah, he's got 'em numbered and cataloged."

"You've heard a few of them?"

"All of them. Twice."

Paul motioned for Mark to follow him. "C'mon, I'll give you the nickel tour."

They stepped into the Control room, a space barely twenty feet across. In the middle of the room were the two periscope wells. Shiny metal shafts, upon which the scopes moved, came up through the deck and disappeared in the shadowy overhead. Behind them were two tables, at which a young man stood, plotting lines on maps.

At Mark's right as he walked in, there sat two men with their hands on black "steering wheels", eyes fixed intently on the panels in front of them. An older, heavier bald man sat behind them. He was leaning forward, forearms resting on the backs of the men's seats. A fourth man sat behind them all at a control panel against the port bulkhead.

Paul pointed at the men with the steering wheels. "These are the helms and planes."

No one looked away at Mark or Paul.

The bald man spoke over his shoulder, without taking his eyes off the panels. "Officer of the Deck. Passing six five zero feet."

Paul whispered, "That's Chief Ramsey--"

The Chief glanced over at Mark and nodded slightly.

"--he's the Diving Officer."

A tall man with shiny black hair and matching glasses stood in front of the periscope wells. He answered the Chief. "Very well. Go to five degrees down angle."

The Chief repeated the order verbatim. He then repeated it once more, this time directed to the planesman, who stammered through a verbatim repeat-back of his own. The young man began to pull his steering wheel toward his chest.

"Watch your bubble," scolded the Chief, "Slow down! Who you think you're racing?"

Paul walked up to the man who had given the order to change the boat's angle of descent.

"MM1 Reed, this is Lieutenant Commander Romero. He's the Navigator. Right now he's the Officer of the Deck."

Reed shook the man's hand.

"New lead ELT?" asked the officer.

"Yes, sir."

"Good. Welcome to *Omaha*."

"Thank you, sir. Glad to be here."

Chief Ramsey's voice interrupted them. "Officer of the Deck. Five degree down angle. Approaching seven, zero, zero feet."

"Very well," Romero said. He turned to Mark and said, "Excuse me, gentlemen."

He reached into the overhead, which resembled a nest of metal snakes, pipes that ran this way and that. He brought back what looked like a CB radio microphone. He clicked it on and said, "Cap'n, sir. Officer of the Deck. Coming to 700 feet."

"Very well," came the CO's voice, made tinny through the speaker.

The CO gave a short series of orders and Paul led Mark over to the starboard side of the space. It was taken up with a bank of four computer screens. They were turned off, with empty chairs in front of them. Paul opened his arms to encompass the whole group of machines.

"This," he said, "is Fire Control."

Mark nodded.

"When it's on, anyway. The screens give us torpedo tube and weapon status, stuff like that. Depending on what we're shooting, there's a few different ways to aim the weapons from here."

Paul tapped the top of one computer. "Except the Tomahawk missiles. They pretty much aim themselves--"

"Don't listen to him!" came a voice from behind the computers, which surprised Mark. The elliptical bulkhead, lined with its rows of silver metal pipes, curved behind the bank of machinery pretty tightly. It didn't look to leave much room.

But then, a little bald man, who didn't quite look old enough to be bald, stepped out from behind the computers, knees bent, hunched way over. He straightened up to a full five foot two or so and smiled up at Mark.

"Don't listen to him," he said again, "He's a short-timer. Heck, he didn't know squat about any of this when we gave him his dolphins. We all just felt sorry for him..."

Paul threw back his head and laughed. Then he play-punched the much smaller man in the upper arm, nearly knocking him over.

Paul had to reach out and grab the man's elbow to keep him upright. He laughed again and said, "Mark Reed, this old codger is SK1 Parmerlee. Been on the boat since it was commissioned, far as anyone knows. He's our Supply boss."

Mark shook his hand and they exchanged the usual greetings.

Parmerlee said, "Well, Mark, if you can remember two things as a Leading Petty Officer, we'll get along fine."

"All right. What're they?"

"Wait!" said Paul, holding up a hand. "Lemme guess, Parm. One is walk-thru's."

Parmerlee nodded and said, "Yeah, I hate it when people think *their* repair parts should take precedence over everyone else's. You need to stay on your Repair Parts Petty Officer. If he does his job right, you won't have any emergencies to deal with."

Paul looked stumped on the second one.

Parmerlee said, "The other one is my Supply lockers. They're all over the ship, even the engineroom. Don't mess with them. Any locker that says 'SK' on it, don't mess with it."

"Ah, he don't mean that," Paul said, "Any SK locker you can get into is extra storage space for you--"

Now Parmerlee put on a look of rage and began punching Paul in the arms and chest. The bigger man backed away, laughing almost hysterically.

Lieutenant Commander Romero cleared his throat. Mark looked over at him. The officer was clearly not amused.

Romero's voice was low and even. "Unless you gentlemen have business in Control..."

"All right, sir, we're on our way," said Paul, who led Mark out the aft end of the space.

MM2 Lawrence proceeded to give Mark what he called his 101-Things-That-Can-Destroy-The-Entire-Boat Tour. Each one, he said, was another reason he was glad to be getting out of the Navy soon. Two decks almost directly beneath Control was the Torpedo Room. *Omaha* was loaded heavily for their

Western Pacific run, a six month cruise known as a WestPac. The Torpedo Room was filled with long, green torpedoes on hydraulic transport skids, about a dozen in all.

"Mark 48 torpedoes," Paul said, "Supposedly, each one carries enough explosive to sink a Russian aircraft carrier."

Reed looked incredulous. He was, in fact. The Soviets had built some monsters during the Cold War, and these weapons really didn't look all that big.

Paul nodded, as if agreeing with Mark's doubts. "Yeah, it's hard to believe. Apparently, if we were to hit them in just the right spot, the carrier's hull would crack under its own weight. Sounds hokey if you ask me. Anyway, one of the drills we run is a Mark 48 Hotrun, where a torpedo gets stuck halfway out one of the tubes. Basically, if that happens, we're dead."

"Oh. Lovely," said Mark.

"Yeah."

Paul walked over to one of the hydraulic skids. Instead of a torpedo, a silver cylinder of the same length was stowed there. He patted it. He said, "Inside this Pringle's can is a Tomahawk missile. This one's not nuclear, of course. If it was, the NucWeps security guard would be emptying a .45 into my chest right about now."

Mark snickered.

"Tomahawks run on JP-5 jet fuel. Any of that stuff leaks out and the whole Torpedo Room goes up in flames."

"Ah."

Paul nodded. He then stamped his tennis-shoed foot on the deck and it sounded sort of hollow. "Under here is the ship's battery. If the ventilation system doesn't work right, the battery liberates gas during charging operations that can build up and explode. Back in '87 or '88, the USS *Bonefish* had a battery fire that killed three guys."

"No kidding. I think I heard about that in boot camp."

Paul walked to the control panel at the forward end of the Torpedo Room. Above it were three silver handles which corresponded to a row of lights. Paul pointed at these. "Hydraulic flood control valves," he said. "Someone calls away flooding in lower level forward, the Chief of the Watch up in Control automatically shuts these valves. These are manual controls, for opening them back up once the flooding has stopped."

Paul looked at Mark and asked, "You ever see a hydraulic system that didn't leak a little bit?"

Mark shook his head.

Paul said, "And you won't find one that doesn't around here, either. How's it feel to know that your submarine's first defense against flooding is a hydraulic system that could spring a leak any time?"

Mark just shook his head again. *Man!* The more he heard, the more the bulkheads seemed to squeeze in around him. He forced himself to take some deep breaths, and his right hand independently clutched his keychain horse.

They finally left the Torpedo Room. They headed aft, down a short passageway. Paul motioned to a closed door on the left, letting Mark know it led to First Class Berthing, where Reed's rack would likely be located. The smell of diesel fuel was stronger as they continued aft.

They stepped into the Machinery Space, or "Diesel". It was aptly named. In the center of the crowded room was a shining diesel engine, with a fresh coat of blue paint. Mark thought it looked as if a large tractor had made an organ donation to the Navy and its heart was now plugged in here.

"Ever hear of a run-away Diesel?" asked Paul as they looked at the silent engine.

Mark let out an exasperated breath. The-Thousand-Things-That-Could-Kill-Us-All Tour, or whatever, was starting to get to him. Mark nodded and said, "It's pretty rare. Throttle assembly goes haywire and the engine revs higher and higher until it finally explodes."

Paul said, "Right. We actually had it happen during an inport test...course the A-div Chief was able to trip the fuel racks off line, and it shut down on its own. That was Chief

Ramsey. Only time I ever saw him run."

Paul laughed, no doubt entertained afresh by the memory. Mark started to feel sick at his stomach.

Paul led him around the large engine to a metal device about four feet on every side. Its face was filled with glass dials, lights and switches. "The Oxygen Generator," he said. "This is how we make fresh air underway. We make distilled water back aft and pipe it up here. The O2 Generator uses electricity to split all the H20's into a bunch of H's and O's. We distribute the oxygen throughout the boat. Course, now you're talking about sizable amounts of pure oxygen and pure hydrogen."

Mark closed his eyes and muttered, "A bomb."

"Hey!" Paul said, laughing again. "How'd you know? You seen one before? 'Cause that's what it's called, The Bomb! That's pretty funny that you knew that."

Mark didn't think it was funny, not at all. Why don't they give guys The 90-Million-Ways-To-Die-On-A-Sub Tour, or whatever, *before* they ask you to volunteer for duty on one? The answer was obvious. Only fools would say yes afterwards. They hadn't even made it back to the Engineroom yet. Mark shook his head.

Without trying, he could come up with half a dozen things that could, conceivably, spell death or disaster in a nuclear power plant. Plus, the Engineroom was where the largest seawater systems were located. A large leak in any of them would mean major flooding and a probable loss of propulsion. Then there were the tanks filled with flammable lubricating oil for the main engines and turbine generators, not to mention the tanks of hydraulic oil, any one of which could function as the source for a very nasty fire, which would poison the enclosed atmosphere of a submerged sub and rob it of oxygen in seconds...

Mark blew out a breath and rubbed his eyes with the thumb and forefinger of one hand.

"Tired? We can go get some coffee if you want," Paul said.

"Yeah. That'd be good."

Up in Crew's Mess, Paul grabbed two coffee cups, white ceramic with a single blue stripe around the rim, from the drying racks located just inside the door to the galley. As he did, he yelled to someone Mark couldn't see. "Hey, Miller, what's for dinner?"

"Cheeseburgers," came the answer, absent of any enthusiasm.

"Dang! Are we ever going to have chicken again?"

"Not till Pearl Harbor, buddy. They didn't have chicken at Guam."

"What?" Paul asked, his face becoming more serious than Mark had yet seen.

"Yeah. We got milk and fruit and coffee filters. No chicken and no fish except frozen fish sticks."

"Dang!"

A frowning, slump-shouldered Paul Lawrence poured the cups of coffee and led Mark to the empty blue tables of the Mess. They sat down across from each other.

"You like the chicken, I guess," Mark said.

Paul shook his head and swallowed a sip of coffee. "Not really. It's just that chicken seems to go away pretty quick on a cruise. In a couple of weeks it's like you're having pork chops and potatoes three times a day. Pork chops and potatoes, pork chops and potatoes...the crazy thing is that they keep posting a menu! It's like, let's find a zillion different ways to tell the crew it's pork chops."

"And potatoes," Mark said.

"Yeah. The old man probably thinks it'd be bad for morale to show some honesty in the menu!"

They both laughed.

Mark said, "That kind of surprises me. I've always heard the sub fleet had the best food in the Navy."

"Oh, they do for the first two days of a cruise. When it turns bad, you're a couple hundred miles offshore and five hundred feet under water."

"Too late to complain."

"Uh-huh. Too late to swim back home."

Mark laughed again. "Well, that does it. My experience here is starting to shatter all the submarine propaganda I've ever heard."

Paul nodded strongly. "That's not the only one that ain't true. Like the one that says that only the cream of the Navy's crop makes it to subs."

"That's not true? I kind of believed that one."

Paul smirked and rolled his eyes. "Not even close. We've got some real winners here, I tell ya. This one kid, Yates, we were in the middle of the Pacific at about two hundred feet. Some guy wakes him up and says, 'Hey, Yates, your mom's on the phone in Control, wants to talk to you'...and he got up and went! Shows up in Control all groggy lookin', asking the Officer of the Deck which phone his mom's on!"

"Oh, no."

"Yeah. Real winners up here."

"I guess."

"Yeah. Another one is the one that says subs are filled with a bunch of flaming gay guys."

"I guess I hadn't heard that one, but I'm glad it's not right."

"Never heard that? You never heard that a sub goes down with 120 men and comes up with 60 couples?"

Mark shook his head.

"Well, it ain't true. Fact, this cap'n's got rid of about five gays in the last two years."

"No kidding."

"Yeah. Never mind about 'don't ask, don't tell'. Parnette won't put up with it."

"Wow."

"Yeah," Paul said, with some enthusiasm. "I heard one of 'em tried to argue with him at the mast. He was like, 'I was born like this. You can't kick me out because of how I was born!'"

"What'd the skipper say?"

Paul's face brightened, as if glad to be asked. When he

spoke for his CO, he straightened up and his voice was much deeper and forceful. "Captain looks at him and goes, 'Son, if you were born color-blind, you wouldn't be allowed on my boat. If you were born diabetic, you wouldn't be allowed on my boat. If you were born with the genetic tendency to consider yourself a chicken, you wouldn't be allowed on my boat. I do not have to allow you on my submarine with all your abnormalities just because you happened to be born that way.'"

"Wow...you're kidding me."

Paul shook his head, grinning. "Course, it remains to be seen who's gonna get the last laugh. I heard the guy went out searching for a lawyer so he could sue the Navy back to three-masted schooner days."

There was some silence, then Paul, his voice lower, even though they were alone, said, "Some people thought Liegert was gay."

Mark was stunned, didn't know what to say.

Paul nodded. "Maybe it had something to do with why he killed himself. I didn't see the note he left, but I heard his wife was going to leave him over it."

Mark nodded a little bit and said, "The captain told me the note said she was leaving because he had an affair."

"Well, I don't know. He never told me he was gay. I don't think he was. But he didn't hassle the guys that everybody knew was gay, y'know? That was different. So...I don't really want to say bad things about the guy now that he's dead, y'know?"

Mark nodded.

Paul went on, and his effort to smile was plain. "It's like, you don't know if maybe the Almighty ain't watching you saying bad things about the dead, y'know?"

Mark swallowed a sip and said, "Well, I don't think anyone's watching you except me."

Paul said, "Yeah. I guess."

They finished their coffee and Paul led him off in search of the Cob, to get Mark his own poopie suits and a rack to sleep in. As they walked, Mark's thoughts strayed to MM1 Liegert, a man he'd never met, and he found himself sympathizing with him.

Whether he'd had an affair, with a man or woman, didn't matter to him so much as the notion that Liegert had been in such despair over his relationship with his wife. She was going to leave him and he couldn't stand it, so he decided to kill himself rather than live with the pain. Mark wondered what that would be like, to be so in love with someone that death would be preferable to living apart from them. Was it even possible?

As they walked, he fished out his keys and looked at the carousel horse again. And he thought then of J.L. and imagined her face on the day they had married. Both images conjured up an aura of magic and fantasy.

Their wedding day. (Like being a little boy, barely more than a toddler, and climbing up, half horrified, on a gigantic, snarling carousel horse...) He remembered never really noticing the emerald green of her eyes *until their wedding day*. The wedding veil had not been able to dampen them. The very notion was ludicrous, like trying to hide flames under a tissue paper. As the minister spoke words, Mark ignored them, too fixated on J.L.. He realized he was obsessed with her, entranced by her, and he wondered if he was going insane over her. Mark had whispered to her that she was the most beautiful woman he had ever seen.

"You don't mean that," she'd responded out of the corner of her mouth, politely keeping her eyes focused on the man who was speaking.

"I do," he whispered. And he did.

Since that time, a lot of words had passed between them, mostly screamed by her at him, granted. He knew that both of them would like to take a lot of those words back, things said with the sole intention of causing pain. Ah, but words were simply sound waves generated by vibrating vocal chords. Those sound waves travel a certain distance and dissipate to nothing. Nothing to go back and grab onto.

The damage was done, like a house-fire several days old, still smoldering. Sometimes a building can be repaired after a fire, and then, other times there's nothing left to do but bulldoze the whole thing, take the insurance money, and run. And maybe there are times when, even if it could be rebuilt, it'd be better not to, because of the painful memories that linger way after the charred material had been replaced...say, for instance, like when a baby has died.

****

The day had gone by with unusual speed. Mark was a little amazed to look at his watch and see that it was 2230, or ten-thirty P.M.. He stood in a space known as First Class Berthing. Paul Lawrence had joked with him that the ride in First Class wasn't much better than in coach. Ostensibly, only E-6's, or First Class Petty Officers, were to bunk in First Class Berthing. Out of the twenty-seven available racks, however, five were occupied by Second Class Petty Officers, as Mark had seen when the Cob (Chief of the Boat) assigned him his.

First Class Berthing was dark except for the muted red "night-lights" in the bulkheads. The smell was dangerously close to that of a locker room. Blue coverall poopie suits hung on pegs outside about half the racks. Shoes were scattered on the floor. From several racks down, somebody was snoring ferociously. *Is that the MGM lion?* Mark laughed to himself and shook his head. The best he could hope for was to get into a shift rotation that had him on watch while this guy was sleeping.

Mark had wrestled his overstuffed green sea-bag full of belongings down from middle-level, where it had been stowed in the Ship's Office until the day's check-in process was completed. Now he stood in front of his new "home". Hopefully it was his anyway...it was too dark to read any of the numbers plated on the front of the rack. His was the middle of three, stacked on top of each other.

He stuck his hand past the blue curtain on the front of

the rack and fumbled for the light he knew would be there. Finally he clicked it on, a small fluorescent bulb. There was his military issue blue and white striped pillow and matching mattress. It was a little unnerving, how small the space was, much shorter and more narrow by far than his rack onboard the *Dixon*. The mattress was on top of the only storage space he would be given, called his "bedpan".

The mattress lid lifted up to reveal the empty compartment, about five inches deep, and as long and wide as the mattress, about two feet by six feet. He didn't know how his entire seabag full of stuff was going to fit in there. He took a deep breath and started unloading.

About a quarter of the way into the job, the door to the berthing space opened, letting in a lot of light and some conversation. It shut again and footsteps approached Mark's rack. He looked up and saw a man in a poopie suit. The man was over six feet tall, gigantic for submarine duty, requiring him to walk with his head bowed down. And he was very broad across the shoulders and chest. The man stuck out his right hand to Mark and whispered out of the darkness, "Are you MM1 Reed?"

Mark shook the hand, which seemed to engulf his own, and whispered back, "Yeah, I am. Who are you?"

"I'm MM2 Lorde. Jason."

"I'm Mark."

"Okay, Mark. Listen, I don't want to keep you awake all night. I had the joy of grading your Radiation Worker quiz. Surprise, surprise. You passed."

Mark snickered. "You mean I can have my own TLD, now?"

Lorde handed him the small black cylinder, a device for recording personal radiation dosage. "Better. You get to be in charge of the whole Radiation Monitoring program, Mr. Leading ELT."

"Nah, nah. The beauty of being in charge is that you get to delegate all those fun jobs to the poor slobs who work for you."

Jason laughed quietly. He said, "Just don't try to get Lawrence to do anything."

"I heard. He's the SNOB, right?"

"He's got short-timer's disease bad. Thinks he already don't have to do anything."

Lorde seemed to want to stay and talk. Although Mark ranked small-talk right up there with infected zits on his list of least favorite things, now he didn't mind. Lorde's unassuming manner was disarming, even as he asked all of the mandatory questions. *Where ya from? Sacramento? Really? I have cousins in Sacramento! Ya married? Got any kids? Really, one on the way?* Mark continued to unpack while answering. He brought a book out of his seabag that caught Lorde's attention.

"A Bible!" Jason's voice almost rose above a whisper. "Oh, man, don't tell me you're a Bible-thumper, please."

Mark hurried to reassure him. "No—no way—really. I guess my wife is, though, just recently. She's freaked out on Jesus. She packed this, wants me to read it, so I can get reborn like she is. Can you believe that baloney?"

Jason just shook his head. Mark shook his own head, too, and tossed the Bible to the very back corner of his bedpan. After some silence, Jason spoke again. "So what's the first order of business, there, boss?"

Mark had been thinking about it, but spoke as if planning his steps out loud in front of Jason. "Well, normally, I'd get a turnover from Liegert. Guess that's not going to happen…especially since I can't contact the Psychic Friends while we're underway. I suppose I need to review several months' worth of logs to get a feel for things. Definitely, I need to inventory the boat's Radioactive Material."

Jason started digging in his poopie-suit pockets. He produced a key and handed it to mark. "That reminds me. You're going to need a key to get into those RAM lockers. The Custody Log is in Nucleonics. Have you been there, yet?"

Mark took the key and nodded. Jason nodded back to him. He shifted his weight from one foot to other and spoke again, his voice lower, more cautious. He said, "I—I guess you know whose rack you got?"

Mark hadn't thought about it, but the answer was obvious. He smiled and said, "Uh, let me guess. MM1 Liegert."

"Yeah, that's right...I just didn't know if anyone had told you yet. I didn't know if you'd freak out about it or anything."

"Nah, that's okay. I'm not religious, and I'm not very superstitious either. Basically, as long as they took his dirty sheets and left his loose change, I'll be fine."

Jason laughed, a little nervously, maybe, then said goodnight and left.

I came to fill Liegert's shoes, Mark thought, *might as well sleep in his bed, too.*

****

In his dream, the man stood naked on the cold, silvery "diamond-deck" deckplates of Shaft Alley. He looked to his right and there was MM1 Liegert, hanging by the neck, very, very dead, stinking. The naked man heard heavy footsteps approaching and suddenly it was like his stomach was in his throat. Panic. He was going to get caught. The suicide note he'd written for Liegert was still in his hand.

He had to try and hide the man he'd killed.

Of course, that was ridiculous. The footsteps got insanely loud, like hammers clanging on an anvil.

Fog descended the ladder from Engineroom Upper Level. Then heavy black boots. It was MM1 Reed. Reed turned around and looked at him. He looked almost sad.

"God knows what you've done," Reed said.

"No, He doesn't. No one knows. And this is a dream."

Reed slowly shook his head. He had been holding something behind his back and now he brought it forward. It was an ax. Its head was dramatically curved, as big as two shovel blades.

"God knows," Reed said.

The naked man looked at Reed, who now wore the black, expressionless hood of a medieval executioner.

Then he noticed the engraving on the side of the ax blade. It said, "Vengeance is Mine."

The man managed to keep himself from screaming as he woke up. He threw the covers of his rack off himself and laid there for a time, sweating and breathing hard.

He couldn't live like this. Maybe he shouldn't. Maybe no one should live, period. The man calmed himself with the thought and smiled in the dark.

Chapter Six

Outrunning death. That's what it felt like.

J.L. barely remembered the ambulance ride. She had been on a gurney next to Rita, where a paramedic was bent over, working quickly and professionally. J.L.'s own eyesight had been blurry. Every few seconds, it seemed, the paramedic looked back over his shoulder at her. He was a native Hawaiian, with straight black, bushy hair brushed back and a tan J.L. guessed was perpetual. He looked comically out of place. J.L. wondered if he juggled flaming torches at luaus in the evenings, then scolded herself for thinking so stereotypically.

She would start to fade out, then he would say to her, "You still here, lady? I need you to stay with me, all right?"

Now she was on a bed in an emergency room. Someone had told her the name of the place, but she forgot it. She looked down at herself and saw that her tanktop had a two-inch wide path of drying blood on it that started at her left shoulder and went almost to the bottom of the shirt. Not to mention the random smudges of blood that were there from holding Rita.

In the confusion and rush of being wheeled into the hospital, J.L. had managed to let someone know she thought she was pregnant. They had taken blood from her right arm. A light had been shined in her eyes while a huge thumb had pushed her eyebrows toward the top of her head. A nurse in a pink smock had placed a bandage on her forehead, in the upper left corner, just below the hairline. They had moved her onto a cold metal table, told her they were going to X-ray her head. A heavy tarp had been draped over her midsection while they did. "Do you have pain anywhere other than your head, ma'am?" someone asked her. No, she didn't think so. She heard somebody mention shock.

Finally, she was put in bed and blankets were tucked in around her. A clear plastic mask was placed over her mouth and nose. The green elastic strap dug into the skin at the top of her ears.

She began to feel more like herself, although her emotions were still a tangled mess. She wondered about Rita. She tried to pray for her. She wondered if the whole mess at the Flea Market had really happened. Of course it had. Why else would she be here?

She looked down at her feet and wiggled them slowly. She could feel the computer disc still inside her pants-leg.

A tall blonde nurse came over to her and took her blood pressure. J.L. thought she looked very tough —very business-like. Around her neck, on a gold chain, was a small golden cross.

"Nice cross," J.L. said weakly.

"Thank you," said the nurse, and her tough face seemed to soften, "You like crosses?"

J.L. nodded.

The nurse adjusted the pillow under J.L.'s head and asked, "Are you a Christian?"

J.L. smiled and nodded again.

Now the nurse smiled, too, and whispered, "I've been praying for you and your friend since you got here."

"Rita...?"

The nurse's face became more serious, the business-like look again. "Your friend is hurt very badly. She's been taken into surgery. Her surgeon is very good. His name is John McDermott. You might want to pray for him, too. If everything goes well, it will probably take them several hours."

Tears welled up in J.L.'s eyes. Without thinking, she tried to blink them back. But, the more she blinked the faster they filled. They spilled over and began running down the edges of the mask she wore.

The nurse looked around and took hold of J.L.'s hand. Softly, she said, "I don't know why any of this has happened to you. But I do know God. And I've seen him do miracles in this very room. Any doctor or nurse who says differently is in denial."

The nurse smiled, and, for an instant, she was J.L.'s mother, tucking her into bed and telling her to have sweet dreams. J.L. nodded and tried to smile.

Two uniformed policemen walked up to the bed, their hats in their hands. The nurse nodded at them, patted J.L.'s hand once more, and walked away.

The police officers could have been brothers. They were both Asian and had roughly the same crew cut black hair. They were the same height, but one was thin and one was thick. The thin one's nametag said, "Phan" and the thick one's said, "Segura". Segura walked ahead of Phan and was trying too hard to smile. He called himself "Sergeant Mike" of the Honolulu P.D. and said he would like to ask J.L. a few questions.

J.L. nodded and tried to sit up a little. She wiped her tears away as best she could.

"We checked your identification, Mrs. Reed," Segura said, "Your husband's in the military?"

J.L. nodded. "Navy."

"Is he on the island?"

"No. He's at sea." As she said the words, she felt very uncomfortable, like she shouldn't be talking about Mark at all. She knew what their next question would be, and she struggled with how to answer it.

"Oh, really? Which ship is he on?"

"Well, he left on the *Dixon* out of San Diego, but he's got orders to go to the *Indianapolis* when he gets back," she said. It was true, without divulging the information that Mark had not wanted to give out over the phone.

Segura's eyes widened. "A sub! I was on the *USS Swordfish,* almost twenty years ago."

J.L. nodded. Segura pursed his lips a little before continuing. "I, um, I need you to try and tell me what happened at the Flea Market."

She took a deep breath, then started. "Rita and I were going to lunch--"

"Rita's the black woman who was with you when the police found you...?"

"Yes. I--"

"Um, do you happen to know Rita's last name? We've got some I.D. on her that says it's Kelly, but the computer is having a hard time matching that name to her Social Security Number..."

J.L. shook her head slowly and said, "Um, no, to be honest, I've only been in Hawaii a few weeks and we met in church...I just called her Rita."

"You were going to lunch."

"Yes, we--"

"Where?"

"I don't remember the name. Some Mexican place on the way to this mall."

"Which mall? Pearlridge Center? Ala Moana?"

"That's it."

"Ala Moana?"

"Yeah."

Segura turned to Phan. "What Mexican places are by Ala Moana?"

Phan looked surprised to have been brought into the conversation. He shrugged and said, "I dunno...there's the Burrito Barn..."

Segura looked back at J.L.. "Burrito Barn?"

"No. They served Shark Tacos--"

Segura's face lit up. He snapped his fingers and pointed at her. "Herve's!"

J.L. nodded.

"I knew it," Segura said, to himself, it seemed. He looked sideways back at Phan and muttered, "Burrito Barn!"

Phan shrugged again.

"Okay, Mrs. Reed, now we're getting somewhere," Segura said, "You're eating at Herve's Hacienda...then what happened?"

Before she could answer, a taller Asian man in a black suit and tie strode up to the officers. He held up a badge with his picture next to it. When he spoke, his accent was much thicker than Segura's. "Gentleman, I'm Special Agent Thomas Kim, FBI. I'm taking command of this investigation due to possible involvement of terrorist organizations pursuant to the Federal Code. I have briefed your watch captain, if you have any questions. That will be all, thank you."

Segura looked offended for a second, then shrugged his shoulders. The officers put on their hats and left. Agent Kim closed up the leather pouch that held his badge and watched them go. He turned around then and looked at J.L.. Although he was not terribly thin, his face was gaunt. The skin of his cheeks was sunken in, as if it was being sucked over his cheekbones. Heavy bags hung under his eyes. Where Segura had maybe tried too hard to be pleasant, Kim tried not at all.

"Mrs. Reed, how much do you know about your friend, Rita?" he asked while producing a notebook and pen from an inner jacket pocket.

Be sober and alert. She thought it was a Bible verse but couldn't remember chapter and verse. Something about agent Kim made her very nervous. "Not much, I guess. Today was only the third time I've ever been around her."

Kim nodded only slightly. "I know it's difficult to accept, Mrs. Reed, but we have reason to believe Rita Kelly is an undercover agent."

The little hairs on the nape of her neck were standing up. She looked down at her hands, and said, "She told me she worked at the Subase..."

"Yes, she does. We believe she may have been gathering intel at Squadron headquarters and feeding it to terrorist organizations overseas."

J.L. thought about Rita in the tunnel at the stadium, less than an hour ago. After shooting the men who were about to kill her, Rita had collapsed and passed out. J.L. remembered how she looked like she had just taken a shower in blood. She remembered seeing the horrible bullet hole in Rita's neck. She wondered what sort of determination, what kind of force of will it had taken for Rita to do what she had done before she faded out.

In that instant, J.L. knew that Kim was wrong. And she believed he was wrong on purpose.

****

The diesel submarine the Americans had code-named *Quiet Tiger* rose to periscope depth. Its control room was lit only by red lights, a trick submarines learned the hard way in World War II. At night, with a ship running as dark as possible, a single cigarette smoked by a lookout could be seen for miles, giving away its position.

Likewise, a submarine puts up a periscope, basically a tube with several mirrors inside it. Its control room is lit normally. The crew thinks, "what the heck, no one's going to see the light, we're underwater for Pete's sake!" But the periscope's mirrors reflect both ways. The man looking through it sees the darkness outside, but the light from the control room is also reflected up, for everyone on the surface to see.

Red light, however, can be spotted from only a fraction of the distance of normal white light. So Americans started "rigging for red" early on. It became standard sub procedure worldwide and remained so even after the advent of fiber-optic cameras.

Quiet Tiger's Captain scanned the horizon through the scope. To the east there was a large freighter, with full running lights on, easily seen against the night, too far away to be of concern, but nothing military was in sight.

He ordered the scope lowered. He gave the order to raise the snorkel mast, start the diesel engine, and commence battery charging operations. He also ordered his communications officer to receive radio traffic.

He read the messages later in his spartan stateroom. The Americans had responded. They were sending the USS *Omaha* to observe his boat's sea trials.

The U.S. Ambassador to South Korea was asking about a fishing troller; supposedly, one of its crew had some American relatives who were worried at having not heard from him in some time. Would South Korea please send out a search and rescue team? Yes, they would. The Captain smirked to himself.

The Americans had communicated nothing to the Japanese about *Quiet Tiger*. Of course, both the American and North Korean submarines had been acquired by the Line 87 net. The Japanese had not told the Americans about his boat, either.

Omaha would be in sonar range in sixteen hours.

Operation Blind Widow would commence upon his acknowledgment of receipt of orders.

The Captain extinguished a Chinese cigarette in a tin ashtray on his stateroom desk. They were really going to do it. A thrill rushed through him, moving from his stomach to the ends of his hair. He had to concentrate to keep his breathing even.

He would play his part. The Americans were responding exactly as predicted. They had swallowed all of the carefully portioned false intel for weeks, and now he would play his part.

Oh, his finger would not push the button, that much was true. That thought, although disheartening at times throughout the past months of planning this operation, was not enough to keep him from feeling giddy over the whole thing as he reread the transmission.

He rose from his chair to go to the Control room and give his radioman a message to send. He hesitated and closed his eyes. He could still remember the sound of his mother's voice and the smell of her clothes on the day that she died. It had taken her nearly two full days to bleed to death. He had been four years old.

Then he thought briefly of the man who should have, by all rights, been his father. That man had been shot to death a year before he was born.

He tried not to think about the other man. But he couldn't help it, and the old anger resurfaced as he envisioned the Japanese slime who had fathered him, or, rather, had impregnated his mother. It had taken him over half a century, but, now, he would have his retribution.

Part Two

"Your enemy prowls around like a lion, seeking someone to devour"

I Peter 5:8

Chapter Seven

"Then there were these two gunshots and the men were lying on the floor. I looked up and there was Rita at the tunnel entrance. She collapsed and was bleeding all over. Then the cops came and the ambulance..."

Agent Kim took a breath and nodded, scribbling something in his notebook.

"Still no indication why you were attacked?" he asked.

"No," J.L. said.

Kim took another deep breath and looked around them. Men and women in green or pink smocks rushed back and forth, mostly ignoring them.

"Did your friend ever say anything? Advance any theories?" Kim asked, looking back at J.L..

"I asked her if it was some drug thing, and she just laughed."

"Let's go back to the point where Rita dropped you off."

"Okay."

"Did she just leave you on your own with no instructions?"

"Right. Why?"

"Oh, nothing. Just seems a strange thing to do."

"Why's that?"

"Well, just seems like maybe she was abandoning you.

Is that what friends do?"

"Maybe she thought the men would follow her and leave me alone."

"Why?"

"I don't know."

Kim looked around again and back to J.L. He glanced at his notebook.

"Mrs. Reed, I must caution you. Rita Kelly will likely be charged with some very serious crimes if and when she recovers. If you know something about her that you are not...*remembering*, at the moment, there is a possibility that you could be charged as an accomplice."

"Accomplice to what?"

Kim's stare grew even more serious, his eyebrows wrinkling toward the center of his face. "Like an incident that took place at the Navy submarine base clinic this afternoon."

She held his gaze. She figured she had to. He was watching to see what her reaction would be, but she was not going to show it. Because what she wanted to do was scream. He was trying to scare her, but what she was feeling was more like revulsion.

She started to wonder how she was going to get away from Agent Kim.

Somehow, he knew exactly what had happened, from the time Rita had picked her up until now. She couldn't put a finger on why she thought that way, but it didn't matter. He knew it all. Rita was not a terrorist. He knew about the bomb that had kept them out of Subase. He knew what the two men with guns had been after. He knew about the disc. And he wanted it. But, did he know she had it?

"I'll get hold of you if I remember anything, Mr. Kim," she said slowly.

He finally looked away from her and flipped back a couple of pages in his notepad. "I didn't get your address, Mrs. Reed."

She thought about it. Did he know it already? "I don't have a place, yet. I'm staying at the Plaza Hotel."

"By the airport?"

"Yes."

Kim closed the notepad. J.L. noticed that he didn't write anything down.

****

Quiet Tiger's radio antennae surfaced from beneath the waters in the darkness. It transmitted a very short message.

The message was received at a radio facility high on a jungled mountain. From there, a phone call was placed to an office building in the North Korean capitol. A man there gave an order to a younger man who sat in front of a computer terminal.

He clicked the computer mouse on an icon that pictured a telephone. The computer dialed a long-distance number. The older man gave another short order back to the radio facility and hung up his phone.

The computer's phone call connected and a simulated ringing sound came through its speakers. The phone clicked and a voice answered in Japanese, "Yokosuka Water Utilities, how may I help you?"

The man at the computer moved the mouse so that the arrow on the screen pointed to an icon of a yellow "happy face". He double-clicked on it. The happy face became a window which prompted, "Run Blind Widow?" The man clicked on the "yes" block.

"Hello? Water Utilities...hello?" came the voice again.

The computer sent an electronic message along the phone line, completely inaudible.

In Yokosuka, Japan, the man who picked up the phone inside the Water Utilities building shrugged his tired shoulders. He hated the night shift. He hated phone calls where no one answered. At least have the decency to say, "Sorry, I got the wrong number!"

Still, it didn't sound like the phone had hung up on the other end. So he said, "Hello," once more and hung up. The computer message got through.

The Water Utilities building was next door to an unla-belled office building owned and operated by the Ministry of Civil Defense. Unknown to any Water Utilities workers, the Civil Defense offices shared their phone lines, at least physically, to make tracing their calls more difficult. Outside calls wanting to reach the Civil Defense offices had to be pref-aced by a four-digit access code, known only to some very high-ranking officials...supposedly. With this code, the Civil Defense phones would ring without disturbing Water Utili-ties.

The computer message, which had been delivered, lodged for a second or two in the main frame of the only Water Utilities computer which was set up for Internet access. That computer was left on, even during the night shift, when only two people were in the building, because every one of the city's potable water transfer pumps and wastewater lift stations was monitored and controlled from there.

The computer's screen-saver program was a slowly changing series of pictures of young Oriental women in bikini swim suits, lounging and smiling invitingly on sunny beaches. It was interrupted for a fraction of a second as the foreign elec-tronic message used the computer to transmit Civil Defense's access code.

Inside Civil Defense, the phone rang, but only once. Not even that...part of a single ring. The electronic binary code thus invaded the phone system and, for lack of a better word, twiddled its thumbs, waiting.

Back at the radio facility on the mountain, a codeword consisting of just two Korean characters was transmitted.

Several hundred miles north of *Quiet Tiger*, the radio message was received by another submarine hovering at peri-scope depth. Minutes later, it lowered its radio mast. Its cap-tain gave an order to descend to two-hundred-fifty meters and called for a bell of ahead flank.

Inside the Engine Control space, four loud bells rang in rapid succession. A young Korean man stood watch as the throttleman spun the silver wheel in front of him counter-clockwise. A hundred and seventy feet aft, a valve connected to that silver wheel by hydraulic linkages opened wide.

The Soviet-made submarine's twin engines were cross-connected for parallel unified operations, so each turbine sucked an equal amount of steam through the rapidly opening throttle valve. The increased flow of steam lowered the pressure in the plant's two steam generators, causing their temperatures to drop.

The steam generators were located just inside the shielding of the submarine's Reactor Space. As their temperatures went down, they made more of a demand on the reactor plant's coolant which flowed through them in bundles of finger thick tubes. As the coolant transferred more and more heat to the steam generators, its own temperature went down, from 540 degrees to just below 500. It became denser as it cooled.

When this dense coolant entered the reactor vessel, the more tightly packed water molecules encountered the randomly flying neutrons, liberated by the fission process, at a much greater frequency. These neutrons bounced off the water's hydrogen atoms and were redirected back into the fissioning fuel, where they went on to impact the bulky atoms of Uranium, initiating more fissions. This increased rate of fuel fissions caused temperatures inside the vessel to increase. Hotter coolant then flowed to the steam generators, which allowed them to keep up with the demand for steam.

This action/reaction process finally stabilized when the engine throttles were at one hundred percent and the gauge in the Engine Control space which monitored reactor power output read 120 Megawatts, enough to power the average American town, and then some.

The submarine traveled almost due east at close to fifty knots. It had gone less than ten miles when it entered the detection range of the Line 87 network. Inside the Civil Defense building in Yokosuka, Japan, a computer screen popped to life in automatic response.

The young employee of the Defense Ministry lazily rolled his office chair back from his desk and craned his neck to look at the screen.

The electronic message stopped twiddling its thumbs and ducked and wove its way into the Line 87 computer hard-drive. One by one, it gave up the codes and passwords necessary to bypass all of the security countermeasures. It took a couple of milliseconds.

The foreign binary code found its home, did its work, and "dissolved". It would be undetectable when the Line 87 computer went through its virus-checker protocol on its regular four-hour routine.

The computer screen developed a sonar image, and the image was accompanied by a series of groans, clicks and whistles. On a yellow backdrop, two pink silhouettes swam side by side.

The Civil Defense employee rolled his eyes. Whales. Ready to mate, no doubt. Sometimes he thought Worthy Wife was a little too good at her job. He sat up at the keyboard and punched in the short command. *Ignore the whales, Worthy Wife, thank you very much.*

Back in the office building in North Korea, the man in charge of the operation chewed on a nail and checked his watch. It had been half an hour. He ought to be hearing something by now--

The phone rang. He answered it. It was the specialist in Hong Kong. He listened. He nodded his head. He said thank you and hung up.

He smiled, spitting out a speck of his fingernail. Part One of the plan was complete, a grand success. He wished he had a drum to beat. *Worthy Wife is blinded*, he thought. *Time to make her a widow.*

****

Mark Reed crawled into the covers of his rack. He pulled the blue curtain shut, and stretched out on his back, looking up at the light fixture that shielded him from the direct glare of the bulb. It looked insanely close to the tip of his nose. *Rolling over in my sleep might be a luxury of the past.*

He turned his head away from the curtain and looked at the inside wall. Fake wood grain seems to be the style around here, he thought. Down by his knees there was a small door in the wall, about five inches square. A padlock was secured to its handle. A metal plate on the door said "SK 3-47A". Mark smiled, remembering Parmerlee's warning about his SK lockers, and Paul's joke about them being extra space.

He couldn't resist. He struggled to roll onto his hip and reached for the handle of the door. He almost laughed out loud when he found that, even with the lock in place, he could rotate the handle just enough--and the locker popped open. Straining, he reached inside and pulled out a plastic bag. He brought it up to his face. It contained a heavy silver metal box with a red and black wire sticking out of it and four gray bolts. He set that down and reached in the locker again.

This time he brought out a small spiral notebook with a blue cover, black pen stuck in the spiral binding. He opened it. On the first page, under the heading, March 12, there was neat handwriting in black ink. It read, "Ever since I got Mia's letter, I've been walking around feeling numb. I go through the motions. I keep saying to myself, *Can you believe it? She cheated on me! Can you believe it? We've got stuff to do. I don't care. I wish it would all go away...*"

Mark stopped reading. This was Liegert's old rack. When he died, he thought, the Masters-at-Arms from *Dixon* had surely come down and taken all of his personal effects off the ship, along with his body. Someone had come and stripped the rack. But why look for any of Liegert's things inside a locked storage locker? Especially inside an SK locker, he thought, in deference to Parmerlee. Well, it was obvious, they hadn't.

Mark looked at the notebook again. No names. It was certainly personal stuff, a journal or something. He thought about what he should do and the answer was pretty clear. He put the stuff back in the locker and shut it. He wasn't sup-posed to be in there, anyway. When they got back to Pearl Harbor, when things slowed down a bit, then maybe he'd manage to re-find it and hand it over immediately. Timed well, it could even be a good career move.

He laid back down and clicked off the light. The man who had been snoring so loudly earlier was still at it. Mark slowly shook his head and closed his eyes.

He thought about the notebook again. He wondered if it qualified as morbid, this undercurrent of desire he had, even now, to read it. Probably. But maybe not much more morbid than sleeping in the guy's rack.

Already, from the first page, there was something about the notebook that drew him. At the same time, he had a strong desire to stay away. Liegert was dealing with the fact that his wife had an affair. Neither one of them was appar-ently very faithful, then, according to the suicide note.

It made him uneasy. The dynamics of Liegert's mar-riage were not so unfamiliar to him after all. Mark had grown up with something similar. As a little boy, he had been able to sense the fact that his father was going to leave. It had been obvious to him for months. Those months had dragged by like an old, colonial winter, and he had been the sole, starv-ing Pilgrim, awaiting the thaw. It had actually come as some-thing of a relief when Dad finally got up the nerve to go.

Mark had not been able to jot down all his thoughts about the ordeal in a notebook. Psychologists were not rec-ommending that therapy for five year olds at the time. But he knew the process. It wasn't pretty.

Mark was inclined to let the notebook lay there. Not out of respect for the dead, but for the damaged.

Even though he found himself now identifying in small measure with the man, at the same time he knew that his sym-pathy for Liegert was evaporating. Liegert's suicide was all about survival of the fittest. Not a whole lot different than the nature shows, when a lioness takes down a slow wildebeest. The whole herd is a lot better off without the sick and the weak straggling along at its fringes. Liegert had made way for Mark, and things would be different. Mark knew he was stronger.

Before he drifted off, his thoughts wandered to his mother and his grandmother. Sad to say, they were weaklings, too. His mom never put up a fight when his father decided to leave them both. So then they had been stuck. They'd wound up having to move in with her mother. His grandmother raised him while his mom spent year after year as a waitress in a hotel restaurant. Grandma was another weakling. Everything she needed, she prayed to God for. He knew she worried about paying the bills and buying food. Even at seven or eight, those things bothered him. But she'd always retreat from reality and sing another chorus of "Amazing Grace."

By the time he entered High School, Mark had decided that if anyone wanted to know what God looked like, they ought to stare at a set of crutches, because that's what God was--a crutch. Mom and Grandma were weak. The crutches fit them. But he was different. He was strong, and he would walk on his own two legs.

Chapter Eight

Two muscular men in green camouflage uniforms walked past J.L.'s bed. They had pistols strapped to their belts and bright silver badges on their chests. She watched them stop a nurse for a moment. She pointed across the room to an older nurse. They walked over to her and talked with her. She spoke just a couple of words to them. They left and walked back across the room to a corner where there were blue elevator doors. One of them pressed the "up" arrow and they waited. J.L. was impressed with how straight they both stood and walked.

Agent Kim had left a few minutes ago. *He didn't seem very happy,* J.L. thought. *But that's okay. I'm not too happy myself. The only friend I have on the island is dying, maybe. Lord be with the doctor and give him full use of his skills and training. My husband is a world away, and not too long ago a couple of guys tried to kill me. So go ahead, Mr. Kim, and be unhappy.*

J.L. lay there and waited. She didn't know what she was waiting for, really. *Isn't that funny? They put an oxygen mask over my face, and I act like I'm chained down until someone decides to let me go.* Funny or not, it felt good to let someone else be in charge of when she should lay down and rest and when she should get up. Let the doctors decide. It's what they get paid for.

A man came over to her. His hospital ID showed a smiling face and the name, Dr. Richard Shickman. She couldn't

114

remember if she had seen him before or not. Probably she had. Who knew? He was a middle-aged man with what looked like a single layer of dark hair and jowls like a cartoon bulldog. "Mrs. Reed," he said. "Congratulations. You were right. You are pregnant."

J.L. closed her eyes. In a second, she recounted for herself all of the circumstances of her life at present. Was it a good thing now to hear the words "You are pregnant?" She didn't quite know why but the answer was, "Yes."

When she opened her eyes, she was smiling. The doctor smiled back. "I see that's good news. I'm glad. You'd be surprised how many young women act like I've sentenced them to death by torture when I tell them they're pregnant."

J.L. laughed and then so did he. "It is," she said, finally. "It is good news."

The doctor nodded and said, "The bad part is that now I'm restricted in what medications I can give you. That's something you need to remember from now on. Whatever goes in your mouth, goes in your baby's mouth, okay?"

She nodded.

"I'd give you some pain killers for your head if I could. Actually, you're not doing too bad. The bump on your head just broke the skin. There's no concussion. In fact..."

The doctor bent over her and started messing with the bandage on her head. She could smell him. *Why do all doctors smell the same? Dentists, too. But dentists smell different than doctors. Definitely.* Doctor Shickman had little black and gray hairs curling over the top of the collar of the white T-shirt he wore under his smock.

He straightened and said, "The laceration is a little less than one inch long and the bleeding has stopped. I can put a couple of stitches in there if you want, but I think you'd be fine with just a bandage."

"That's fine."

"Just a bandage?"

"Yeah. Thanks."

He nodded. "How are you feeling otherwise? Nauseated, trouble breathing?"

She shook her head. "I'm getting a little warm."

J.L. nodded to the blankets piled on top of her. The doctor felt her forehead with the back of his hand and put his stethoscope, draped over one shoulder, into his ears. He moved the covers down and put the end of the scope on J.L.'s chest for a few seconds. He nodded his head and put the scope back over his shoulder.

"I was a little concerned that you might have been going into shock. Your skin was cool and moist when you got here and your blood pressure wasn't doing too good. Human body's the darndest thing. We had a hang-glider pilot in here once. Dove off the mountains on the North Shore and his glider just collapsed. Guy fell like three hundred feet onto a beach. Broke his neck, arms and legs, punctured both lungs. He lived. Going through rehab, probably surprise us all and walk again. On the other hand, we had a guy, was cutting his lawn in sandals. Whacked off his big toe with a weed eater, nearly passes out at the sight of his own blood, stumbles inside and dials 9-1-1. They got a bandage on it, stopped the bleeding, but the guy freaked out, went into shock--and, bang!" said the doctor, snapping his fingers, "the guy dies in the ambulance right as it pulls up."

J.L. shook her head.

"Darndest thing," the doctor said. "Well, Mrs. Reed, since you're a military dependent, I shouldn't really be treating you anyway. And since you've just got a cut, and you seem like you're calmed down, I'm going to go ahead and release you. Okay?"

"Sounds good. Thank you, Doctor."

They made her sign her name to a form before they let her go. The nurse complained about the "ration" they were going to get from the Navy for treating one of their dependents in a civilian hospital. The bill wouldn't be paid without a Congressional hearing, according to the nurse, who, even though she was complaining, seemed nice enough.

J.L. found her way through the hospital from the ER desk to the main desk in the front lobby. She asked about Rita Kelly. She found out she was in Operating Room 2 and she got directions. When she got there, she saw the double white doors and the sign above them: "#2 OR", and the two muscular men in camouflage uniforms standing one on each side, feet shoulder-width apart, hands held behind their backs. One of them was black, and one was white. The black man smiled at her briefly and the white one nodded to her in acknowledgment.

She raised a hand a little higher than her waist and waved at them nervously. *That was dumb*, she thought. *Should've just said hi.* There was a small, empty waiting room across the hall from the operating room. She was about to go in there, but found herself walking up to the two men. The white man lowered his hands from behind his back and brought his feet together. When she was still ten feet away, he said, "Is there something I can do for you, ma'am?"

Something in the tone of it also seemed to say, "Please stop where you are, ma'am."

She stopped and rubbed her hands in front of her. "I was just going to ask you if you knew whether or not they were operating on Rita Kelly in there."

The white guy looked a little surprised. "Yes, ma'am. But you're not...*family* or anything...are you?"

The black guy smiled big. He looked like he was trying to keep from laughing.

"Well, no. Not family. She's my friend is all," J.L. said.

The white guy seemed aware of his partner trying not to laugh at him. He straightened up and said, "We've been sent on order of Admiral Crabb to keep all visitors away from Miss Kelly, ma'am. That's all I'm allowed to say."

J.L. nodded and began to back away. She asked, "I don't guess you've heard about how the operation's going, have you?"

"No ma'am."

"Okay. Thanks."

"You're welcome, ma'am."

She went into the waiting room and sat down. A television was mounted on the opposite wall. It's sound was turned down. She had to walk up to it to turn the volume up enough to hear.

She actually didn't notice what was on. It was just noise for her. She sat in the big chair all alone and rested her chin in her hand. She closed her eyes and prayed for Rita. In fact, Rita consumed her thoughts. *It's not even possible, is it?* She shook her head, providing her own answer. *There's no way Rita planted that bomb. If she did, would that mean that the guys who shot at her were the "good guys?" Why the heck would the good guys try to kill me? It was too ludicrous. Rita was one of the good guys.*

At some point, she noticed her legs were falling asleep. She got up to walk around a bit, which she did, but not without pain. She felt a bulky pressure on her ankle, and looked down. The disc. Later, she would think about simply handing the disc to the military guards and telling them the whole story. But, by that time, it would be too late.

****

J.L. had read every magazine in the waiting room and watched three consecutive reruns of "Happy Days" when she decided to change the channel. The first channel she turned to was a 24 hour news service.

There, under a caption that said, "Pearl Harbor, Hawaii, Earlier Today," was an aerial view, probably taken from a helicopter, of a parking lot surrounded by trees. A column of thick smoke rose from a crumpled mess of a car and people in white Navy uniforms ran back and forth. A fire engine was pulling into the parking lot, lights flashing.

"December 7th, 1941," came the voice of an unseen male anchorman. "That was the last time a bomb was unleashed against the United States Navy in Pearl Harbor. Until today, it seems. Those bombs fell from fighter planes of the aggressive Japanese Empire and brought about the beginning of American involvement in World War II and devastated the Navy.

"Latest reports say that *this* bomb, a car bomb, was detonated by a Korean-American named Kenneth Sung, a former employee of the Navy Exchange, apparently as an act of revenge and hatred. No one was killed in this bombing. However, if you'll look in the upper right portion of your screen, you will see the Navy's Branch Medical and Dental Clinic. Unconfirmed reports say that up to a dozen sailors and Marines received injuries ranging from lacerations to broken eardrums as a result of the blast."

The picture changed to a frontal of the anchorman, a thin man with perfectly set reddish-brown hair and a pair of reading glasses with gold frames. He held some papers in his hands, low enough to let his silk tie remain visible. He flashed a small smile and nodded seriously. Suddenly his face expressed solemnity — or grave concern.

"I'm Peter Sandage with today's ongoing story. A carbomb exploded in the Navy clinic's parking lot at about one o'clock Pacific Time. Almost immediately, Honolulu newspapers and radio stations began receiving calls claiming responsibility, most from radical Hawaiian separatist groups.

"Police, however, were suspicious of the validity of these claims. The car was traced and found to belong to a former manager of the Navy Exchange, a military-run discount store. When police and FBI agents arrived at Mr. Kenneth Sung's apartment, they found him dead, from an apparent self-inflicted gunshot wound. Although no word has been released about the presence or absence of a suicide note, the police have speculated publicly that Mr. Sung was despondent over the loss of his job and a recent divorce.

"Police also confirm that the Navy has been besieged by a rash of bomb threats.

"However, we have just received word of a new development in the story, and for this we go to Franklin Martinez on scene at Pearl Harbor. Franklin?"

The scene shifted again, and there was a large Hispanic man in a ridiculous blue Hawaiian flower print shirt and a red tie. He held a microphone in one hand. His other hand was up against his ear. A breeze was blowing his hair around as he stood on a sidewalk lined with full, green trees.

"Yes, Peter," he said. "I'm here just up the street from the Naval Medical and Dental Clinic where the bomb exploded. FBI and forensics specialists are still combing the area and have roped off a very large portion of it. I can look and see from here, every once in a while they will stop and very carefully lift something off the ground, or the street, and seal it in a plastic bag--"

"What's the new development, there, Franklin?" Peter asked.

"Right, Peter. I have been told, the press has been told, that there is apparently some evidence that Mr. Sung may have been in contact with the Communist Chinese government, possibly working as a spy here of some sort--"

"A spy!" Peter sounded like a kid on Christmas opening a present and liking what he saw.

"Yes, Peter. In fact, I'm now joined by Special Agent Kim of the FBI."

J.L. sat up and her mouth dropped open as Agent Kim moved into view and stood beside Franklin Martinez.

"Agent Kim, please, if you will..." Franklin said, shoving his microphone roughly under Kim's chin.

"Um, yes. When something of this nature happens, of course you hope that it is the work of a single deranged individual. Unfortunately, we have come across some documents owned by the late Mr. Sung which indicate that he may not have acted alone, and that there were plans to detonate a similar bomb at Philadelphia Cove."

Franklin's face contorted into a mask of confusion. He pulled back the microphone and said, "Philadelphia? Philadelphia Cove? Agent Kim, I grew up on this island and have never heard of a place called Philadelphia Cove."

Kim nodded with sympathetic understanding and said, "Philadelphia Cove is a code-name for a particularly important weapons loading bay here on Oahu...however, this operation was still in the planning stages."

Franklin smiled and hogged the mike again. "So, no more bombs today, then?"

Kim tried to smile. "No. No, I don't think so."

"Agent Kim, I believe you were saying you had a picture for us? One of the suspects involved in the bombing?"

"That's right. We have a few eyewitnesses of the bombing here and an incident involving a lot of gunfire a little later in Pearl City in which two men were killed. We have faxed a composite drawing to all local and national news media, as well as airports and hotels in the area."

The view shifted back to Peter in the studio. He said, "Ladies and gentlemen, this picture comes to us from the FBI. It is suspected that this person was involved in terrorist activity earlier today in Pearl Harbor, Hawaii. Okay? Let's see it."

J.L. almost fainted. It was her face.

Chapter Nine

Mark Reed dreamed. Being jolted awake by an unfamiliar voice calling his name made the dream hard to remember. There was only one image he recalled. Other than that, it was all just emotion and feeling, tough stuff to keep a hold on as you're waking up.

The image was of J.L., dressed for summer, standing on the sidewalk. She was wearing a white sleeveless shirt and the golden curls of her hair blazed with a sort of metallic fire in the sunlight. She held his baby, a girl apparently, in a pink blanket, its head resting in the crook of her left arm. J.L. was saying good-bye. The thing that haunted him about the image was the smile on her face. He knew his wife was strong and independent, a prerequisite for a Navy wife, certainly...but this smile went beyond that. This smile said, "Mark, I love you, but we really *will* be better off when you're gone."

Then there had come the whisper. "Psst. Um, Petty Officer Reed...Petty Officer Reed?"

Mark realized with some confusion that the whisper was not part of the dream and he struggled out of it. He woke up in the darkness of his rack, to the dirty-socks smell of the berthing space.

"Petty Officer Reed," came the insistent whisper again.

Reed snatched aside the curtain that enclosed his rack. A shadowy form stood close enough to touch with his elbow, had he wanted to. "Yeah?" Mark said.

"Um, sorry to wake you up, Reed...welcome to the sub fleet...the Officer of the Deck wants you up in Control."

Mark felt like he had just gone to sleep. "No kidding? Is my mom on the phone up there?"

"Huh?...Your mom...?"

"Never mind. It's a joke I heard. I'll be right there."

The shadowy figure walked away. The door to berthing opened, letting in light momentarily, then shut. Mark thrust his left arm outside his rack, where it came under the red light of one of the "night-lights" in the bulkhead. He looked at his wristwatch in that light. He had been in his rack for an hour and five minutes.

He walked into the Control space after getting on his poopie suit and some shoes. The current Officer of the Deck was his department head, the Engineer, Lt. Commander Bushler. He was one of the few officers that Paul had introduced without offering snide comments about him after they had left. Paul had said Mr. Bushler was "the real deal." The Navy would like everyone to believe that each of its officers was as smart as Mr. Bushler. Mark's first impression of him had not contradicted that analysis.

The Engineer was a soft-spoken man. He nodded a lot in place of the word, "yes." Bushler knew he was brilliant, Mark guessed, and believed you'd come to understand that too, eventually, so he didn't have to try and prove anything.

The Engineer was standing in the forward starboard corner of Control, looking at a computer screen mounted about six and a half feet off the deck. The screen displayed the rippled, vertical rows of green computer light which formed the visual representation of whatever the sub's passive sonar system was hearing.

After a few seconds, he lowered his gaze and looked toward Mark. Reed wasn't sure he'd been noticed, but then the Engineer motioned to him slightly. Reed went.

Mr. Bushler was about to speak to him when the Diving Officer, a chief Mark hadn't met, announced, "Officer of the

Deck, my depth is one-five-zero feet, zero bubble."

With all the apparent thought of someone ordering lunch from a drive-up window, Bushler said, "Very well. Chief of the Watch, to Maneuvering, make turns for five knots."

The Chief of the Watch, a black man who sat facing the port wall, answered without looking back. "To Maneuvering, make turns for five knots, aye. Starting the trim pump."

He flipped a black switch on his control panel and a green light came on next to it.

"Very well," Bushler said in a low monotone. He turned back to Mark.

"Petty Officer Reed, I woke you up because we're about to perform an infrequent evolution which you are going to be required to observe for your submarine qualifications. If you don't get it done now, it may be some time before you get another opportunity."

"Oh, no problem, sir. I appreciate it. What are we doing?"

"Petty Officer Gulledge will escort you," Bushler said, turning away from Mark and motioning to a thin kid in thick glasses, who grinned and waved.

It was apparent the conversation with the Engineer was over. Mark might have been offended had he not still been so sleepy. He marched off after Gulledge.

Gulledge took him down to the middle level, down the longest passageway in the sub, unimaginatively known as the Middle Level Passageway. They went through a door labeled "Crew's Berthing," into the dark, where they confronted a much worse smell than First Class Berthing. Gulledge had a small flashlight attached to his belt and he turned it on, cupping a hand over it to muffle the glare.

As they walked toward the forward end, between the racks stacked three high, brushing past hanging poopie suits and accidentally kicking shoes around, Gulledge whispered over his shoulder, "Have you heard of a Telescoping Array?"

"Huh-uh."

"It's basically just a sonar buoy attached to a retractable arm that comes out of the nose of the boat."

"Nope, never heard of it."

They came to a bulkhead at the end of the rows of racks.

"This is as far forward as you can go, at least when we're underway. In dry-dock, we have to actually go inside the nose-cone for maintenance," Gulledge said. He turned off his flashlight and flipped a switch on the bulkhead. A bright white light shone straight down from the overhead.

From the bottom rack at Mark's feet, a blue curtain jerked back. A crew-cut head with eyes squinting against the light came out and faced them. The head said, "What the heck, Gulledge?"

"Sorry, Joe," Gulledge said. "We're scoping in a few minutes."

"Oh," the head said, and returned out of sight. The curtain closed behind it.

Gulledge squatted down and opened a square "lid" in the deck. Mark joined him. Inside the exposed space was a black metal cylinder about six inches in diameter which looked to extend horizontally both forward and aft. Gulledge pushed a button next to the cylinder and a small screen lit up with three digital zeroes in a row.

There was also a sound-powered phone in the recessed space. Gulledge picked it up and spoke into it. "Control. Scoping Array. Phone Check."

Mark couldn't hear the response, of course, but Gulledge nodded and then said, "Control. Scoping Array. Scoping Array manned for deployment."

Gulledge lowered the phone and looked at Mark. "It'll be a little bit," he said. "We have to rig for ultra-quiet."

"What's that mean?"

"Oh, just that we're going to do our best not to make noise. Any maintenance that involves moving tools around has to stop. They shift all the equipment they can to slow speed or reduced frequency. They get people back aft to man the phones so no shipwide announcements have to be made.

That sort of thing."

"So...is this array thing better than regular sonar or what? Why do this?"

"It's better. And worse. See, the scope goes out two hundred feet. The arm it's on consists of about two dozen sound-silencing joints. Then, once they energize the array, " Gulledge said, bringing his hands together as if cupping an imaginary basketball, "the buoy itself sits inside this magnetic cage, see, that lets water flow through it. When they turn it on, the magnets fire up and suspend the buoy so that it's not in contact with the arm at all."

"No kidding."

"Yeah. So, while it's suspended like that, you can get some really long-range images and you get to take these sonar snapshots of your own submarine from the outside. It lets us check ourselves for sound-shorts and noisemakers before we head into some place where we know we're going to want to be really silent."

The phone squawked. Gulledge answered it. "Scoping Array."

Gulledge paused, listening, then said, "Deployment of Scoping Array started, aye."

Gulledge pointed at the row of three zeroes. They were not zeroes anymore. The number clicked up, showing the progress of the Array's deployment, at about five feet per second.

Gulledge put a hand over the mouthpiece of the phone and said, "We're just here in case."

"In case what?"

"In case the arm breaks or something." Gulledge pointed to a red button on the side of the cylinder. "That's the emergency release. If it gets stuck, we can't do much about it except let it go. Million dollars down the drain."

"Wow. That's not good."

"Eh...no big deal. They take it out of the Cap'n's pay." Mark smiled.

Gulledge said, "That's why we don't use it much. You

have to stay at a certain depth and you can't go over seven knots. Sometimes even a bad current can damage it."

"Too high tech to use very often?"

"Something like that."

When the Scoping Array's digital indicator read, "1-9-9" Gulledge said, "That's as far as it goes. Since the first time we deployed it, it's never gone the full two hundred."

Gulledge led Mark back up to Control and turned him over to Mr. Bushler. Again, the Engineer had little to say, and Mark left shortly, noting that he only had three hours left until he was supposed to meet MM2 Lorde in Engineroom Upper Level, where Mark would begin standing watches "under instruction" as the Engineroom Supervisor.

****

The man who killed Petty Officer Liegert sat in the space called Nucleonics. It was the laboratory for the reactor plant; a four foot by six foot enclosure almost completely made of stainless steel. One continuous steel countertop circled the space at waist-level, taking more than twenty square feet of room. This countertop combined with shelves and cabinets of steel, peppered with yellow and magenta trifoil warning labels, to leave the human occupant precisely enough room to turn around.

He had locked himself in and now sat on the one stool, his arms resting on the counter in front of him. He stared straight ahead. That's what it looked like anyway. In reality, his gaze was directed backward. It was a waking dream, one that he had on occasion. More frequently on this Westpac. He had hoped that doing away with Liegert might stop these episodes.

For a while it seemed to work. Now they were back, with an intensity and a sense of horrible reality that they had lacked before. Even though the air conditioning in the enclosed space kept the room in the low sixties, sweat was breaking out on his forehead and around his temples as he saw…and remembered.

There was Mom. He was six, and she was drunk out of her mind. Her eyes glassy, watery, a stupid, senseless grin on her face as she ignored him and sung with the radio.

"I'm hungry, Momma."

He had to repeat it three times. The song was over and she finally heard him.

She was irritated. She didn't want to hear it from him. Was it her job to put food in his little, stupid mouth? Is that why she existed? Hadn't she breast fed him for three years? And now he still wants her to feed him? Didn't he just eat yesterday? Now, shhh! Shut up! This is my favorite song. Go on. Get out of here!

He walked slowly to his bedroom. Hands balled up in fists. Whole face and ears felt on fire, tears seeming to fly out, not just fall. He was unable to say anything. He shook all over. When he did speak, it was a hiss through clenched teeth that blasted spit everywhere. "I hate her. I hate her!" Then a new thought. "*Die! Die! Die!*"

Dad wasn't home yet. So he waited and seethed in his room. Hours passed. He couldn't hear Mom anymore. Just the radio, the sad country music she loved. At some point, he had thought about pouring himself a bowl of cereal, but… there was something about his rage. Something almost sustaining about it. He wasn't hungry anymore.

More hours, and the sun went down. The radio station's FCC license curtailed its signal strength after sunset, so the music stopped.

He left his room. No lights were on in the house. Only the sound of the radio static was present. *Mom?* There was no answer. He found her on the bathroom floor. She was there in her underwear. The medicine cabinet was open. Bottles and pills were scattered all over the floor. He had thought she was dead.

She opened her eyes, halfway. She looked very sleepy and very scared, all at once. She raised her hand toward him, but it fell back down. She said his name, slurred.

"Call...the police...you've got to call...police." Tears
ran down her face. She whispered his name and cried,
"Please...I've done something...really stupid...you've got to
call..."

He stood there, motionless. His wish for her death was
coming true. It had been a prayer, really, and God had heard
him and was pleased.

She tried to get angry but lacked the strength. He left.
He passed by the telephone in the living room and left it sitting in its cradle. He went into the kitchen with a profound
sense of calm and satisfaction. He made himself a peanut
butter sandwich. While he did, he could hear her. Every once
in a while, she called to him. Vomiting once. Moaning. Calling.

He took his sandwich and walked outside. The sunset
was gorgeous and he distinctly remembered looking at his
hands in its light. They seemed to glow orange with the glory
of God.

He went to the backyard and sat in the single swing.
The bathroom window faced the yard. Now the sounds she
made were muffled. It got dark and she stopped calling.

From there it blurred. Dad driving up, turning off his
headlights. The door opening. Dad screaming, calling out his
name in a panic. The police, the ambulance, the sirens, lights,
the hurrying around. Standing at the edge of her grave days
later in a little suit and tie. Knowing right there, at six years
old, that God had given him power over his Mom's life.

He had enjoyed it, and he had been thankful.

****

Kevin Bushler leaned over the charts at the Quartermaster's table at the aft end of the Control space. The Diving
Officer continued to make reports to him, which he continued to acknowledge in a "ho-hum" sort of way. Oh, he heard
them all, and he cataloged them in his brain, somewhere, but
they were not his priority. The maps were. The maps and the

radio message traffic he held in his hands.

There was *Omaha* on the map, to the south and west of the southern end of Japan. And there, a couple of inches north, was the spot where they anticipated interception of *Quiet Tiger*. Well and good.

What bugged him was the message that military satellite recon had picked up two North Korean cruisers leaving their national waters under heavy steam and heading almost due east, toward Japan.

The last time *Omaha* had come out of a shipyard period, to go on sea trials, three surface ships escorted them. Of course, had *Omaha* had some terrible accident during submerged ops, there was precious little their "skimmer" escorts could do for them, except maybe mark the spot where they went down, just so that any later memorial structure would be placed accurately. Still, it was a nice gesture, a *routine* gesture. And, granted, we're talking about a radically different culture with the North Koreans, and a navy with much more limited resources. Still, *Quiet Tiger* had no skimmer entourage, and it bugged him.

And why had the American surveillance/"fishing" boat apparently met with an inglorious end? Bushler looked at the spot where they would meet *Quiet Tiger*, and the place where the North Korean skimmers were running, a good distance away...and it bugged him.

With reluctance, and some concern over exactly what he would say, Lt. Commander Bushler decided to have the Captain wakened.

The Captain came out a few minutes later, still in his khaki uniform. He owned no poopie suits —on purpose. He always stood out from the rest of the blue-clad crew that way. He talked with Lt. Commander Bushler over the QM table and the maps. No one was allowed to stand close enough to them to hear their conversation. They seemed to argue, then began to agree.

The Captain sent the lowly Messenger of the Watch, an eighteen-year-old, to wake up the XO, Mr. Shelby. Shelby joined their conversation after several minutes.

Finally, they broke up, like football players coming out of a huddle. The Officer of the Deck ordered the Scoping Array retracted and stowed.

The Captain then nodded to him. Mr. Bushler said, "Chief of the Watch. Man Battlestations."

The order was acknowledged and the alarm was sounded.

****

Mark had just crawled back into his rack when the 1MC blared, "Man Battlestations!"

He immediately heard the sound of naked or sock-clad feet slapping down on the tile of the deck around him and the lights came on. He hauled himself out of his rack as well and put his poopie suit and shoes back on. Mostly, he tried to stay out of the way. The men around him all knew what they were doing and where they were going. He did not, not yet having been assigned a spot or duty during events such as Battlestations.

Everyone ran out ahead of him. He walked up to Crew's Mess. About twenty men sat at the tables there, a comical bunch. None of them quite had their eyes fully open. Several heads featured hair flying in haphazard directions. Yawns were plentiful. He heard a couple of them ask, "What's this about?" No one had an answer.

A very large guy sat at a table, eyes red and drooping. The white stencil lettering above his left breast pocket said, "Lorde". Mark grinned a little and sat down across from him.

"Jason?" Mark asked.

The big man looked up at him. "Ah, MM1 Reed."

"Yeah. You look different in the light."

"Yeah. You look better, too."

Mark smiled. "I didn't say you looked better."

Jason snickered and nodded his head.

"Jason..."

"Yeah?"

"Why in the world are we at Battlestations at this time of the night?"

Jason shrugged his shoulders. "Either we're being shot at or the old man just wanted to make sure everyone was awake so he could talk to us."

Mark nodded.

About a minute passed, and then Parnette's voice came over the 1MC. "This is the Captain. If I could have your attention for just a moment."

Jason motioned to the overhead with one upraised palm as if to show Mark, "What'd I tell ya?"

"We are approaching our designated target area where we are scheduled to intercept the North Korean submarine I briefed you all about. Some satellite pictures we have received have given us reason to suspect that its sea trials may not go the way we thought. Our plan is to continue on and monitor the North Korean just long enough to ascertain what the real nature of the situation is; then we may head North to take a look at some naval maneuvers the North Koreans are conducting up there.

"We are nearing the zone of our original operation, so the plan is still to conduct a few drills on the morning watch, charge the battery and empty our tanks. We should get quiet around noon and stay that way for four and a half weeks.

"By the way, Battlestations was set in two minutes, two seconds. That's not bad, but we need to do better. I apologize for the hour of this announcement, gentlemen, but I figured, if I have to be up, the rest of you should darn well lose sleep, too."

The men in Crew's Mess generally all laughed and shook their heads. The Captain went on. "Secure from Battlestations drill."

Jason and the rest of the men in Crew's Mess lumbered to their feet and began dragging back toward their racks. Jason muttered as he left, "Gee, thanks, Captain. My life is greatly enriched because of this."

Mark checked his watch again. Was it worth going back to his rack for just a couple of hours of sleep? Probably not, he conceded to himself. He went anyway.

****

The telephone was answered and a voice came back. A young man said, in a British accent, "Empress Hotel. May I help you?"

Agent Kim said, "Room 209."

"One moment, please."

As the phone rang, Agent Kim thought ahead to the day when Hong Kong would revert back into Chinese control. No more British accents from hotel employees. He smiled at the prospect and wondered vaguely if the Blind Widow operation would change the politics between China and England enough to interrupt that. He didn't get to continue the thought. The phone was picked up.

"Hello?"

"Kim."

"Wait."

Kim waited. A series of buzzings and clicks, much like the sound of a fax machine, came from the room in Hong Kong. Kim smiled and shook his head. This guy was good. He probably could've demanded more money to betray his country. He'd have been worth it.

"Okay. The line's clear," came the voice of Reggie Nelson.

"Listen," said Kim, "we've got a minor situation over here."

"What kind? How minor?"

"Sung and Kelly."

"What about them?"

"Sung had the whole thing."

"What? How?"

"Don't know how, yet. A hooker in Waipahu, maybe.

It leaked, okay? Nothing like Blind Widow is gonna go off with zero leaks, you know that."

The man in the Empress in Hong Kong cursed softly.

Kim said, "We got Sung."

"Dead?"

"Yes. But he was in contact with Major Kelly when we found him."

"What does she know?"

Kim forced himself to laugh a little bit. It would put the Hong Kong man at ease, hopefully. "It doesn't matter. She won't ever talk again."

"Sheesh! You killed Kelly, too?"

"Not yet, but she's shot up pretty good. Still in surgery. If we're lucky, she'll die on the table."   Kim took a breath. "That's not the end of it, though. Kelly made a disc. We have no way of knowing how much is on it."

"Where?"

"I don't know. We had her car bugged but that wound up being useless to us."

"Oh...you're kidding. Tell me you're kidding me."

"Stuff like that happens. You know this. Why am I telling you this?"

"Okay, okay...we know nothing. So now what?"

"So, I'm thinking she's given the disc to another girl, a civilian. A Navy wife."

"You're kidding. Are you kidding me?"

"Shut up! Are you going to freak out here? Do I need to give Lee a call or what?"

The man's voice came back, lowered an octave or two, much more even. "I'm fine. So now what?"

"I've handled it. I've spoken to her. She's not saying anything. She's scared to death."

"You've spoken to her? Why haven't you killed her?"

Kim shook his head. Maybe this guy was being paid too much after all. "I might remind you, I'm an FBI agent. Generally, we are not supposed to go around shooting Navy wives for no good reason, especially not in the Emergency

Room of the largest hospital in Honolulu."

"Well...get the Lum brothers to do it. That's what they're there for, isn't--"

"Shut up, you idiot! The Lums are dead."

"Wha...? You're kidding me."

"Shut up. I've got the situation under control. The whole island thinks she's a domestic terrorist, now. If she shows her face, the police will snap her up. If she's got the disc when they do, they know to turn that over to me immediately."

"Yeah? Why didn't you just arrest her there?"

"Because all we need is for her to call an attorney who wants to get his face on the news channels. This island is crawling with Hawaiian separatist groups who'd like nothing better than to cast aspersions on a federal agency, especially the FBI...listen, I spoke to her. She is young, and weak and scared. If she shows her face, we've got her. If she hides, even better. We only need her to stay down for two days. Then, who cares whether or not she has the disc or what it says?"

"Yeah. I guess so."

"Of course. Now just pass the message on. Bottom line, we are still green on Blind Widow over here. Okay?"

"Yeah..."

"Okay?!"

"Yeah! Okay, okay. You're the fed. Okay."

Kim hung up the phone in police headquarters, Honolulu. He checked his watch. Time to go pay Mrs. Reed another visit.

Chapter Ten

The small-framed woman with short, brown hair skulked around the corner, her back to the bulkhead. She held her pistol pointed up, next to her cheek. The beads of sweat on her face reflected the blinking, red lights around her. The sound of her breathing seemed to fill the place, just a notch or two below outright panic. After a few seconds of staring down the dark passageway, she apparently decided the coast was clear and moved forward slowly, almost tiptoeing.

She had gone a few feet when a pipe running along the floor of the passage sprung a leak behind her. An angry plume of white steam shot up and formed a large cloud. She screamed a little, whirling around at the noise, her gun extended in both hands.

Predictably, painfully so, it was then, as she was lowering the weapon and almost laughing at the steam, that something began to uncoil itself from the tangle of pipes and electric conduits in the dark overhead. Its first tentacles lowered without a sound to the deck, just over her shoulder, followed by its spiny, scaly eight-foot tall body, topped with a head crowded with spikes and fangs.

Had she heard it? No, but her expression made it plain that she sensed it. Her slumping shoulders straightened. Her lips were pursed tight. Her eyes strained to see over her shoulder while her head stayed facing forward.

The woman drew in a breath and screamed. Not a

scream of terror; more like a battle cry. She spun around, again extending the gun, and pulled the trigger. Red blasts of sparkling energy flew from her pistol, making a noise that combined thunder with an electronic screech. In rapid succession, the blasts impacted on the monster's torso and produced a Fourth of July spray of white sparks, and dark pieces and parts that J.L. guessed were supposed to be chunks of the evil creature.

Some people in the theater cheered. J.L. was not one of them.

She sat against a wall, toward the back, as far away from everyone else as she was able. The closest people were a teenage boy and girl, sitting in the last row. They had been about as engrossed in The Outpost as J.L., which was not much at all. The movie had attracted only about half a housefull. It was not J.L.'s typical cinematic choice. In fact, she had chosen it out of the three playing at Waikiki's Cinema Plex for a singular reason: It was the longest.

When she had seen her face on the television in the hospital room, her stomach sank. Once, in the eighth grade, she had tried to shoplift a candy bar from a convenience store in Amarillo, Texas. Her friends, Marcy and Renea, did it regularly and never got caught. J.L. was a lot worse criminal than they. No natural talent, maybe. Whatever the reason, the old man, ancient really, had spotted her right off. She could've outrun him if she had tried. But she couldn't move once his ancient eyes had fixed themselves on hers.

He had cocked his head to the side and looked sad. He raised a finger and motioned for her to come near. She had gone, her chin resting hard on her chest. She realized she might be in some legal trouble, but the thought of having her dad find out about this made her queasy. With good reason, as it turned out...

The sight of her own face on television, connected with words like "terrorist plot" and "despicable act" had produced similar feelings in her today. She knew she was innocent, but the feeling was there nonetheless.

She thought that the guards at Rita's operating room had not seen the television picture. Still, she had started trembling and knew *that* fact, combined with the two-inch wide column of dried blood on her yellow tank top, might just arouse some suspicion.

She had considered throwing the computer disc at them as she fled from their sight. Maybe they would become curious enough to send the disc straight to the office of Admiral Crabb. *Yeah, right.* She couldn't take a chance on them maybe stumbling into doing what she wanted them to do. Rita had risked way too much for that disc for J.L. to simply hand it over to some enlisted grunt and hope for the best.

She had walked quietly, but quickly out of the waiting room and avoided eye contact with the guards. She continued walking like that until she reached the bottom floor of the hospital and went out the front doors. The sky had darkened and it was cooler than when she'd last taken note of the temperature. The buildings around were highlighted with the pink hue of approaching sunset. She didn't notice that, though. She had looked for a cab.

She almost started crying when she saw that none were in sight. But then she spotted one, a dark green four-door with a white top and a lighted "TAXI" sign on its roof. She had debated where to go. The hotel? No. Agent Kim had her hotel room number. She decided to go downtown, into Waikiki. She'd been on the island long enough to know that Waikiki on a weekend evening would be shoulder-to-shoulder with pedestrian tourists.

She'd been correct. She walked through the crowds, again trying to avoid looking at anyone. She couldn't help noticing, though, that she was being noticed.

On the sidewalk, there was a guy in a bear costume, handing out green fliers advertising Bully McGiver's Bar and Grill. He yelled, "Go to Bully's!" much louder than he had to, to everyone who took a flier. Farther down, a woman with long brown hair stood in a top-hat and tails...well, almost. Her outfit was a standard tuxedo up top, but ended at the waist. From there down, she wore an astonishingly high cut bikini which sparkled with sequins, black fishnet hose and dazzling red high heels. The lady smiled at the young males passing by, and would motion with a flourish to the black double doors beside her. The doors said, "Fancy Dan's Exotic Dancers."

A chubby man standing about five and half feet tall, wearing wire-rimmed circular glasses, brushed past J.L. in great haste. He, too, wore a large, black top-hat plus a black cape. In one hand he carried three bowling pins. In the other, silver metal rings. Late for a juggling date, naturally. A rather homely woman followed him, in a plain white T-shirt, no bra, and red shorts. A little farther down, a man stood on a corner with a megaphone and an open Bible. The area around him was about the only place that was not crowded at all. "I know you don't like to hear it," J.L. heard him say, "but I'm here to tell you that there really is a hell, and you don't wanna go there." Someone threw a styrofoam cup full of ice and cola at him as J.L. passed by. He ducked it smoothly, not missing a beat. "That's okay. I love you, buddy. So does Jesus!" he yelled into the crowd.

In all that, J.L. was almost amused at how much she was noticed. She could see people pointing at her out of the corner of her eye. Her first order of business had thus been to buy a T-shirt, plain and dark, which she threw on over the tank top. She removed the square, white bandage from her temple. She bought a blue baseball cap and stuffed as much of her hair as possible underneath it.

She had found herself at the movie theaters and decided that she needed some time to sit and think, and pray. It turned out well. She got there near the beginning of the science fiction/horror flick, which looked to run almost two and a half hours

She had been encouraged at how her brand new attire had stopped all of the pointing fingers and double-takes. Had any of those who noticed her seen her picture on T.V.? If so, would they connect her to it? She realized she couldn't control any of that and tried to stop worrying about it. The concession stand in the theater lobby was not crowded and she was hungry, so she spent an obscene seven dollars on two hotdogs with cheese, then sunk into the dark as best she could.

As she sat there, staring blankly at the screen, she found herself puzzled. Her intuition, or whatever, about Agent Kim had been right on, no doubt about that. He was something other than he seemed. She was certain of two facts. He knew her name, and he knew she was innocent. And, yet, he had put up her picture as a suspect in some terrorist plot and had *withheld* her name. For the life of her, she couldn't figure out why.

Her eyes filled with tears as she stared past images of spaceships, like fish in an aquarium, maneuvering in a field of stars and blackness. She angrily blinked these tears back. They were an irritation she didn't want to put up with.

She deserved it all, anyway, didn't she? Sure, she did. What did she think, anyhow? She was going to give her life to Jesus, make some emotional vow in a moment of sorrow and disgust with herself, and He would make it all better? He would turn Mark around, too, give them a new baby, maybe a little house with aluminum siding and a white picket fence, and let them live happily ever after? *C'mon!* She knew, yes, she did, that she deserved nothing like that.

She deserved what she was getting. *So stop your baby-crying.* But then she couldn't stop it at all. It was a struggle just to muffle it enough to keep from attracting attention in the midst of the stereo sounds of laser battles and the growls of alien monsters.

God doesn't want us to hate people, she thought. *But, I hate my father. I hate him for all the times he yelled at me, not at my brothers, but at me, yelled like his heart was about to explode, yelled about nothing, yelled about me doing normal four-year-old girl stuff like using real cups for my tea parties with my stuffed animals; and, for the way he yelled at mom, all the time, called her a stupid goyim whore (I was nineteen before I realized goyim meant Gentile and not "adulterous"!), for the way he used to humiliate her in front of us*

kids, proving how much smarter he was than her, for making me
believe she really was an idiot, for making me hate my own mother.
God says I'm supposed to honor my husband, but I haven't.
I just became my dad. I yelled and yelled and yelled, letting Mark
know just how clearly I knew that he was an idiot after all, blaming
him for his schedules which he had no control over, blaming him for
holidays he had to work, for being at sea on our first anniversary, for
leaving me alone so many times.

The yelling progressed, and she didn't know why. At
first, maybe it was simply all she knew...that's how her own
parents had related. Maybe the screaming was a weird way
of saying, "I love you." It wasn't long before it was obvious
that was wrong. There was nothing loving about it.

Mark's even temper through all of it just enticed her to
turn up the volume a little more, to get a little more vicious, a
little more personal, just to try and get him as worked up as
she was.

The coup de 'etat occurred on a hot night in San Diego.
She'd been in top form. Mark had walked in a little late.
Hadn't bothered to call. Dinner had cooled. That was all it
took, and she was off to the races. The louder she screamed,
the more quiet he got. A sailor through and through, he'd bat-
tened down the hatches and planned to ride out the storm.

Enraged, she had launched a coffee cup at his head
without thinking about it. It missed him by a mile and detonated like a porcelain grenade against the kitchen wall, spraying shrapnel everywhere.

A neighbor had heard the whole thing. And maybe the
neighbor had even gotten used to hearing her voice through
the walls that separated their military housing units, but the
sound of kitchenware exploding had been too much.

Military police arrived within minutes. That single
incident had very nearly ruined Mark's whole career. Oh,
he'd have continued on and done well, of course; there was
no way for Mark Reed to do otherwise, but getting kicked
out of Navy housing, or ordered into some kind of counsel-
ing program, would've been maybe just enough to edge him

out of consideration when the Review Board started picking Chiefs from among the First Class Petty Officers.

Although Mark had never said anything, they both knew that she had crossed some sort of line with the coffee cup. The yelling and screaming had nudged its way into the realm of physical violence, reaching a crescendo worthy of her father's approval.

God wanted her to respect Mark, but she had not. Not even close. When she got into one of her screaming moods, she could be counted on to say things that shocked even herself after she calmed down. She might threaten to have an affair, threaten to kill him or have someone else kill him, threaten to spike his food with cocaine just to get him busted on a drug test. Insane times, that's what they were.

She thought about Rita. She thought about holding her. About how she had looked like she had been dipped in a tub of red dye. And she thought that the bullet in Rita's neck should, by all rights, be in her own. She didn't deserve to live. She deserved to be like Megan.

Before they had been married, but after they'd gotten "serious" about their relationship, they had talked about children. How many? Boys or girls? What names do you like? Mark had shrugged his shoulders and sipped at his soda, like he was embarrassed to admit he'd thought about it. Then, he'd said he sort of liked "Megan" for a girl's name.

They had separated for two months after the Night of the Flying Mug. He had not scolded her, never yelled back.

In a rare moment of introspection during their time apart, she had felt sorry for her actions, and had gone to some lengths to apologize and try to win Mark's trust again. When they did get back together, she got pregnant.

A trip to the hospital and one ultrasound later, and J.L. had decided to name the baby Megan. The baby was Megan, Mark's girl. For J.L., she symbolized, maybe, reconciliation. When she told Mark about it, they both cried. It was the only time she'd seen him do that.

Just two days later, at a beach near their home on base,

she'd felt ill. A storm came up out of nowhere about that time, and they had left in a rush. It came down in torrents, turning the afternoon into night. Something had seemed to put a hand in her insides and crumple everything at once, like a football fan with an empty beer can.

They had gotten to the Navy medical center in time to save J.L.'s life. Everything imaginable had gone wrong inside her, it seemed. She had nearly bled to death, slipping in and out of consciousness. During an "in" period, she'd seen a nurse rush out of the room, where lots of people were crowded over her, all talking at once. The nurse had a blue cloth in her hand, cupped there, and a little reddish glob in its center. So tiny. So very tiny. And blood everywhere. No one had to tell J.L.. She had known. Megan was gone.

In a way, Megan had taken Mark with her. It was never the same after that day. Megan had been a cruel hoax, a little ray of sunshine that shone for a moment then disappeared forever behind a dark cloud. Now the cloud was all there was, and all there had been for the last year.

She hated her dad. She had destroyed her marriage with her own hands. Surely Megan had represented God's retribution against her. Surely. Megan was dead because of J.L.'s wickedness. Were it not for her failures, maybe God would have let Megan live.

Now, wasn't it just wishful thinking for her to "come to Jesus?" She does all of this junk, then goes down to the altar at one church service, confesses her sin, and some guy who hung on a cross two thousand years ago is supposed to be able to change her? To erase her past? To forgive? It was ludicrous.

If anyone deserved to be nailed to a cross, it was her. Not Him.

****

Admiral Crabb sat at his desk in the office building which jointly provided spaces for the administration of submarine Squadrons One and Seven. Normally at this hour he would have been alone in the building. Now though, weekend or no, the place was lit up and buzzing. His was a dark office, with a plush blue carpet and wood-grain paneling. The doors of a wooden cabinet opposite his desk were open, revealing a television screen.

Crabb pointed a remote control at the TV and pushed a button. The picture froze. A single horizontal static line bisected the image of the composite drawing of a woman he didn't know. His eyebrows moved in toward his big nose and he blew out a breath quietly.

There was a knock on the frame of his office door and a Commander in working whites stepped inside. "Admiral, sir," he said, holding up a sheet of paper. "All sub crews have been recalled, minus one guy on *Sam Houston* who they haven't been able to get a hold of yet. Emergency reactor startups are completed on all but *Corpus Christi*, of course, but the drydock has gone to Defcon four around her. *Indy's* the only boat with special weapons on board. They report situation normal. All boats still manned to repel boarders, no unusual activity reported. No divers in the water. They're all just...waiting on your word, sir."

Admiral Crabb nodded and rubbed his forehead with one hand. "What news on Philadelphia Cove?"

The Commander shrugged. "Recon Marines have swept topside for devices twice. Underwater Demolition Teams are diving the harbor. PacFleet says he can get us a SEAL Team here in three hours if UDT needs assistance."

Crabb shook his head quickly. He had the expression of a man who's just taken a swig of lemon juice.

"You said *Indy's* got specials?" Crabb asked.

The Commander nodded. "Just one."

"Anyone else with an operational load of weapons?"

The man checked his clipboard. He shook his head. "Just *Sam Houston*, sir."

The Admiral turned his head to look at the frozen picture on his television again. "Dennis," he said, "A bomb goes off at the clinic. NIS says the threat to Philadelphia Cove may be hot and live. And what do we do?"

"Well, we wait to make sure everything's kosher."

Crabb turned back to him. "That's right. We sit here, almost completely unarmed, and check for lint in our collective belly button."

The Commander looked surprised. Crabb asked, "How much credibility do you think this Philadelphia Cove thing would have had, say, yesterday? Before a bomb went off?"

"Zero."

"Exactly. But now that a real life bomb has exploded on Navy property, the guys at NIS are puckered to maximum. Meanwhile, no ship in Pearl Harbor can get any weapons loaded."

The Commander nodded.

"Dennis, I want you to call in the storekeepers."

Now the Commander was shocked.

Crabb said, "You heard me. I don't care what time it is. You get those shore-duty pukes out here now. I want a 60-day stores load done on *Indy* and *Sam Houston*. I want it in four hours. Get a hold of Harbor Services. I'm gonna need two tugboats. Commander, I want these two submarines in the water by oh-three-hundred hours, or I want somebody's butt gift-wrapped on my desk."

"Yessir."

"As soon as they're gone, I want those tugs back here pulling out *Fargo* and *Albuquerque*. I want them headed for Philadelphia Cove."

"Yessir."

Crabb dismissed the Commander, who walked out smartly.

When he was gone, Crabb looked up again at the drawing of the young woman. He looked down at his desk, where a manila folder, bordered in fire-engine red, lay open. On the top was a picture of Kenneth Sung. The late Mr. Sung, he thought. Darn fine agent. Sung was a wrinkly faced man of about sixty. He looked like a guy you'd find selling fresh fish from a pushcart in Seoul. Under Sung's picture was his service record. POW during the Korean conflict. How in the world he got out of that alive was a mystery, Crabb thought. Nearly thirty years working for the CIA since then.

Beneath all of Sung's information was the same sort of stuff for Major Rita Kelly. Admiral Crabb shook his head. Sung and Kelly had worked for three years to build contacts and sources that would allow them to monitor the attempts of the smaller Pacific Rim nations to get their hands on nuke weps from the cash-strapped former Soviet Union. All for nothing, now. Sung's dead and Kelly probably will be... Crabb picked up his phone and hit a speed-dial number that he rarely used.

"Yes, this is Admiral Crabb at Subase. Get me Tom Gentry."

After some seconds, the Admiral smiled and said, "Busy, Tom?"

The Admiral nodded his head. "Look, buddy. I've got some information about the bomb that you boys over there are gonna want. No, I need to see you in person. Right. Right, bending the rules a little bit," Crabb said, glancing up again at the TV screen and the pencil line drawing of a young woman he didn't know. "But I need a favor for it."

****

He couldn't help it. He couldn't go to sleep knowing it was just a matter of minutes before he would be getting roused again to go on watch. So Mark fished MM1 Liegert's notebook out of the locker in his rack again and began to read.

Today I read about the first murder in the history of the world. It's in Genesis. Cain and Abel, the first brothers, went out into a field and Cain killed him. It boiled down to jealousy. God was nicer to Abel than he was to Cain. Cain couldn't stand it.

Fine and dandy. That's understandable. Stupid, but under-

standable. Like God wasn't going to be just a little mad about the whole deal!

What got me was that Cain had a conversation with God about the whole thing prior to the murder. He asked God why Abel got treated so well. Basically, God says, look, you are a sinner. Stop sinning and things will be cool. But, then, God told Cain that sin desired him. Sin wanted Cain. That seems really strange to me, and yet it seems right somehow, too.

Do I follow sin, or is it after me? Because I've noticed that when I do mess up and do something wrong, even though it seemed like it was something I initiated, once I've done it I don't feel like I'm satisfied ...I feel like I've been captured. So, it's like, did I get what I wanted, or did sin get what it wanted?

He was stunned. *Liegert was some sort of religious guy?* Mark shook his head and closed the notebook. It fit. Mark had been right all along. Liegert was weak, limping along on the God-crutch, finally brought down by suicide. And, maybe in a weird way, Liegert had been right...sin got him. Grandma used to say, "The wages of sin is death."

Mark opened the notebook again and turned the page, leaving Liegert's musings about Cain and Abel. The sentence at the top of the page stunned him in a different way.

Mia had an affair, and I can't change that, or change her, or fix everything, but I realize there is one thing that I have to do--I have to forgive her. I have to be willing to give up my right to be furious. I've done some things in my life that I deserve to die for, according to God's law, but Jesus Christ didn't kill me--he forgave me. I've got to do the same thing. I know that isn't going to make my marriage suddenly heal itself, and Mia may decide she really wants to leave for good. And I know it's not going to be an easy thing to do: the thought of her and another man sets my brain on fire. But my own peace, with myself and with God, depends on me letting it go.

Anger and hatred and revenge seem really attractive to me right now, though. This is going to take a long time. Maybe my *anger is a little like Cain's jealousy of Abel. I think I want it, but the truth is, it wants me. I don't know.*

This was disturbing. Liegert had, in two short paragraphs of talking to himself, wiggled out of the view of him which Mark had been so certain of just seconds ago. If J.L. had cheated on him, he knew, about the most coherent thing he'd likely put on paper was a flood of the worst profanity he could come up with, mixed with threats and promises of vengeance.

He knew he would be thrown into a panic if J.L. cheated on him, and here was this guy he had pegged as a weakling, calm and collected. And if he was thinking irrationally, in terms of the Bible and Jesus, at least his thoughts were in some semblance of order. Liegert had taken a page out of Mark's own playbook by deciding to let his thoughts triumph over his emotions.

Mark's image of Liegert had changed, so much so that he became puzzled by one thing. The suicide. Why would a man of apparently strong faith, a guy who could think his way through something as emotionally threatening as adultery, then go kill himself?

Mark's grandma had not killed herself. The thought repulsed her, in fact. He remembered her final years. Her body had been overrun by arthritis. One of the cruelest ways to go that there is, he thought. The disease won't kill you, at least not before it's made every waking moment an exercise in the experience of agony.

He had asked her himself whether death wouldn't be better than prolonged, constant pain. She had laughed. No, no. She said that she would thank God for every day she drew breath, knowing it was more than she deserved, and if she were reduced to only being able to *think*, she would pray, she would worship. She would do what she was created to do. She would love her family.

And she did; even at the end, when doctors said the pain she suffered was "blinding", Mark had known that he was her chief concern.

Mark looked at his watch. He realized that he no longer considered his grandmother a weakling.

Chapter Eleven

Liegert's journal:

Paul's short-timer's attitude may be getting the best of him. I can't say that I blame him. It'll be nice to transfer to shore sometime, or get out for good. I can imagine that it's hard to keep focused on the job at hand.

Paul screwed up the Discharge Log again. That's three times since we left Pearl. I don't know how he's doing it. It's like it's almost on purpose.

How do you make the exact same mistake three times in a row on something like that? Paul's not inexperienced. He knows how to do his job. He's simply getting lazy, I think. I think he's guessing about the density compensations. He gets close, sure. But that's not what Congress is going to want. Close may count in horseshoes, but not in calculating the amount of radioactive water discharged to the environment!

So this is the third time I've had to take the Discharge Log down to him on watch in Engineroom Forward and have him rewrite the whole thing. The Engineer was not pleased. He asked me if I thought Paul should be written up for it. I said no. Eng said he was at the end of his patience. One more stupid mental error out of Paul on this cruise, and he wants me to write him up.

I tried to relay this fact to Paul. I tried to let him know I got the Eng to back off this time, that I didn't want to write him up.

He flipped out. "Write me up then, you jerk!" He threw the

Discharge Log into the Feed Pump bilge. Guess I caught him at a bad time. Something about it really ticked me off. I feel like it was only God's grace that let me speak evenly to him.

I said, "I don't know what's up with you, Paul. I don't care, really. But I want that Discharge Log clean and dry and spotless and perfect by the time you get off watch."

I left and he cussed at me the whole way.

I don't know what's up with him. He had the Log all fixed on time, though.

****

Casualty drills are to a nuclear submarine what insulin shots are to a diabetic. Not pleasant, not fun, but absolutely essential.

Admiral Hyman J. Rickover had made sure of that. Years after his death, all nuclear power sailors are still aware that Rickover believed the axiom, "Practice makes perfect."

Rickover had been handed the reins of the Navy nuclear power program at its inception. Until his death, the nuclear fleet was his baby. He was politically savvy, even though he knew enough to stay out of overt politics himself. He knew that building a nuclear fleet was, at the get-go, a thin-ice proposition.

Hollywood was already producing movies about ants the size of sixteen-wheelers and other terrifying prospects, all resulting from some government experiments with "atomic research." Rickover knew that one serious, or even close-to-serious, incident with nuclear power would kill the whole concept for the Navy. This notion was vindicated by the manner in which nuclear power was made off-limits to the US Army after an accident resulting in multiple deaths at SL-1, a nuclear plant in the desert of south-east Idaho.

Two nuclear submarines had been lost, it's true. But neither one was due to an accident with the reactor plant. The USS Thresher and the USS Scorpion are still on the bottom somewhere.

After sending down a crew in a Deep Submergence Vehicle to investigate, the official story on *Thresher* was that she died because of water. Not water outside, but probably inside, as in flooding. Specifically, she died because of water in the air.

The theory was that she began to take on water from some source, the exact location being irrelevant. She tried to perform an Emergency Main Ballast Tank (EMBT) blow to recover, which involves blasting high pressure air into huge tanks filled with water just inside the sub's outer skin. Force all that water out quickly enough, and the reduced weight causes the sub to rocket to the surface.

Supposedly, though, *Thresher*'s high pressure air had too much moisture in it. The effect of blowing air through an orifice, such as an EMBT valve, is that the temperature plummets. The water vapor in *Thresher*'s air first condensed, then froze. The ice quickly blocked the airway into the tanks. She filled with water from the flooding and sank. Submarines are now careful to keep their high pressure air bone dry.

The story on the *Scorpion* is more mysterious, with the cause of her demise officially unknown. Rumor is that sonar pictures of her dead hull reveal a huge hole in her side. A hole from an explosion that, apparently, blew from the outside in. Legend has it that there are two Soviet submarine hulls resting on the bottom not far from her.

Despite these incidents, the Naval nuclear program went on. Rickover knew, though, that he had not been given a blank check, nor any guarantees concerning the longevity of his pet project.

And so the little Admiral insisted on the best, most intelligent officers for his program. But that was not so new and innovative as his insistence upon recruiting the most intelligent enlisted men as well. Rickover distrusted automatic equipment. To the greatest extent possible, he wanted control over a nuclear plant to be in the hands of trained men who knew how to think.

A vital part of that ongoing training was casualty drills.

The Admiral didn't just want eggheads; he wanted eggheads who could think under pressure, with speed and precision. The "Admiral's Interview" was also part of that. More dreaded than any exam, by far, was the one on one personal interview. Rickover continued this practice, as long as his health permitted, with every single nuclear-trained officer prior to allowing that officer's graduation from his program.

Hyman Rickover was a diminutive man, but his vulture-like features combined with his legendary perfectionism and temper to make him the consummate intimidator. And he knew it. He wanted it that way. In his Interviews, his whole desire was to shake his young candidate to the greatest extent possible, and only then ask one doozy of a question on atomic theory. The Admiral could, and did, terminate candidates right then and there, depending on his mood and his opinion of how well they reacted to pressure.

Whether apocryphal or not, one particular story was told over and over on the *Omaha*, about one officer's Interview with the Admiral. The handsome Ensign in dress whites strode into Rickover's office and came to attention in front of his desk. The Admiral didn't bother to rise from his burgundy leather chair, but simply sneered and said, "I don't think I like you. But I'll give you a chance before I flush your career down the toilet. You've got exactly thirty seconds to make me mad."

The Ensign paused just long enough to absorb the challenge, scanned the room and then strode over to a bookshelf. He picked up a model ship-in-a-bottle, four feet long, two feet high, a huge, ornate three-masted sailing ship. He threw it on the floor without ceremony or hesitation, where it shattered into a zillion pieces.

Redness surged into the Admiral's face. He hissed through clenched jaws, "Get out!"

The Ensign received word minutes later. He had passed his Interview.

The drills had the same purpose. That is, get the operators used to pressure. Make sure they can perform mistake-free under it.

Omaha was running some pretty advanced drills when Mark Reed came onboard. His first day on watch in the Engineroom, under instruction as the Engineroom Supervisor with MM2 Lorde, convinced him of that.

The first one had started out as a simple "Flooding in Engineroom Lower Level." The Drill Monitors, off-watch engineering department personnel in red hats, had stationed themselves at all three levels. At a predetermined time, the Drill Monitor in Lower Level opened up a low pressure air outlet, which made a horrendous roaring noise.

The Engineroom Lower Level watch, alerted by the roar, charged into the space, known as Propulsion Lube Oil, or PLO Bay, to find the Drill Monitor waving a green plastic trash bag and yelling, "Cold, salty water! Cold, salty water!"

The Lower Level watch giggled at him, and then assumed a thoughtful pose, chin in hand. "Hmmm. Sounds like a fire to me!"

"No, you idiot!" yelled the monitor, "Flooding!"

The Lower Level watch took off, forward into Main Condensate Bay and grabbed the 2JV phone. He spoke into it over the noise of the venting air, "Flooding in Engineroom Lower Level! Flooding in Engineroom Lower Level."

Maneuvering went on to alert the entire ship, and so it started. Mark had a hard time keeping up with Jason Lorde.

This incredibly large guy flew up and down the ladders that connected the levels. From Upper Level, down some stairs, then a vertical ladder to Lower Level, to find and isolate the source of the simulated flooding, back up two vertical ladders to the manual controls for the Main Seawater Hydraulic Flood Control Valves, where they simulated re-opening them (since Maneuvering had simulated shutting them), back down to make sure flooding had not been reinitiated, all the way back up to instruct the mechanic standing Engineroom Upper Level to write up a Tagout order which would help ensure the flooding didn't get restarted by someone turning the wrong valves, into Maneuvering with the

Engineering Watch Supervisor, Senior Chief Markiss, to report to the Engineering Officer of the Watch. (Where exactly was the flooding, could it be repaired underway, how long would repairs take, and were there any propulsion restrictions as a result of the new Main Seawater system lineup.) Ten minutes never passed so quickly.

But that had not been the end of it. According to the drill scenario, the flooding in the PLO Bay caused electrical grounds in the main propulsion lube oil pumps. The grounds led, inevitably, to electrical fires, which soon had the whole bay engulfed in flames. This, of course, led to a loss of propulsion lube oil, so that Mark and Jason had to assist the Throttleman in Maneuvering in performing an emergency stop on the Main Engine Shaft, to eliminate the chance of running the multi-million dollar main turbines without oil.

This means the Throttleman spins shut the Ahead throttle while opening the Astern throttle. Steam is applied in the direction opposite the current shaft spin. As the Main Engine Shaft slows down, the Throttleman applies a low balance of Ahead and Astern steam to keep the Engine from moving at all, at which point it becomes the mechanic's job to engage the Main Engine Locking Device. All done while wearing Emergency Air Breathing Apparatus's (EAB's) because of the ongoing fire drill — the Rickover Legacy.

Thirty minutes later, the Engineer's voice came over the 1MC speakers, saying, "Secure from Flooding in Main Seawater, Fire in Propulsion Lube Oil, and Loss of Lube Oil drills. Drill Monitors prepare for drill set two."

Mark followed Jason's lead, pulling the black, rubber EAB from his face. Lorde's big face was now outlined by a thick red indentation where the breathing mask had sealed to it. Mark almost laughed about it, but knew the same was true of his own face.

Engineroom ventilation fans were secured during the fire drill, to minimize the spread of the simulated toxic gases, and the temperature in Upper Level was now over one hundred degrees.

"Get the fans back on!" Jason shouted to the Upper Level watch, who was already getting it done. Jason's poopie suit was marked by large dark spots around the neck and underarms. His hair was matted to his head with sweat.

After all of the damage control equipment was put away, Mark and Jason went to the water fountain in Upper Level and took some long drinks.

"Can I ask you something?" Mark said.

"Sure."

"What did you think of MM1 Liegert?"

Jason was still trying to catch his breath, but he said, "We got along fine. Why?"

"Well, I mean, was he good at his job and all that?"

Jason shrugged. "Sure. Probably wasn't the best ELT in the world, but he was good. Why? What've you heard?"

"Oh, not much. Just some conflicting opinion about him."

"Oh, yeah?"

"Yeah. The old man said he may have killed himself because his wife was leaving him over an affair he had, then someone else told me he was maybe gay..."

Jason shook his head, no. "He wasn't gay. Who said that?"

"Paul Lawrence."

Jason smirked and rolled his eyes. "Don't listen to Lawrence, man. Those two never liked each other. They came onboard together about four years ago. Liegert made MM1 and Lawrence never did. So Liegert got the Leading ELT job instead of him. Paul's just sore about it."

Mark nodded. "Do you know if Liegert was a Christian?"

"Yeah, well, he said he was. I don't know. He didn't try to cram the Bible down anyone's throat, y'know?"

"Yeah." Mark looked at his white tennis shoes, thinking, and then said, "I didn't think Christians believed in suicide."

The 2MC, the all-stations address system confined to

the Engineroom spaces, blared, "All Ahead Flank!"

Jason shrugged and started back toward Engineroom Lower Level. Over his shoulder, he said, "Yeah, well, maybe Liegert wasn't really a Christian."

They were off again. Mark followed Jason in a "controlled fall" down two ladders into Engineroom Forward, where the watchstander was turning the switch to start a second Main Feed Pump to answer the Ahead Flank order. Mark bumped his shin, hard, on the lower lip of a hatchway as they bolted aft from there. No time to cuss about it, though. He gritted his teeth and half-limped as fast as he could to keep up, as Jason helped the Lower Level watch get all of his pumps shifted to fast speed. Then they scrambled up the ladder into Shaft Alley. A drill monitor stood all the way aft, by the hydraulic pumps. He waved at Jason and Mark as they entered the space.

"What are you doing back here, Paul?" Jason asked.

The drill monitor was Paul Lawrence, who was, true to form, grinning. "Oh, just causing trouble. I've got eighty days left in this man's Navy. Might as well be the biggest pain I can be."

Mark said, "That sounds familiar. Isn't that what they say in the Army commercials?"

Paul threw back his head and laughed, almost dislodging his Drill Monitor baseball cap. "Something like that, boss. Heck, if they'd said, 'Be the biggest pain you can be' I'd've joined the Army right away."

"You'd be their poster child," mumbled Jason. It didn't seem like he was trying to be funny.

"Get a life, Hayseed," Paul shot back. He wasn't being too funny, either.

The ship suddenly took a severe down angle. Paul smiled, having already braced himself, as Mark and Jason struggled for a moment to find things to hold onto.

The 1MC blared, "Jam Dive! Jam Dive! Loss of rudder and planes in Control. Maneuvering, answer Back Emergency! Jam Dive!"

"You jerk!" Jason roared.

Paul laughed and said, "Hey, ain't my fault. The CO approved the drill set. Complain to the Eng if you want!"

Jason struggled uphill a couple of feet closer to Paul, where he punched a latch on a gray locker mounted near the shaft. The locker flew open, revealing itself as a "book", with metal and laminated pages attached to the hinge. Jason snatched out one of the laminated sheets and began reading it. His hand reached for an orange T-handle valve. Paul stopped him by grabbing his wrist, and said, "Simulate, Jason. It's a drill."

Jason growled at him and pushed past. He let the sheet direct him to the (simulated) turning of valves, two at waist level, one up high in the overhead, one down by his feet, one that he had to snake his arm in between two silver pipes to reach.

Senior Chief Markiss arrived in Shaft Alley, spitting out expletives about the angle and the drill set and the Engineer and the Captain and the whole Navy and just about everyone else currently using up air on the planet. "You got local control yet?" he yelled to Jason.

"Yeah! That's the last valve!" Jason answered.

Paul whistled. They looked at him. He was tapping his toe on the silver deckplate and pointing down.

Jason cursed now and pushed him out of the way. He bent down and lifted up on the hinged plate. There was a little orange valve, and he simulated turning it. Paul laughed and said, "Now, you got the last valve!"

Senior Chief Markiss jerked up a 2JV phone and spoke into it loudly. "Maneuvering, Watch Supervisor. Have established local control of planes in Shaft Alley."

The angle of the ship leveled off within seconds. The Engineer's voice came over the 1MC. Even with its amplified blare, he sounded disinterested. "Secure from Jam Dive drill. Secure from Engineering drills. Drill Monitors, assemble in the Wardroom in five minutes for critiques."

Senior Chief Markiss climbed out of Shaft Alley by the

port ladder to Engineroom Upper Level, still railing against college graduates with commissions and ambitions, the worst of whom were, without question, Annapolis grads. The Engineer was an Annapolis grad.

Jason seemed to take the whole drill set as an affront. He fumed quietly. Paul followed the Senior Chief up the ladder. He spoke back to them over his shoulder, "Excuse me, gentlemen. I have a date in the Wardroom and then a date with my rack."

When it was only the two of them, Jason put up his right hand and patted a light fixture. "This is it," he said. "This is where Liegert hung himself."

Mark was a little shocked at Jason's willingness to just blurt that information out.

Jason nodded, maybe to himself, and went on, "He used a marlin line. Can you believe that?"

"That's what I heard the morning it happened. Must've hurt."

Marlin line is only about an eighth of an inch in diameter. It's presoaked and treated in a type of tar, or pitch. On a submarine, it can be found in a Damage Control tool bag, along with blocks of wood and other materials that might come in handy when you're trying to patch a hole in something.

"Yeah, I guess."

Jason lowered his head and quickened his pace to leave.

****

Agent Kim parked his navy blue government sedan on the first level of the parking garage, attached to the back side of the Plaza Hotel. He thought about parking out front, but decided that he could be here a while.

The garage was well lit against the darkness. A nice cool breeze blew through, since the sides of the parking garage were open to the elements. The breeze brought a freshness

Kim noted but didn't stop to enjoy.

A bright, open hallway was next to the elevator doors. Big letters on the wall said, "Lobby" and a red arrow pointed down the hall. He went that way.

He passed a small laundry room on his right, then the hallway became carpeted and the walls were more finished than the painted concrete of the garage. The hall opened up to a small lobby. Only two chairs and one large plant were in the middle of the room. He went to the front desk and flashed his badge at the Filipino woman with long, straight black hair who was manning it.

"Excuse me," he said, "My name is Special Agent Kim."

"Oh--um, yes," she said, her eyes blinking quickly, "Wh-, what can I do for you, sir?"

This was going to be easier than he could've hoped. The girl was terrified. A big badge that says FBI and the words "Special Agent" often seemed to shake ordinary people.

"I need to get a key to Room 412, if I may."

The woman paused, blinked some more. Kim could almost see her thinking, *This is highly irregular.* So he prodded.

"I'm in the middle of a very serious investigation. Maybe you've seen something about it on television."

She stared blankly. Maybe it wouldn't be so easy after all.

He took a breath. "Ma'am. I have reason to believe the person staying in Room 412 is in a great deal of danger, and if I don't get in there and find some way to get in touch with her..."

The woman's lips formed an "O", and she shuffled some papers on her desk. She produced a key with a blue tag marked 412. She started to hand it to him, then brought her hand back, frowning. "Do you need a warrant to go in there?"

Kim smiled, fantasizing about punching her in the nose. "Are you going to demand one?"

She started blinking again. "Well...no, I don't guess so--"

Kim reached over the counter and snatched the key, still smiling. "Well, I guess that's your answer, then."

He walked into the dark room and decided he had just learned two things. For one, Mrs. Reed had not been here all day. The curtains were drawn wide and the air conditioner was off. It was stifling. Next, he figured that meant she had seen her picture on TV and was too frightened to come back here. He smiled. He flipped the light switch and checked his watch. Twenty-four more hours like that, and he would not care whether he saw her again, ever.

He let the door close behind him, and then began opening drawers. They were empty.

He found two suitcases, one large, one small, lying open. Mrs. Reed had not unloaded her suitcases into the dresser drawers. She didn't plan on staying long. By the way the suitcases were packed, he learned that Mrs. Reed was organized and methodical. He dumped them both on the bed.

There was nothing of interest. Unless, of course, you're into groping women's underwear. Some other time, maybe...

On the small, round table, there was a Bible. It was on top of a pad of notebook paper and an old hardcover book. He moved the Bible and read the paper. It was filled with a woman's handwriting, and began, "Dear Mark." He read the whole thing.

She was apologizing. She was sorry. She had lost both her parents, and she didn't want to lose him, too; not now, not with a baby on the way. Kim's eyebrows went up at that. Then, the best news of all. She was tired of being alone. She knew no one. Well, almost no one. There was Rita. Kim smiled. She was still in surgery last time he'd checked, but it didn't look good. She'd met Rita at church. Kim stopped smiling. From what he knew, churches were often filled with people.

They were often filled with not just any people, but with gooey, doting people. People who love to feel like they are helping other people. And, from what he had heard, churches often had pastors. Sometimes they were the worst. Like kids who want to bring home every stray dog, every bird with an injured wing. This information was not calming to Agent Kim, and he stormed out of the room determined to do something about it.

****

Agent Kim knew her name. And still he had put her face up on that television screen as if he did not, as if he had not spoken to her. She had to conclude this: it was all right with him if she didn't get caught right away. It didn't make a heck of a lot of sense, but that's where she was in her thinking.

J.L. thought that maybe the way to foil him was to turn herself in. *If he doesn't want me caught too soon, maybe I ought to give him what he doesn't want.* But Kim was in charge of the police, at least in this matter. She'd heard him claim command. Even if the police were not with Kim in whatever he was doing to her, she knew that he would be put in charge of her whenever she was caught. He would get the disc.

But Agent Kim could not get the disc. She could hide it somewhere and then turn herself in, she thought. Then, while they're holding her, the disc sits in its hiding place and Admiral Crabb doesn't ever get it. No, there was no way around it. She was going to have to get the disc into Crabb's hands herself.

J.L. came to this conclusion as her cab pulled up to the front of the Plaza Hotel, illumined against the night by several sunken lights, projecting up from the landscaping, upon the building's entrance. The cab driver was a large Samoan man (was there any other kind?) with shoulder length black hair in tight curls, almost an afro. He was braking to stop in front of the Plaza's double glass doors.

"Um, y'know what?" said J.L. "I'm sorry to be a bother,

but do you think you could go on around to the parking garage?"

The man looked back at her. He shrugged and started accelerating again. "Chure," he said. "If dats mo betta fo you, iss mo betta fo me."

J.L. hoped that meant, "Yes." He was going in the right direction, at least.

The parking garage was four stories high. It would've been the largest building around in several of the towns near where she grew up in Texas. Its design would only work in Hawaii, or a place very similar, though. It was open to the elements on its sides. Now, florescent lights, hanging from the underside of the enormous concrete layers, lit each level.

She felt her stomach sink. This was a dumb idea. The cops would be here. They'd be watching the place where they knew she "lived."

Or maybe not, she thought. Agent Kim had withheld her real name, even though he knew it. Maybe he had withheld this information as well. Yeah, she thought, he almost had to. If he gave out her hotel and room number, it was a matter of checking the registrar to find her name. He obviously didn't want that happening for some reason.

Still, J.L., she scolded herself, *that's an awful big risk to take for*—Now her stomach felt worse. In her room was clothing to change into. She could do something with her hair, maybe, or figure out somebody to call on the phone without people looking at her. Then, for the second time that day she found herself asking who she thought she was kidding.

It was about the movie theater. It was about sitting there and realizing how little she deserved anything from God but what she was getting. It was about coming to the conclusion that maybe her faith was just plain stupid after all. It was about doubting whether or not Jesus Christ would, or even could, be anything real for her.

There was a time, after Megan had died and Mark had left, that she had simply sat down and looked at the palms of her hands. She had been struck at that time by how small they were. They were normal-sized, of course, but really, that meant they were small in the whole Great Universal Scheme Of Things. They were small and powerless. Worse, they were empty. They would remain that way, she had been certain. They would never hold the baby she had lost. The knowledge of that emptiness had become a physical ache in her knuckles and wrists.

She looked at her hands now. There was a similar ache, and when she realized why, she felt silly. She ached for her Bible. To have it in her hands, to feel its weight, to open it and rifle the pages, hearing them ripple by, and smelling the ink. It was silly, she knew, but once she got it in her hands, it might be a while before she actually settled on a page and started to read.

God would be there for her, in those pages. And that was silly, too, she guessed. *Isn't God everywhere? Well, yes, He is.* But she needed to hear Him, and that is where she knew He would speak. He would speak to her as a Father. And that, in itself, would be a novelty. (Hearing a father speak like a father, that is, and not like some tyrant.) She needed to get back, right with God, if she was going to go on.

The cab lurched to a stop, startling her.

"Da kine parkin garage," the driver announced cheerily. He leaned over to look at his meter on the dashboard. "Dat be eight-pipty-tree, mo betta."

J.L. scrounged around in the darkness of the back seat. She pulled a bill from her fanny-pack and handed it over the front seat to the man. "There," she said. "There's ten—I think that's a ten—yeah, o.k., um, keep the change. Thank you very much."

"Mo betta!"

****

Kim took long strides out of the Plaza's elevator and headed back toward the parking garage. He went swiftly enough to stir up the air around him and begin to smell himself. That only made him angrier.

How many churches were there on the island of Oahu? About a billion? He felt vaguely like a volcano, ready to go off at any second. Come to think of it, wiping out entire regions filled with cities and civilizations sounded pretty good to him at the moment. He almost smiled in spite of himself.

His hard-soled shoes echoed loudly on the concrete as he walked to his car. It was dark, even with the lights on, even with the lights reflecting off the hoods and windshields of every car in the place.

He was glad to be carrying a weapon. He was the hunter, to be sure. Absolutely. Still, it was dark. And who knows, really? So, he was reassured by the very slight bulk and weight, nearly imperceptible if he didn't think about it, of his shoulder-holstered, Vector CP-1 9mm pistol, illegally imported from Austria. The thought comforted him.

He was still thinking fondly of it when he started his car and began backing out of his parking space. He thought of the CP-1's futuristic molding in black polymer, of how the grip was ergonomically designed, and of how the frame seemed absent of any harsh lines or sharp corners...Suddenly there was a glare of light and the blast of a car horn, accompanied by screeching tires.

Kim slammed on his brakes, jerking himself deep into his seat. He craned his neck in time to see a red Camaro pass him rather quickly. The passenger flipped Kim off on their way around his bumper. The Camaro was headed higher up in the garage, and he needed to go down. Too bad, he thought.

He finally got backed out of his space and started down. He rounded a corner, near where the elevator door stood. In the heat of his anger, he was going faster than he needed to and his tires squealed on the concrete.

He completed the turn and could now see the entrance/exit of the garage. He stepped on the gas as he barreled through the last, dark corridor of automobiles. In fact, he was going so fast that he very nearly missed noticing J.L. Reed, who walked up toward the elevator.

He cussed loudly and slammed on the brakes. His tires protested and the car skidded several yards. *Had that really been her?* He looked back when his car finished convulsing its way to a stop.

It was her, all right. Even from fifty or so feet, and in the half-dark, he could tell that. She had turned around and now was simply standing there, looking at him. Their eyes met, but neither one of them did anything for several seconds.

Then she was off, running up for the elevator.

He cussed again and turned back around in his seat. He tried to slam the car's automatic transmission into reverse, but he went too far, into park. He stepped on the gas pedal and, of course, went nowhere as the engine raced high.

Kim forced himself to ease the lever down from park into reverse. He held the wheel with his left hand, and threw his right arm back over the seat, straining to look behind him.

Mrs. Reed had reached the door and was wildly slapping at the top button beside it. Kim shoved the gas pedal down as hard as he could, and the tires screamed at him again. By the time they gained traction, she was running again, headed up higher in the shadowy structure.

She was gone around the corner. Kim thought about trying to get his car turned around, but the space was too cramped. So he kept going in reverse. He wished that his window had been down. He wanted to be able to hear her footsteps, if at all possible. There was no way to deal with that now without stopping, though.

To his irritation, he did have to slow down for the corner. He was not, after all, a stunt driver. There was no way he was making a 180 degree turn like that doing about twenty miles an hour backward.

Then, as he came out of the turn, an alarm sounded. It was a car alarm from up ahead. A horn was repeatedly honking, and car lights were flashing. He kept driving, but slowed down as he closed the twenty-or-so feet to the upset vehicle. She had been here. She had tried to open the door and hide herself inside.

Kim slowed to a stop as his car came opposite the alarming Cadillac. He put his car in park and stepped out. He scanned the darkened area, now lit up at intervals by the Caddy's flashing red brake lights. She hadn't gotten in there, but she was here somewhere. It was too far to the next turn up ahead. She had not made it that far. She must've realized she couldn't and started exploring other options.

Kim took out his CP-1 and held it pointing up in his right hand. He slowly began walking up toward the next turn, in the narrow space, barely enough room for cars to pass each other, between the two rows of parked vehicles. To his left was the outside row, and beyond that, the half-high brick wall and open space, the Hawaiian night sky. The alarming car was in the right hand row, along the inside of the garage.

He smiled as he walked, looking carefully to his left and to his right, between each car. After a little while, he decided it was laughable, and he did laugh. It was purposely very loud, just so she could hear him over the infernal, rhythmic honking.

"Mrs. Reed!" he called out, as loudly as he could.

There was no answer but the honking horn.

"Mrs. Reed, if you are this stupid, to come back to your hotel room, then you might as well give it up right now!"

Still only the honking, echoing.

He smiled and shook his head, even as he continued to bend over and try to peer into the darkness underneath the cars.

"Mrs. Reed! I am putting my gun away now." And he did. "So why don't you just come out. Or, better yet, why don't you just throw me the disc? If you do that, then I will leave you here."

Except for the horn, there was only silence. Then, without warning or fanfare, the horn stopped and the lights quit flashing.

"Well, it's about stinkin' time," Kim muttered in the new stillness. He turned around. There, right beside his own car, he saw something move. He was sure of it. A shadow had darted into the outside row of cars right next to his own.

He grabbed his gun again and began walking in that direction. The urge to run was nearly overwhelming. But if he ran, so would she. So he walked.

Less than ten feet from his own rear bumper, and almost positive he could see a shadow crouched behind a compact car, Kim was bathed in white light. He whirled around, to the shriek of tires. A car was coming his way from up higher in the garage, and obviously having a hard time trying to stop. Kim and his car were right in its path, taking up the entire passageway.

He shielded his eyes with his gun. Through the glare, he could see that it was the red Camaro again. The driver's right arm was stiffened against the horn — one continuous blast. The passenger had leaned out the window and was flipping Kim off, yelling obscenities.

Kim lowered his weapon and aimed it at the driver. Within seconds, the Camaro started backing away at a high rate of speed. The passenger ducked below the dashboard.

When Kim turned around, the shadow he'd thought he'd detected by his car was gone. He held his breath and listened. Only the engine noise of the Camaro, getting farther away — no footsteps.

He bent down as low as he could and scanned in all directions. All he saw was tires. He straightened up and cursed under his breath. He put his gun back in its holster.

He walked between a couple of cars in the outside row, up to the waist-high wall, and looked out. He leaned over the edge and looked down. There was only pavement and mani-cured grass with lots of shadow. It was a long drop. Twenty feet or so, at least, he guessed.

She was not there. But if she had made that fall and then got up and ran off, she was a heck of a lot stronger than he'd given her credit. He slapped the wall's thick, concrete column, which supported the next level, in disgust and went back to his car. He drove off slowly, his eyes open and alert. She was gone.

****

"Martha, come look at this." Ted turned away from the window. His wife, Martha, was sprawled on the bed of their hotel room, lit only by the happy, dancing lights from the television. She had not even bothered to take the camera from around her neck.

"Martha!" he said again, sternly this time. "You've got to see this."

He heard Martha begin snoring. *Sheesh*, he thought. *Take her to the mall, and she'll go continuously for two, three dozen hours or so. Take her on one whale-watching tour, one heck of an expensive hour, let me tell ya, and she's out like a light.*

Ted shook his head in mild disgust over his wife of forty-three years and turned back to the window. He looked down at the parking garage. *You hear all the time about how crazy folks are in California. But they've got nothing on Hawaii,* he thought. Even in his head, he said it like a Bronx-accented version of, "How are ya?"

On the outside of the parking garage there was a woman, apparently. *Hard to tell, these days. All the men wanna look like broads.* Anyway, the *person* had long, blonde hair and seemed petite. She clung to the outside of the structure of the garage like she was doing a Spider Man imitation. He had watched, open-mouthed, the entire time.

It was a dumb coincidence, really, that he had gotten up from watching "Wheel of Fortune" and went to the window. Further dumb luck that he had looked down at the parking garage, of all places. He had watched the girl hop up on one of the low walls of the place. With only some hesitation, she had grabbed onto one of the vertical columns between the window spaces and thrown her leg around. He'd watched her tennis-shoed foot slip a couple of times before she'd found some support.

But when she did, she had started to climb up. She had just gotten her knees about even with the underside of the next level when some guy, apparently looking for her, maybe he'd seen her, had stuck his head out and looked over the edge.

Ted had actually knocked on his hotel room window. Of course, there was no way the guy could've possibly heard that. But if the dark-haired man had happened to look at him, Ted had been ready to point at the sky and mouth, "Look up!"

So Ted watched, and Martha snored, while the girl struggled up to the next window space and hauled herself back inside. When she was gone within the shadows and out of sight, Ted turned around and shook his head and said, "Darn crazy Hawaryans!"

****

Two hours after a young, pregnant woman had crawled to safety on the outside of a parking garage, a man woke up in his living room chair, where he had fallen asleep with a book in his lap and the television turned on.

I ought to just give up and go to bed, thought Robbie. The images on his TV screen had been a meaningless jumble for quite some time.

It was that darn book again. It was making him think about his little church. It was making him worry about most of the members of his congregation, people he'd grown so close to over the years, that he knew for a fact they meant more to him than most of the members of his own extended family. They loved him that way in return as well. But, he thought, *they'll only take so much...that darn book!* He shook his head slowly and smiled in spite of himself.

Thirty-two years in the ministry, and one darn book comes along and turns everything upside down. He had been preparing for an adult Bible study series on St. Paul's letter to the Romans. Someone, he couldn't remember who (not a member of his own church, though...maybe the guy at the bookstore), had recommended an old book by Charles Hodge.

He'd picked it up and started reading it. It was tough. The author had lived before television, obviously. Hodge actually expected folks to be able to hold onto a single train of thought for more than thirty seconds. Worse, while you're straining to hold onto the one, he introduces about three more; and for the rest of the long chapter, you're not going to understand what in the world he's saying if you haven't kept 'em all straight!

That darn book, Robbie thought again. He'd have put it away after the first three pages if it hadn't become a matter of pride for him. He was, after all, a veteran preacher of the Gospel. He was not altogether unfamiliar, therefore, with theology. Then, aside from the technical rigor it brought, Hodge started boldly proclaiming ideas that Robbie had never previously given much thought. He knew enough to recognize them as old-fashioned Calvinism. And he had a lot of really clever answers he routinely used to dismiss Calvinism...but Hodge would not go away. Robbie kept going back, if only to figure out exactly why Hodge was wrong.

Darn book. Robbie finished it last month. It had upset his whole nice world. He was getting ready to retire. He didn't need this.

He still believed Hodge was wrong, but admitted that he was not smart enough to say why. Which was a cop-out, he knew. Truth was, Robbie was scared stiff that Hodge might, in fact, be right. That would mean that the choice-centered Gospel he'd preached for the last three decades was faulty. Not a comforting thought to an old man.

Of even less comfort was the certainty that not one individual in his congregation had read Hodge, or would. If the tenor of Robbie's preaching changed, as a result of trying to communicate what he thought he'd learned, well, now, that was not going to go over very well, even with the friends who loved him. Oh, they probably wouldn't fire him, he knew.

How could they? It was his church. But they'd start asking him what he planned to do with all his time once he retired. The hints would begin to drop.

Robbie's stomach started hurting. Time for his late evening Tums. But he was too tired to get up. I'm going to fall asleep in my chair again, he thought; then wake up at three in the morning, to find that this station is running some masterpiece like "Biker Chicks on Mars." And then I'll be forced to watch it all because my lower back will be so kinked-up I can't move...again.

And, when I'm walkin' all hunched over tomorrow, JoAnna ain't gonna be any bundle of sympathy. She'll say, "Mercy, Robert, you're an old fool, you know that?" and then he'll say, "I believe you been tellin' me that since I was young, old woman."

Then she'll say, "And it hasn't helped at all, now, has it?" That's the way it always worked, and he had yet to figure out any decent comeback once it came to that.

So Robbie laughed a little to himself and hit the off button on his remote. He squinted his eyes and muttered, "Oh, oh, oh," as he fought valiantly to climb out of his recliner. When he was standing on his feet, victorious, he smiled and whispered, "Thank you, Jesus."

Robbie took tiny steps in the dark, even though he had his living room layout memorized. "Thank you, Lord, that my back still works...a little."

There was a soft knock at his front door. It made his stomach want to jump up into his throat. The knock came again, and he started for the door.

He unlocked it and opened it cautiously. At first, he didn't see anyone in the dark, but then he realized there was someone there, dressed in dark clothes, someone who had started to walk away, but was coming back.

It was a little white woman in a baseball cap. Robbie turned on his porch light and both of them squinted in the glare for a moment. Did he know her? He couldn't tell. She didn't look well, though. Dark, heavy bags hung under bloodshot eyes.

"Um...Pastor?" the girl said, almost whispering.

"Yes, ma'am? What's going on, child?" he asked.

"Um...you probably don't remember me, but--"

He pointed a finger at her. "J.L. Reed. Richards? Reed?"

She laughed a little. He was glad to see it. "Reed," she said.

"Yeah, you sat with Rita Kelly last two Sundays."

"Right...wow, I didn't think there was a chance you'd remember me..."

He tapped his temple and smiled. "Mind's still strong. 'Bout the only thing that is."

She tried to smile again, he could see.

"What's the matter, child?" he asked again.

Tears rolled down her face. She sniffed and said, "I need help."

Chapter Twelve

After his watch was over, Mark went forward and ate lunch. It was pork chops and potatoes. He ate quickly. There was a myriad of administrative details he had to wade through. The brass here would almost certainly not rush him, but he wanted to be done with it all by the time they thought to mention it.

Less than fifteen minutes after leaving the Engineroom, he was back, in Upper Level. He had the RAM, or Radioactive Material, notebook. It would allow him to find the scattered storage lockers, in order to do an inventory. *See the world! It's not just a job. It's an adventure!* He smiled and shook his head as he trudged aft past the main engines. Those recruiting commercials never showed guys doing the tedious parts of their jobs. Like RAM inventories.

But then, it wasn't adventure that had made him join, so that was all right with him. He had joined because, in his estimation, the Navy, more than any other branch of the Service, meant leaving. Operational Naval units don't sit at military bases for months and years on end. They shove off. They get up and go. That attracted him, because that's what he was after. He had been ready to leave.

Leave for where? He questioned himself. *Anywhere.* Because anywhere is not nowhere and that's where he had been.

He spotted the silver locker he'd been hunting. It was about two feet on a side and hung up against the port bulkhead, about five and a half feet off the deck. It was set behind the 1.6 thousand gallon per day distilling plant, or "Still"; and so he had not seen the yellow and magenta tri-foil warning label until he was practically face-to-face with it.

He brought out the key Jason Lorde had given him, already attached to his key ring. He raised it halfway to the lock, then hesitated. The padlock was in place, through the locker's turning handle, but the mating piece meant to hold the handle still had broken off its light weld. Technically, if he wanted to get technical, this represented damage to a Radioactive Material Storage Area. But did he want to get that technical?

Brand new on board, brand new to submarines, he was the rookie., the new guy. If he made a big Radiological Control issue out of a broken handle…he'd get branded immediately, not as a stickler for detail (which he admittedly was), but as the surface-sailing radcon geek who was way too uptight. He looked back up forward, where the Upper Level watch was leaning against a handrail, drinking coffee, staring sleepily at the starboard main engine. The mechanic was ignoring him.

Mark opened the locker. There was a yellow plastic bag inside. The plastic was especially thick; but transparent, so that the contents could be viewed without opening it. It was a shiny metal pipe assembly, about a foot long. The bag was twisted closed on top and sealed with green duct tape. There was a RAM tag, which identified and cataloged the item.

"Yep," Mark said to himself, "Mare Island Naval Shipyard sample rig. Hottest thing on the boat outside the Reactor Compartment."

Mark had brought a beta-gamma detector along, to see that the radiation levels on the tag actually matched the levels coming off the item. He held the cylindrical probe up next to the bag. The needle on the dial face immediately rose.

Mark whistled when he read the meter's final number. He grabbed the top of the bag, around the duct-tape seal, with his left hand and lifted it out. Several things happened at once. Almost as soon as he hefted the weight of the metal assembly, he felt a deep-striking pain in the fingers of his left hand.

He also noted the presence of two, orange radcon gloves sitting loose where the bag had been. Then, as he grimaced at the pain in his hand and knew that something was terribly wrong, he saw that the bag was tearing. And that was ridiculous. These bags are specifically made for toughness. The pipe was not *that* heavy!

There was not any time to panic. The bottom fell out of the bag altogether and the sample assembly fell with it. It clanged on the deck, simultaneous with Mark's first drops of blood.

His ears felt overheated, as embarrassment began to mingle with the pain in his hand. He dropped the remaining part of the bag, and it surprised him by "clanging" a little as well. He looked, and protruding from the bag was a knife blade, now stained red. It had been sticking up against the bag seal, and hidden by it as well.

He clenched his left hand in a fist, as much out of anger as to stem the bleeding. That action wound up stopping neither the fury nor the blood. His palm was dripping red onto the floor and down his wrist toward his elbow.

"What in the …?" The Upper Level watch approached, alerted by the noise.

Mark whirled around without moving his feet, to minimize the spread of dust-borne contamination. "Stand fast, Upper Level!" he said hotly.

The mechanic froze.

When Mark spoke again, it was the professional in him, rising to the occasion. "Upper Level, we have a potentially contaminated spill with an injured man here. But before you alert Maneuvering, I want you to redirect this ventilation duct so it's not blowing this stuff around."

Mark motioned with his left elbow to a large pipe coming down out of the overhead. The mechanic nodded, shaking. He moved forward and pushed the vent duct in toward the center of the boat.

"Thank you," Mark said slowly. "Now, do you have any rags with you?"

The mechanic nodded and pulled a white cloth from his hip pocket. Mark said, "Now throw it to me."

The mechanic did what he was told, lobbing the rag underhanded. Mark stuffed the rag in his left hand and clamped down on it. The watchstander ran off to find a 2JV phone. Mark cursed himself under his breath. After Maneuvering announced, "Spill! Spill! Spill!" and went on to give the known facts of the casualty (including, "The injured man is Petty Officer Reed!"), he cursed himself again.

Spill with Injured Man! How many times had he run that drill? About a zillion, but never as the dumb, injured idiot. Always as the Radcon expert who comes in to save the day. All he could do was wait for his fellow ELTs to respond to Maneuvering's cry for help. They would come and rescue their new, brave leader. He cursed himself again.

*Gee, Captain, sir. This sort of thing's never happened to me before. Honest. Cross my heart and hope to die. I'm really very careful about radioactive contamination. Really I am...Yessir, I'll be a **great** Leading ELT for ya! I want to be a Chief!!* He cursed again.

A minute later, Jason Lorde, Paul Lawrence, and the Doc came pounding aft to deal with the situation. As the two ELTs donned yellow protective clothing, Mark lowered his head and cursed a final time.

Then, as the radiological commotion around him kicked into high gear, he thought, *Wait a second. What in blazes is a knife doing in a bag with the MINSY rig? That bag didn't fall apart. It was cut.*

Now he was mad.

Two hours later, Mark sat in the *Omaha's* Wardroom. It was about half the size of Crew's Mess, but only had one large table. A three-inch band of white gauze was wrapped around the fingers of his left hand.

Framed pictures adorned the wood-paneled walls. They were all of *Omaha*. *Omaha* at her commissioning, the whole boat set on roller tracks, ready to be pushed into the water; her nose-cone specially painted with a stars-and-stripes design. *Omaha* running on the surface, photographed from a helicopter. *Omaha* emerging nose-first from the sea, foamy water spraying everywhere.

Mark sat at one end of the rectangular table. Closest to him on his right, the Engineer was pouring over a large, black technical manual. Mark was familiar with it. "Radiological Controls." He could see that Mr. Bushler was opened to the section dealing with incident reports. The Eng was writing notes onto a yellow legal pad.

Commander Shelby sat next to Bushler. His right elbow was propped up on the table, and he held his chin in his hand. His stare was rather blank. Waiting.

The red-haired Doc sat, hands folded in his lap, across from the Eng, and a young-looking ensign sat next to him. This was the CRA, Mark's division officer. Mark had spoken to him briefly. He could tell the junior officer really didn't know much about supervising ELT's. Mark had promised to help him along.

The aft door to the Wardroom opened, and the CO stepped in.

All the seated men started to their feet, but the CO waved his hand and muttered, "As you were."

They all sat back down as the CO pulled out the chair across from Mark.

The CO never looked at Mark, but said, "Go ahead, Eng."

Bushler cleared his throat and looked up to address the group. "Gentlemen. There is no way around this. A spill does not automatically require the submission of an Incident Report, nor even does a spill with injury."

The Engineer looked at Mark over his glasses.

"But," he said, "skin contamination, with or without injury, does."

Mark knew that already. He saw Parnette sigh and lower his head.

The Eng went on. "We are here to collect statements from those involved."

He nodded to Mark, who then retold the story of how the spill happened. When he was finished, the Engineer said, "CRA?"

The young, blonde ensign looked surprised to be called upon. Flustered, he held up some over-long stapled sheets of paper.

He said, "According to the radcon logs, MM1 Liegert performed the last Radioactive Material Inventory two months ago."

He flipped a few pages and stopped at one and pointed to a place. "No anomalies noted."

The Captain shook his head and shifted forward in his chair, frowning. "CRA," he said, and Mark could tell by the tone that this was the bad cop. "Do you mean to tell me that Liegert failed to note the fact that he sliced the MINSY rig's bag? Are you saying he failed to note the fact that he taped a knife to it in the hopes of gigging the next man?"

The blonde man's complexion reddened and he stuttered, "No...sir....I....he noted..."

"He noted what?" Parnette asked, leaning toward the officer.

The answer was a whisper. "No...no anomalies...sir."

Parnette closed his eyes and fell back into his seat. The XO was staring up into the overhead, rubbing his neck with his hand a little too deeply.

Mark sat forward, "Um, excuse me, sir," he said.

Parnette opened his eyes. "Yes, Reed."

"Sir, I don't think Liegert did this. In fact, I don't think an ELT did it at all."

Parnette blinked. "Why not?"

"All the ELT's have keys to all the RAM lockers, sir.

The lock on this one was busted."

The Captain tilted his head a little and widened his eyes.

Mark said, "Plus, I'd bet anything that the gloves left in there were left by whoever did it. No one except the ELT's has got access to the radioactive waste bin. I think the guy who did this raided a spill kit and got out the pair of gloves. He was smart enough to know he would need them if he was going to be slicing that bag open. When he was done, he couldn't just throw hot gloves into a normal trash can."

The CO nodded once and stared at the table for several seconds. Then, he shook his head. "No. Whoever did this was not rational. Why'd he put on gloves to take an action that could potentially contaminate the whole boat, including himself? This was not something planned out rationally. It was done randomly. A random act of violence toward whatever sucker happened to inspect that locker next."

He looked directly at Mark. "Sorry, Petty Officer Reed. You were the sucker."

Mark tried to grin slightly, even though he was not in a grinning mood.

Parnette continued. "Not only was it a random act of violence. It was an act of sabotage against my boat. I don't believe I like that very much, gentlemen."

The CO looked around at the men, who all seemed to do their best to look like they agreed with him. Parnette said, "I think whoever did this was beyond caring. He didn't care about Omaha, and he didn't care what happened to him. In the last two days, we've received proof that Liegert was at that point. He didn't care anymore. He was feeling destructive. It just happened to turn inward on him."

Shelby was nodding now. Something about it didn't seem right to Mark when compared with what he had read in Liegert's journal. Should he say something about that? Who knows, he thought? He could just as well be wrong about the guy. Besides, the issue of "who-dun-it?" was secondary in his mind right now. The real question was about the extent of the consequences.

The Engineer spoke again. "Corpsman, would you please relate your actions in this matter?"

The Doc shifted in his seat and croaked, "Well, any casualty with injury has got to be weighed. Which is worse, the casualty or the trauma? In this case, I could see that Reed had used a rag to help stop the bleeding and wasn't in danger. So the radiological casualty took precedence, and I just kinda stood there and waited until it was my turn."

The Engineer nodded.

"Then, when they were frisking Reed out of the spill area, the rag was hot."

"Contaminated?" asked the Eng.

"Right. I had them frisk his hand right then."

"And?"

"And," the Doc said, looking over at Mark as if to say he was sorry, "there were counts...about three hundred counts above background."

The Engineer scribbled down, "300 cps > bkg."

"Then, we bagged up the patient's hand and transported him to Nucleonics, where we flushed out the wound into the contaminated sink with deionized water."

Mark sat stunned. *The patient's hand?* In all the commotion it hadn't occurred to him until now. This incident was going to become part of his permanent record. When the Doc had run the cold water into his wounds, that had been painful. Painful enough to nauseate him in fact. But this...this was worse.

He could feel the blood draining from his face. No First Class ELT looking for his Chief's anchors was going anywhere once the Review Board saw that he had actually been injured and contaminated in a spill, prompting an Incident Report to the Secretary of the Navy.

It wasn't his fault. But that wouldn't matter. There would be plenty of other First Classes in front of the Board who had nothing like that in their records. The Board would not care why.

The Doc kept on talking. Mark's right hand, almost of its own volition, found his keys in his front pocket and clutched the metal horse. He squeezed it hard.

My career, he thought, *has just ended. Liegert is dead, but I am destroyed.* Mark only heard the Doc in a tangential fashion.

"The water flush, along with some swabs, eliminated the counts in the wound areas. However, the flesh itself may be shielding some betas. There's no way to know. My recommendation is that we keep Petty Officer Reed out of the Engineroom, at least until the wounds have solidly scabbed over. Until that time, I need to unwrap the dressing at least daily and frisk the wounds again to see if any further contamination gets pushed to the surface by the healing process."

The Captain sighed and nodded his head. He said to the Eng, "I guess we're in need of yet another Leading ELT for a while."

The Engineer nodded and addressed the CRA. "Petty Officer Lawrence?"

The CRA agreed. "He's next in line, seniority-wise."

Mark became aware of his death-grip on the carousel horse and released it, angry with himself. There was nowhere to go to get away from this. The horse could not magically transport him somewhere, to some fairyland where his career was still viable. He wanted to punch somebody, only he didn't know whom to punch.

But he would find out.

When he left the Wardroom, Paul and Jason were waiting for him in Crew's Mess. Jason handed him several sheets of radiological survey results, the paperwork aftermath of the spill. Mark looked them over, still disgusted with himself, and put his initials on each page in the blanks labeled, "Leading ELT Review." Mark handed the papers to Paul.

"How's your hand?" Paul asked.

Mark shook his head sharply, dismissing the question altogether. "Cap'n thinks Liegert set the whole thing up. Part of the self-destructive thing he had going."

Jason asked, "You don't?"

Mark shook his head again. "No. I don't."

Both of the other men's looks said, "Well, who then?"

Mark said, "I intend to find out who did it. When I do, they're going to wish I hadn't."

Part Three

"Evil pursues sinners"
-Hebrew proverb

Chapter Fifteen

Reggie Nelson sat at the desk in his room at the Empress Hotel in Hong Kong. His head still hurt and his own smell offended him, a combination of body odor and vomit. What a night it had been.

He had taken the hydrofoil across Hong Kong's famous Harbor as soon as it got dark. That had been pretty cool. The coolest part was watching all the junks scramble to get out of its way as it headed over to Kowloon. Their little lanterns swung crazily as the wake of the hydrofoil tossed them up and down for several seconds.

It was also cool to be the scrungiest dude on the boat. Everyone else was dressed in formal attire. Asian men taking their ladies, for a price, no doubt, to the Kowloon side for a night of gambling and casino-hopping. They all looked at him, down their noses, and it made him laugh. He was confident he was carrying more cash than any of them.

Now, the night was a blur. A blur of bad luck and worse champagne. It was so bad, in fact, that he had switched to beer, even though the added formaldehyde made him want to gag. He forced himself to get used to it. Now he was paying for it. He had learned one thing on his ventures outside the United States, but he doubted it was the sort of tidbit that would profit him later in life. It was that there is no hangover like a formaldehyde hangover, and no diarrhea like

Asian beer diarrhea.

It was going on noon. Had he missed the point of contact? He hoped not. The people who were supplying him with cash and a room in Hong Kong didn't seem like they'd be very understanding about these things.

He turned on his computer and got the modem going. He entered his commands and waited. Ten seconds later, he had access to Japan's Line 87, Worthy Wife net. The characters were all Japanese, of course, but so was his keyboard.

That had been one of the things that had attracted the North Koreans to him. His dad had been employed with the Federal Government as a diplomatic aide to Japan. They'd lived there for years, and he'd learned the language.

He typed in a request for a current summary report. Worthy Wife was monitoring one hundred and thirty-four civilian ships of various sizes. There were a smaller number of various military surface craft, including the two North Korean cruisers heading straight at the Japanese mainland.

But what he was concerned about was the *Omaha*. And there she was, right about where he figured she'd be. That's cutting it close, he thought. *Omaha* was only minutes away from normal passive sonar contact with *Quiet Tiger.*

Fate was smiling on him, without a doubt. If he'd slept another half hour, he'd have botched the whole deal. Mr. Lee would not have been happy.

He backed out of Line 87 and punched in the commands to dial up Mr. Lee's office.

****

Mr. Lee had still not been overjoyed to only have a matter of minutes to get *Quiet Tiger* her instructions. But he had dealt with it, and with the miserable American boy. He would continue to deal with him, at least for a little while. Then, the boy would become irrelevant.

Quiet Tiger was surfaced and snorkeling, waiting for word to begin her "sea-trials." They received the message and dived. Her captain knew that she was an old boat, and that, as an old woman's bones creak and whine, so did she. He would not have to make any extra noise for the *Omaha* to hear him.

So he gave command to carve circles in the water at thirty meters. He was not ready to take her much lower than that.

He checked his watch. He needed to give the Americans at least thirty minutes.

He thought about his country. How proud he was. His was possibly the only nation on earth with people noble enough to make Communism work. The poverty and famine festering within her borders like open sores were not her fault.

The blame was rightly placed at the feet of South Korea, the apostate puppet of the West. The South had continued an unending, covert push to subvert and destroy the glorious aims of the North. The South didn't care how many people were killed in the effort, how many North Korean boys and girls starved as orphans in the streets. The South ignored her own corruption and grew fat on the delicacies of Western capitalism.

The ultimate sign of degeneration in the South was her total reconciliation with Japan. She was a whore in the palace of the emperor in Tokyo. She was a most-willing Comfort Woman.

The South paid no attention to history. She forgot. She accepted riches in exchange for her forgetfulness.

He would not forget, ever. He would not forget his mother. Or her husband, the man who should have been his father. He would not forget the stories his mother had told him. They were so vivid in his brain, he was sure he actually saw the things that happened before his birth.

The man who should have been his father had been bayoneted by the soldiers of the Imperial Japanese Army. His crime? He had a beautiful wife and the soldiers wanted her. He could see the man in farmer's clothes, grabbing at his blood-soaked belly with both hands, falling into the very land he was farming.

They had made his mother a Comfort Woman. Thinking about it made his hands shake, because he could see everything, even though she had never told him those stories. He could see the dirty, sweating Imperial soldiers backhanding her across the face. He could see her fall onto the grimy mattress, could see them tear at her clothes, could hear her screaming at them.

One of them, who knows which, had impregnated her. At some point, they grew tired of her and let her go. She had given birth to him. She should have discarded him. It would have been understandable. But she did not. She had raised him and loved him.

The soldiers came again one night. One of them recognized her and began laughing and boasting to his fellows about the last night he had spent with "this Lilly." They had attacked her. He was four years old. They ignored him, and he watched the whole thing.

When they were finished, one of them, still laughing, drew out a pistol and shot her once in the abdomen. The Japanese man looked down at him and just smiled. The soldiers went away.

It took her a long time to die. He had crawled up next to her. He said nothing. He did not cry. She draped an arm around him and sang a lullaby until she could not sing anymore.

Now the Captain checked his watch again. It had not been half an hour, but he could wait no longer. Most times, when he thought of his mother, he was sure he could feel the spirits of his honored ancestors surrounding him, crying out to him for vindication. He gave the order to surface.

****

Omaha had been rigged for Ultra Quiet for forty minutes when the com system between the Sonar Room and Control squawked. The voice from Sonar was quick. Almost impossible to understand unless you know what you're listening for. Mark didn't know what he was listening for, but he was learning.

The Engineer had decided that, since Mark was not going to be headed Aft for some time, he might as well learn his roll as part of the Special Tracking Party. When this was stationed, the regular practice was to take the Engineroom Supervisor and the Auxiliary Electrician from their watches and bring them up into Control, where they could assist the Quartermaster. Their job was to simply keep independent track of numbers that appeared on a screen at the Fire Control Station, and to feed these to the QM at his request.

"Con, Sonar, have a new submerged contact bearing three-two-two, range five thousand yards. Believe contact is a submarine. Designate contact *Quebec One.*"

The XO, Commander Shelby, was the current Officer of the Deck. He walked over to the single sonar screen at the front of Control and looked at it for a few seconds. He grabbed the CB-radio type transmitter from beside the screen and spoke into it, "Sonar, Con, aye. Get me a classification."

"Con, Sonar, aye. The computer's working on it."

"Sonar, Con, very well." The XO put the mike back.

Mark noticed the Engineer coming up the aft ladder from Crew's Mess. Bushler saw him and asked, "How is your hand, Petty Officer Reed?"

Mark smiled and said, "Good as new. Ready to go back to work."

Bushler's lips turned up slightly. It might have been a grin. "I believe that the Doc will have the final say on that one."

The XO met the Eng on the periscope dias. The Engineer handed some papers to him and said, "I agree with your assessment, sir."

The XO nodded. "We've just now acquired her."

"Con, Sonar," came the metallic voice again. "The computer had to go way back for this one. *Quebec One* is a

French diesel boat, circa 1955 or so."

The XO acknowledged the report. He and the Eng looked at each other with raised eyebrows. The XO spoke into the mike again. "Sonar, Con. How sure are we about that? Has the boat been modified at all?"

"Con, Sonar. Not that we can tell, sir. It matches the profile."

The Eng walked back over to where Reed was stationed at the QM's table. This time he was definitely smiling. "No shielding."

"Sir?" Reed asked.

"The battery technology that India has been developing involves the capture and conversion of gamma rays liberated in the process of normal radioactive decay."

Mark knew what that meant. All radioactive decay gives off energy of some sort. That's what's unhealthy about it, like a sunburn. "Like solar energy gets converted to electricity through photovoltaic cells?"

The Eng nodded. "The impediment to doing this with radioactive decay has always been with the sensitivity needed in the cells. And, of course, to have a strong battery, one would need…"

"A whole lot of powerful radioactive material," Reed offered.

"Exactly. And you would not be able to shield it in the same manner as our reactor. That is, close up and tight. You would require a different geometry with the material than if fission was the goal."

"So, this boat doesn't have shielding?"

The Eng shook his head. "Even if one removed the conventional battery from an old diesel submarine, you would not then have the space required for both the new equipment, and what amounts to a small reactor compartment. I believe that would require extensive modification to the submarine's hull. Our own Navy did this sort of modification in order to construct the first generation of ballistic missile subs. We took fast-attack boats, cut them in half, and then welded the two ends onto a complex of missile silos."

Mark smirked and nodded, recalling the stories he'd heard about that while a student at the Navy's Nuclear Power School. "And since that modification hasn't been done here?"

"Either," the Eng said, "*Quiet Tiger's* crew will be dead from radiation exposure in short order—or, she does not possess the experimental battery the intelligence suggested."

Mark pointed at the spot on the map where the Eng had told him before of the North Korean cruisers. "So, these ships you were wondering about? Is *Quiet Tiger* a decoy, meant to hold us here while they go and do their thing?"

He nodded. "That is my thinking."

"Captain in Control," someone announced. Mark looked up and saw Parnette and Shelby walking over to the maps.

"Sirs," the Eng said to them with a nod.

"Why don't you let him know what we're talking about," said the XO.

"Captain, sir, I may be speaking prematurely, but I don't think so," he began, taking off his copper-framed reading glasses. "I suspect that *Quiet Tiger* is a decoy. We are the only American fast-attack boat in the region, and as long as we stay around them, we are conveniently occupied."

The CO smirked, but kept listening. "What's on your mind?" he asked.

"As I told you last night on the midwatch, I am first of all concerned about the lack of surface ship escort for the sea trials of what is ostensibly the shining star in the North Korean Navy."

The CO nodded and said, "Right. We agreed there could be a couple of different reasons for that. We said we'd watch *Quiet Tiger* and then zip up and check on those cruisers if we had time."

The Eng acted like he didn't hear him. "The second thing that has puzzled me is the disappearance of the 'observation' fishing troller coincidental with *Quiet Tiger's* launch.

Why would North Korea destroy that boat now, when it's been there for months? Of course, I'm assuming it is gone because it was destroyed. But why?"

"Just to thumb their noses at us. They know there will be no retaliation," said the XO.

The Eng nodded. "That is certainly plausible. But I am thinking this: Satellite recon picked up their cruisers, but we don't have satellites that can track submerged targets."

"Another submarine?"

"Yes, Captain. That is my thinking. I am proposing that the two cruisers in fact are escorting a North Korean submarine, but not *Quiet Tiger*, and not here. Our observation boat was in a position to watch that second sub launch before the depth would permit a safe dive."

"That goes counter to all our intelligence. And South Korea's as well," the CO said.

"I would concede that. We don't know how the *Quiet Tiger* intel made it around, over, or through the DMZ to a topless bar in Oahu, but I admit that it tends to undermine my theory. But I have more questions."

"Let's hear 'em," said Parnette.

"Well," he said, motioning to the papers in the XO's hand, "you saw the radio traffic. They say their battery system is in need of eighteen hours worth of repair. Since when do you send a prototype submarine to sea with her main power plant in need of eighteen hours of repair? That could merely be a delaying tactic to keep us here."

"C'mon, Eng," Parnette said, "Something could've busted already. We're talking about the ship building techniques of a communist country on the verge of starvation and a forty-year-old boat, here! It ain't exactly Newport News Shipyard."

"Granted," he answered. "But think also about their supposed nuclear battery. Think of the shielding a battery of this sort would require. The boat we're tracking is an unmodified diesel from the Korean War era. How long is it? A hundred, a hundred and fifty feet? Where is the shielding?

Where is the battery stored?"

The two senior officers stared at each other. The CO said, "You guys are convinced we're in the wrong place?"

The Eng nodded enthusiastically. "I am, sir."

The CO nodded himself, less enthusiastically. "So what is it you want to do about your theory?"

Shelby spoke up, saying, "Well, sir, I think it's reasonable to assume that if *Quiet Tiger* has been given eighteen hours for repairs, she will take at least that. I think we should zip north at flank speed for nine or ten hours. Take a long-range snapshot with the scoping array at that time. That should just about let us get a picture of whatever is in the area of those cruisers. If we're wrong, then we have time to get back and reacquire *Quebec One*."

The CO was quiet for a moment and then took a deep breath. "Officer of the Deck," he said.

"Sir?" Shelby said, straightening his back a little.

"Mr. Bushler here is going to give you a new course to follow. Do what he says."

Shelby smiled and nodded. "Aye-aye, Cap'n."

At that, all three officers left the QM table to Mark and the on-watch Quartermaster, a Second Class named Kresge. Kresge was busy drawing with a pencil and a straightedge. Mark was dumbfounded.

He said, "Did you just hear all that?"

Kresge didn't look up. "Yup."

Mark had to laugh at his nonchalance. "That conversation would probably be classified so high the Pentagon wouldn't let anybody but God and the President know about it."

Kresge shook his head and kept drawing. "Nah. Just the President. God wouldn't pass the background check. Too much past contact with foreigners."

Mark could only shake his head. Kresge said, "Welcome to submarines."

Chapter Fourteen

J.L. wiped her nose for the hundredth time. The tissue had gone above and beyond the call of duty. "All for this," she said, setting the 3.5" computer disc down on the table in front of her.

Pastor Robert (he preferred Brother Robbie) and his wife, JoAnna (who was the only person on earth who refused to call him either "Robbie" or "Brother") sat stunned and speechless. J.L. simply looked at them, giving them time to let the whole story sink in. JoAnna had gotten out of bed and was wearing a bathrobe.

She had made a big pot of hot chocolate for them all, listening in while J.L. related recent events to Robbie at the kitchen table. Robbie's skin was a shade darker than the drink and his close-cut hair was all gray, as was his mustache. Though he was going on seventy, there wasn't much in the way of wrinkles in his face. JoAnna was a thin woman. Her hair had not yet gone completely gray, but she did have some dignified wrinkles. Her skin was a little lighter than Robbie's. The husband and wife turned to stare at each other.

JoAnna rose from the table. She asked J.L., "Which hospital did you say Rita was at?"

J.L. shook her head. "I really don't know. It's just a few blocks away from the main drag at Waikiki."

"Community General? Or was it Presbyterian?"

"I'm sorry, Mrs. McClain. I really don't know."

JoAnna's face softened as she turned away and picked up an enormous phone book from the kitchen counter. "That's all right. I'm sure we'll find it."

Robbie stared at J.L.. She was reminded of the way that Agent Kim had tried to read her face. Now, though, she was hoping to be as transparent as possible.

"That's quite a story, young lady," he said, smiling slightly.

"I know."

"Are you sure it was your face on the T.V.?"

"Yes, sir."

"Really? Sometimes those drawings don't look like nobody at all! Look like some high school art class, just tryin' to figure out where to put the eyes and all that."

She laughed a little, which surprised her. Something about the McClain house made it hard to stay tense. "No, I'm sure it was me. Especially since they basically connected me to Rita when they showed it."

Robbie nodded. He said, after some silence, "Means this FBI man ain't quite right, huh?"

"Yeah, I think that's what it means."

"What if you just mailed the disc to somebody?"

J.L.'s face said, "Huh?"

"Well, if you got rid of it like that, maybe some of the heat would go away. Maybe this Kim guy would go off chasing the disc instead of you."

She nodded. "I think that could be true. But...I don't know...whatever happens, I can't get the picture of Rita out of my mind after she saved my life. She was so bloody. She had no business doing anything other than lying down and dying...but she got there and saved me. She went through a lot for me, and I don't think it would be right for me to take the easy way out if it means being careless with this."

She pointed at the disc that still sported Rita's bloody thumbprint.

Robbie nodded, eyebrows raised. "That takes a lot of courage. And a lot of faith, to say that."

J.L. said, "No. I don't feel very full of either one of those right now."

Robbie smiled big. Bigger than he should have, she thought. Like he thought he knew something she didn't.

"So what do you want to do with it?" he asked.

She shrugged, and turned her mug of hot chocolate around slowly. "I think...I think I need to put this disc in Admiral Crabb's hands myself and tell him where it came from."

"How you gonna do that?"

"I don't know."

JoAnna came back from speaking on the phone. She said, "Rita's in Community General. She's just out of surgery. In critical condition. The doctors...the doctors say she's got about a fifty-fifty chance now."

Brother Robbie smiled gently. "I guess it's a good thing we don't believe in chance, then."

J.L. could see tears welling up in the older woman's eyes. Robbie reached up for her hand, and she squeezed his in response, placing her other hand over her mouth. Then she sat down next to him, straightened up with obvious resolve, and said, "Robert, I want to go be there for her."

He chuckled and said, "Who you talkin' to, old woman? Someone who doesn't know you at all? Of course, we're going."

Then he looked at J.L. and said, "But, first, we need to get our visitor taken care of for the night."

JoAnna apparently knew what that meant, even if J.L. didn't. Robbie and JoAnna reached their hands across the table to her. She took them. Their hands were warm and felt so much stronger than her own.

Robbie bowed his head and prayed, "Dear Lord, Your eyes are upon us now. And I know, Lord, that You have brought this girl to us for a reason and so I thank You. Thank You for making us able to help her, even in a small way. Father, I pray You would descend on J.L. right now with your Spirit of peace, and that You would calm her busy mind. I pray that you would surround her this night with the protection and fortification of the Heavenly hosts; that you would set a hedge around her as she sleeps. Oh, Lord, we lift our voices to You now for Sister Rita, as well. We ask that you would heal her broken body, Lord, and care for her. In Jesus' name, Amen."

JoAnna said, "Amen."

J.L. wept. She could not stop. Maybe she really had gone crazy.

JoAnna put an arm around her shoulders and led her down the hall to the guest room, where she turned down the covers on a small bed and laid out another bathrobe, retrieved from the closet. She let J.L. know she was welcome to take a shower, and that there were fresh towels in the bathroom.

"You sleep tonight, child," she said as she closed the door behind her. "And don't be afraid anymore. Ain't no one messing with this house unless the Lord gives permission… and He ain't givin' permission to nobody."

When J.L. was out of the shower, she heard the McClains drive off in their car. They had accepted her, brought her in, and made a place for her. If they could do it, suddenly it wasn't such a stretch to think that Jesus could, too.

She pulled the light covers over her shoulders in the dark, and when she slept, her dreams did not disturb her.

****

Omaha secured from Ultra Quiet and went to Ahead Flank. She passed by *Quiet Tiger* at a range of three-thousand yards.

It hadn't mattered whether they were rigged for Ultra Quiet or not. Contrary to gathered intelligence, *Quiet Tiger* had not been fitted with the latest in passive sonar. In fact, she had no passive sonar at all.

Passive sonar is like sitting in a dark room, watching a burglar enter with a flashlight turned on. You'll see him a long time before he'll see you. Active sonar, the reverberating ping of the WWII movies, is the flashlight. Maybe you'll get lucky and point it in someone's face right off, but, more likely, you're just going to succeed in giving away your own position.

So *Quiet Tiger* sat silent, pretending to have passive sonar, while Omaha charged by, making all the noise in the world.

The North Koreans had known this would be a gamble, but their bet was hedged. Because they did collectively have passive sonar, in the form of Japan's Worthy Wife.

The American in the room at the Empress Hotel watched the whole event unfold, courtesy of his uninvited link with Line 87.

He was a little bit perplexed. None of his instructions from Mr. Lee mentioned what to do if *Omaha* broke off *Quiet Tiger* after just two hours. *Omaha* was at 800 feet, going 38 knots. Now, the distance between the subs was growing at an alarming pace.

Shaking, he backed out of Line 87 and hit the button to dial Mr. Lee.

Minutes later, the following message was received by *Quiet Tiger.*

"The American has broken off its surveillance and is heading into the Blind Widow operation area. It is several miles from your location, moving at more than double your top speed. Abort your mission and return to port."

The North Korean captain guffawed after he read it and tried to hand it back to his radio officer. Some sort of joke. But the officer would not take it. The officer would not look at his commanding officer. The officer looked worried.

The Captain reread the message four times.

At the end of the fourth, when it was apparent the words were not about to change or fade away, the Captain addressed his crew. He commended them. To a man, they had performed their duties in a manner reflecting gloriously on their nation and their ancestors.

He gave his second-in-command control of the bridge. He ordered him to return the ship to port.

He looked straight ahead of him as he walked into his stateroom and closed the door. *That was it. It was over.* He had been given one assignment. Delay the Americans. They had not been delayed.

He thought about his ancestors, a line of very proud and noble people — on his mother's side, at least. He could feel their spirits surrounding him now, could sense their deep disappointment. They had all lived honorable lives. They had been stripped of their honor by the Japanese. Fate had left it up to the bastard son of that honorable line, tainted with the blood of the vilest of enemies, to reclaim that honor.

Not only would his hunger for vengeance remain forever unsatisfied. His mother's family would stand dishonored for all time. And that was the deeper hurt.

He jammed the barrel of a pistol into the soft flesh under his chin and pulled the trigger.

****

Four hours later, Mark finished his watch in Control. He went to his rack and tried to get some sleep — no success. He decided to read in Liegert's journal.

Why would God love me? If I'm going to believe my Bible, then I must believe that He does, but why? What is it about me that earns His love?

Jesus taught that if we are obedient to his teachings, then the Father will love us and answer our prayers. That sounds like a relational sort of reciprocating love that I can begin to understand.

But what am I to make of Paul's teaching that God loved me, a specific individual, before the creation of the world, before I existed, and while I lived a life of rebellion? While I was a sinner, God loved me.

Nothing I have done merited that love. In fact, if we're talking about merit and what I deserve from God, then I'm getting exactly the opposite of what is "just." All I have ever earned is His wrath. But He chooses to love me instead.

I guess maybe that is the point. He chose. He chooses. He loves me because He wants to. That seems to eliminate me from the equation. That's a good thing, I think. As long as I know that He loves me purely based on His own good pleasure, any boasting on my part is disqualified. All I am left with is an overwhelming sense of awe. Maybe bewilderment is a better word or astonishment.

It's funny to think that this one decision God made, to love me, motivates not only Him, but me. It motivated Him to do what was needed to cleanse me of my sins, to remove from me the wrath that I deserved. That happened on the Cross. And it motivated me, eventually, inevitably, to turn to Him and honestly desire to do what pleases Him.

How do I communicate that? How do I make people understand when I talk to them about Jesus Christ that I'm talking about a relationship based on God's love, and not about handing them "The Truth," not about changing their doctrine, so much as changing their hearts?

****

Agent Kim drove up to the gate of the Military Housing area in the community of Ewa Beach. He followed the instructions on the sign by the guard's booth. It said, Slow Down-- Dim Lights--Have ID Ready.

A Marine in green camouflage manned the booth. A service .45 was holstered at his side.

The Marine stepped out of the booth and up to Kim's car as it stopped. Kim rolled down his window and flashed his badge.

"What's your business, sir?" the Marine asked.

"I'm Special Agent Kim. I'm investigating the shooting of Ms. Rita Kelly, who worked at the Navy Subase. I need to go through her house."

The Marine shook his head. "I'm sorry, sir. All military facilities on the island are at an elevated Defcon due to the bombing yesterday. If you are not in actual pursuit of a suspect, I'm afraid I can't let you in."

"I'm FBI, corporal — Federal Bureau of Investigations.

Just who do you think is going to investigate a bombing of a federal installation?"

"I don't know, sir."

"I am, that's who."

"I'm sorry, sir. I'm going to have to ask you to turn your vehicle around now."

Kim looked ahead. There was no physical gate. Maybe he could just go--. He noticed at the edge of his vision, the Marine moved his hand stealthily to the grip of his weapon, unsnapping the leather strap that secured it.

Kim put his car in reverse and rolled up his window. He cursed to himself. He smiled at the guard as he left.

The guard watched the red tail-lights for several blocks, then went back into the booth. There was a yellow note stuck beside the phone. He dialed the number on the note.

"Naval Investigative Service, may I help you?" came the answer.

"Yes, this is Corporal Washington at Ewa Beach Housing Gate. I need to speak to a Commander Gentry."

Gentry took only seconds to pick up. "What do you have for me?" he asked.

"Yes, Commander, sir," the Marine said. "I was told to call if contact was made with FBI Agent Kim, so..."

Gentry asked for the details and seemed happy to get them.

****

Hours later, *Omaha* went to Ahead One-Third, to periscope depth at 1547 local time. She stuck up her radio mast and received traffic.

The Captain read it first, in his stateroom. Upon comparing the radio message with his Ship's Log, he found that the North Korean cruisers changed their course and speed just twenty-one minutes after he had broken off the observation of *Quiet Tiger*. Parnette was not a man who believed in coincidence. The cruisers were now heading south at an estimated speed of 45 knots, by satellite photos. He felt safe in making some assumptions.

One, the North Koreans knew about *Omaha*. Possibly, *Quiet Tiger* had acquired them when they were close. And two, it was looking more and more like Mr. Bushler had guessed correctly. Maybe *Quiet Tiger* really was a decoy.

He left his stateroom. Parnette went to the maps. He handed the message to the Quartermaster on watch and pointed at a particular line. "Here," he said. "Update the cruisers' positions, please."

"Yessir," the young man said, who then went to work with a pencil and a straight-edge, using the numbers provided by the satellite.

The CO motioned to the current OOD and updated him on the situation. "Keep the boat at PD. Limit speed to cavitation."

"Aye-aye, Captain," the officer said, and gave the appropriate orders.

Cavitation is a bad thing, generally, from a submarine's point of view. The screw which propels the ship acts like a giant centrifugal pump, using its spinning blades to move water around. In a centrifugal pump, the center of the blade assembly, or "impeller", becomes a low pressure area, the suction of the pump. Water is sucked into it. Then the artificial gravitational force, created by the spinning, throws the water to the edges. This is the centrifugal pump's discharge.

If water temperature is high enough, and the suction pressure low enough, water entering that low pressure center area can begin to form bubbles of water vapor. The force then throws these bubbles to the outside of the impeller, where the pressure is much higher. The vapor bubbles collapse violently. In a pump, this phenomenon sounds like a bunch of marbles being shaken in a coffee can.

Cavitation can happen on a sub's screw the same way, and the sound is a lot worse. So it's avoided, religiously. There are even self-monitoring sonar devices that will signal an alarm if and when it happens.

Parnette stuck his head inside the curtain leading forward from Control into the Sonar Room, where three men sat in a row in headsets, facing green monitors. The CO said, "Sonar Supervisor, be aware, you should be acquiring two surface contacts in a few minutes. There may also be a new submerged contact with them. Keep your ears open."

"Aye, Cap'n," said a man seated on a high stool behind the three.

He walked back into Control, and said to the Officer of the Deck, "Go to Battlestations."

****

Mark did more reading. Hopefully, he had told himself, it'll put me to sleep:

I talked with Paul in the lab today for a long time. In almost four years, it was the first time we really got to just talk. I've kind of sensed that he's pretty uncomfortable with the whole topic of religion. But then, he brought it up. I've been thinking about what he said ever since. If I understand him, he's got three major issues with Christianity.

#1. He says Christians think they're better than everyone else. I said I would agree that there may be some who think that. But, then, there are a heck of a lot of arrogant atheists walking around, too. I asked if he'd ever read any Carl Sagan. He said no. I told him he ought to before he goes with the notion that Christians have a monopoly on snobbery. I said what is true is that Christians know that God expects them to live up to a higher standard than most people will accept, and maybe that's what he's talking about. And, I think its only since I've been a Christian that I truly realize how wicked I am, or can be. I'm better than no one--I'm just as bad, which is precisely why I need the forgiveness of Jesus Christ.

#2. Paul can't believe in a good God who allows so much sin. I said, Who says He's allowing it? He hates it! Paul said, Well, why doesn't He do something about it, then? I said, He already did. Jesus Christ died on a cross because of sin. It was God's way of dealing with it. We talked about Judgment Day, when every wrong

will be made right. Well, at most, he said, that means God doesn't like evil. Still, I don't see why He allows it to continue instead of waiting for Judgment Day. I said that was the final solution, but that God has presently chosen to combat evil by the same means in which evil is committed...by human hands. God seeks that His people would oppose and combat evil. So I told Paul that when he starts questioning God's "inactivity" against evil, he better watch out: God may question him in the same manner.

#3. This was the lamest one. Paul says he can't have faith in a God he can't see. I said, Let's change the subject--do you believe in UFO's? He said yes. Ever seen one? No. Why believe, then? Because lots of folks have seen them. So you believe in what you haven't seen based on someone else's testimony? He was smart enough not to answer. He said, with all those planets out there, billions of billions, isn't it arrogant to think we're alone? I said, with all those planets and galaxies interacting perfectly, each one in its own course, so that the whole universe is like one enormous Swiss watch, isn't it arrogant to look at that obvious design and refuse to acknowledge a Designer?

Finally, I asked him, if I could absolutely prove to you that Jesus is God, would you serve him? He said, Honestly, probably not. I said, Then maybe your problem isn't with being convinced, it's with a refusal to submit. I thought that would make him mad, but he only said, You may be right. I think there's hope for him.

Mark was amazed. No Christian had ever challenged any of his own arguments like that. He found himself wishing he could meet Liegert and talk to him.

It didn't sound like there was any deadly sort of antagonism between Lawrence and Liegert. They disagreed. That much was obvious. But, if Liegert's account was accurate, they were civilized about it.

Mark thought along these lines for a while, then became engrossed in his own problems. There was J.L. and the new baby. Enough to fill a book right there, he thought. But, now there was the spill and his injury. There was the certain damage to his career.

He wound up not sleeping at all. The alarm sounded, and he had to get up. The Engineer had got him placed in Control again for Battlestations. He wondered sarcastically what big announcement the Captain had for the crew now.

****

The American in Hong Kong went down to the lobby of his hotel and threw a fit — stomping, screaming, spit flying. Reggie had a blast.

The Empress Hotel staff were mortified. Two Chinese men in formal white shirts and black bow ties ran from behind the front desk, and approached him, eager to please. Eager to make him stop screaming.

"This is a second-rate dive!" Reggie yelled, extending an upraised index finger as high above his head as he could, striking a Patrick Henry pose.

They asked what the problem was.

"What's the problem? What's the problem! I'll tell you the problem. How is a businessman like myself, an international entrepreneur, supposed to conduct business in the Ninety's with a single phone line in and out of the room? A room I'm paying a lot of cash for, by the way! Can you answer me? Can you? I want you to book me in a hotel that can get me a second phone line!"

They scrambled around like a, like a...*Chinese fire drill*, he thought. "What are you running in this place, a Chinese fire drill?"

They went very fast and were very apologetic. They would get him another phone right away, of course. They had one on a long cord they could string in his room immediately. Was there anything else?

He was about to say no, but then said, "You've let my wet-bar run dry again, too!"

They promised to fix that as well. He laughed all the way up in the elevator.

When he got to his room, a Chinese boy who was gasping for air was waiting at his door, holding a white phone. The cord went across the hall, under the door to another room.

"Wow!" the American said, laughing. "You just ran up all those stairs?"

The boy nodded, still gasping.

"Now that's service!"

The door at the end of the hall, marked "Stairs", burst open and another boy ran toward them carrying a large silver tray loaded with three cans of beer and several miniature liquor bottles. A handwritten note in the middle said, "Our Compliments".

Now he was ready. The staff boys left, and he called up Worthy Wife on one phone line and dialed Mr. Lee on the new line. He popped the top on a can of Foster's Lager, smelling the formaldehyde, and got comfortable. This was going to be the best video game he ever played.

Chapter Fifteen

Mark got to his spot at the table in Control as the Captain announced, "I have the Con."

A young man wearing a sound-powered phone headset announced, "Maneuvering reports Battlestations manned aft."

"Very well," Parnette said. Mark saw him check his watch and shake his head slowly.

"Con, Sonar. Have two surface contacts, bearing zero-one-three, range five thousand yards. Designate contacts November One and Two."

"Sonar, Con, aye," said Captain Parnette into the microphone.

Control was rigged for red, and the Captain ordered #2 periscope raised. The port periscope went up, the interface assembly coming out of the deck to stop at chest height.

Parnette crossed to it, folded down the handles on its sides, and bent over to put his face on the eyepiece. He walked around in a circle with it once, quickly.

He moved the scope around to forward again and waited a few minutes. Mark could only wonder what he was seeing.

Finally, Parnette said, "Mark target number one."

The Captain pushed a button with his thumb that took a zoom photograph of the ship. A member of the Battlestations tracking party, a senior Fire Control Technician, said, "Mark target number one, aye," and wrote down the digital readout above the Captain's head, which showed exactly where the scope was pointed.

Parnette moved the scope slightly and repeated the process, saying, "Mark target number two."

Then he stood straight and ordered the periscope lowered.

"Diving Officer," he said, "Make your depth six-nine-two feet, five degree down angle, come left three zero degrees to course three-three-zero. Ahead standard."

While the flurry of verbatim repeat-backs was going on, the CO turned to Mr. Shelby and said, "I'm tempted to launch a flare over their bows."

Shelby grinned. "Just gonna skirt around them?"

"Yeah. Boring is best."

"That's what my wife says."

Mark blurted out a laugh at that. Both officers turned and looked at him — neither smiled. He decided he should keep quiet.

A high-pitched whistle suddenly surrounded them, seeming to come from everywhere at once. Its pitch varied and changed. It lasted about five seconds.

The Cob was the Diving Officer. He turned around with wide eyes. "What the...? They know we're here? They're going active already!"

The Captain said, "Thirty degree down angle. Ahead full. Minimize cavitation."

The boat angled down, as it had during the Jam Dive drill, until standing up was like being on a steep roof top.

"Con, Sonar, *November One* has changed course, new heading three-zero-zero!"

The CO looked at Shelby, who was frowning; then made his way to the Control sonar screen. Mark watched him blink his eyes several times, as if trying to make sure he was seeing things correctly. "Sonar, Con, aye," Parnette answered.

He turned and looked at the XO. Shelby said, "One of them is on an intercept course."

Mark studied the Captain's eyes. They told him that this was neither expected, nor good. Mark's stomach churned. He would've preferred a simple announcement.

****

The American howled his laughter. His computer screen showed three blips, each with a single Japanese character next to it. *Omaha* was the southern-most, moving diagonally toward the upper left of the screen. One of the two above it moved almost straight to the left. The other was now changing course. Instead of moving straight down, it was starting to come left slightly.

"No, that's good," he said into the phone. "They haven't changed course yet. They're passing one hundred fifty meters in a hurry. Speed...looks like thirty-one knots. Go get 'em, boys!"

He finished off the Foster's and reached for a San Miguel.

****

The *Omaha* leveled off at 692 feet. It was Parnette's depth of choice, in deference to her hull number.

"Con, Sonar, range to *November One*, one thousand yards."

"Sonar, Con, aye."

"Con, Sonar, course change on *November Two*. New heading two-zero-five."

"Sonar, Con, aye."

"They're trying to flank us," said the XO.

"Tell me how they're doing it, and I'll field promote you," the CO said, deadpanning.

Then he said, "Diving Officer, come to starboard, new heading zero-five-zero."

"Come to zero-five-zero, aye."

The boat leaned to the right, like an airplane executing

a roll. Mark braced himself with his good, right hand on the QM's table.

"Easy, easy!" said the Cob to his helmsman.

Then, the Cob reported, "New course is zero-five-zero, sir."

"Very well. All Ahead Flank."

****

Reggie laughed some more. The *Omaha* was now heading toward the top, right-hand corner of his screen. He threw back his head and yelled, "Yee-haw, cowboys!"

Into the phone, he said, "Okay, I got a change for you. She's heading northwest now, speed's 36 knots and rising."

On the other end of the phone, the message was translated into Korean and relayed to a man speaking into a radio. The message went out almost instantaneously.

****

"Con, Sonar, *November One* new course one-eight-three. November Two is slowing and turning."

"Sonar, Con, aye," Parnette said, slamming the mike back into its holder.

"What do you think, Cap'n?" Shelby said.

"Nothing to think! They've got some kind of great passive sonar. That's all there is to it."

"We've had zero intel like that."

"Yeah, well, I'm about ready to declare intel useless."

The Captain took a deep breath. He said, "All stop. Cob, use the boat's drift to get us as low as you can. Chief of the Watch, trim us up at twelve hundred feet if we get there. Send the word to all stations. I want absolutely no noise from anywhere. Nobody passes gas without my permission."

****

"Oh, don't just stop! Keep running! C'mon..."

Disgusted, he spoke into the phone. "She's stopped.

Yeah, that's what I said. She's going deeper, just now passing three hundred meters. What? No, no, your north boat is right on course. Yeah, start slowing down, or you'll pass right over it."

He waited a couple of minutes, then said, "Whoa, there ya go. Yeah, that's it. She's at 337 meters, just sitting there. Take her. She's yours."

****

Nobody said a word in the *Omaha* control space. Some of the younger men looked up at the overhead. A Quartermaster named Joe Garcia crossed himself. Mark was tempted for an embarrassing moment to do the same, in spite of the fact that no one in his entire family was Catholic. But he had heard all the clichés about Foxhole Conversions, and he was not about to do that. God was still a crutch. That wasn't going to change now.

"C'mon," the Captain whispered. "Get creative or get off the pot, here, gentlemen. What's it gonna be?"

They waited.

"Con, Sonar! We've got splash noises! Repeat, splash noises! Times two...Times three!"

Parnette yelled to the XO, "Emergency Flank! I want tubes one through six loaded now!" then, to the Diving Officer, "Hard right rudder!" Then, to the Chief of the Watch, in case the coming depth charges were sonar guided, "Launch noisemakers now!"

Omaha leaned hard to the right and there was a sensation of picking up speed.

Seconds passed and then the CO grabbed the mike and growled, "What about it, Sonar?"

"Con, Sonar...I got nothing, Captain! No Actives, no detonations...They're coming straight down!"

Parnette slammed the mike home and turned to the XO. "To all stations, prepare for impact!"

Shelby gave the message to the Chief of the Watch, who passed it along.

The three depth charges had all been programmed for 337 meters. They exploded precisely, within two seconds of each other.

It felt like one explosion on *Omaha*. The deck seemed to move about a foot and a half to the right instantaneously. Mark never even felt himself come off his stool. He did, though, feel himself hit the deck and slam into a locker against the sub's port bulkhead.

The XO and CO were the only ones in Control left standing when it was over. The Cob had fallen out of his chair. The helmsman and planesman were strapped in, or they would have gone as well. Joe Garcia was screaming. He was on the deck, grabbing at his knees. Mark realized right away what had happened to him. He had heard about it in Damage Control training some years back. Garcia had been standing with his legs straight when it happened. Both knees were dislocated, now.

Mark got up and helped another man drag Garcia to the ladder that went down to Crew's Mess and the Doc's office. As they did, the Chief of the Watch reported, "There is a steam leak in Engineroom Upper Level. They think it's minor and can be isolated. Request the man in the Steam Suit lay aft."

"Very well, send the Steam Suit aft," the Captain said.

Of course it was a minor steam leak, Mark thought, with some sarcasm. Tests had indicated that a major leak would kill all Engineroom watchstanders in less than fifteen seconds.

The XO said, "It's like they can see us!"

The CO nodded. "We have to be quicker."

****

The three explosions had appeared on the screen like quarter-sized circles, overlapping, which blotted out both the North Korean cruiser and the *Omaha*. They faded after several seconds.

The American's enthusiasm returned. He sat up in his chair and set the half-empty San Miguel can on the table.

The *Omaha's* blip was still there, moving at a solid forty knots, just to the south of the stationary cruiser, and curling toward it. He whooped and raised both fists in the air, leaning his chair back.

He said into the phone, "Hey, you missed! How could you miss?"

His eyes went wide after a closer look at *Omaha's* numbers. "Holy Cow! You better get that thing turned around! She's coming up...fast!"

****

Omaha was pushing a 45 degree up angle. Parnette had taken matters into his own hands by ordering an Emergency Main Ballast Tank (EMBT) Blow.

The Chief of the Watch had thrown the two "chicken switches." Automatically, valves were opened in all the ballast tanks, allowing air compressed to over three-thousand pounds per square inch to explode into them. This evacuated the water, which normally filled them, in an instant. Omaha was rising like a balloon full of air in a bathtub.

The CO shouted instructions as they rode the boat to the top, "Fire Control, standby! I'm gonna want a snapshot on tubes five and six right away! Chief of the Watch, get those tanks refilling as soon as we're there!"

The Engineer was there, beside the CO, and he whispered, "This may be a bad time, Captain. But destroying a cruiser on the high seas is an act of war...not that I disagree with your decision, of course--"

The CO stared at him, almost blankly. "Mr. Bushler, peace time or not, a ship has got the right to defend itself. We can't hide, and they can outrun us. We've already taken battle damage after an unprovoked attack in international waters...I think it's just a little late to become a pacifist, Eng."

The Cob said, "Here we go!"

****

On the bridge of the North Korean cruiser, in the deepening darkness of the sunset, only two men saw *Omaha* emerge. The round, midnight black nose burst through the surface and soared almost thirty feet straight up. White water sprayed away from the sub, like ashes shrugged off by a Phoenix. Before those men even realized what they were watching, the nose tipped toward them, until it splashed down in another white explosion, leaving the *Omaha's* sail clearly visible.

The North Koreans who had been manning the depth charges scrambled toward the deck guns. *Omaha* was close enough for them to see the white 692 emblazoned on her sail.

****

"Torpedoes away, Captain!" yelled the young man at the Fire Control Computer.

"Diving Officer! Hard port rudder! Ahead Standard!"

The CO walked over to the Chief of the Watch and said, "Get those tanks filled, Chief, or we're all dead, okay?"

"Yessir!" The Chief's hands flew over his control panel.

"And make sure they're starting an air charge aft."

"Yessir!"

"Con, Sonar, time to torpedo impact, ten seconds, nine, eight, seven, six, five..."

They all waited.

"Con, Sonar, two detonations!"

The Control space filled with cheers. Mark's were among them.

Parnette ordered the scope raised. He looked into it. He said, "One target has been hit."

Mark detected a note of business-like satisfaction in his voice. Parnette spun the scope around, looking aft. Very quickly, then, he slammed the scope's handles back into their storage positions. "Lower scope!"

Omaha rocked port and starboard on the surface, and that was not good for Mark's stomach either. There was a sound like muffled thunder, and the sub leaned hard to port in response.

"Emergency Deep!" the Captain yelled.

Shelby looked over at him.

Parnette said, "Tell me again why they thought aft torpedoes would be a bad idea on 688's."

Shelby shrugged. He asked, "Are we heavy enough to dive yet?"

Parnette shook his head. It wasn't a, "No" shake, but rather an "I don't know."

Mark held the carousel horse in his hand without realizing it. He was new to submarines, but understood the implications of staying on the surface while a cruiser fired deck guns in their direction.

****

"Yeah! Yeah!"

Reggie was jumping in the air. It wasn't a return of patriotism. Hardly. It was simply lack of loyalty to his current employer. It was merely the novelty of it all.

On one jump, his right knee contacted the table. His can of San Miguel tipped over, splashing all across his laptop's keyboard.

He stopped jumping and started cussing. His hand lunged for the can, to right it, but ended up knocking it instead. It spun on its side, spraying beer in a circle.

He lunged for it again, with both hands this time. He missed it again and knocked the phone cradle off the table and onto the floor. He cussed some more.

He backhanded the beer can onto the floor.

Reggie picked up the phone and yelled, "Hey! They're diving again--"

He pulled the receiver away from his ear and looked at it. He put it back to his ear. There was a dial tone. He screamed a cuss word at the top of his lungs.

He reached for the phone cradle, picked it up and started to redial the number.

On the next to last number, there was a loud pop. A plume of white smoke coughed up from his combination laptop/processor. The screen went black. He thought about trying to get it going again and worried vaguely about the possibility of electric shock. His fingers shaking, he dialed the front desk and politely asked them to call him a cab.

****

When they reached three hundred feet, the CO took the mike and said, "Still no course change?"

"Con, Sonar, November Two still on coarse three-two-five. Speed five knots."

"Sonar, Con, aye."

The Captain listened as the trilling whistles of active sonar came in five seconds bursts, one right after the other. They weren't even close.

"What do you think?" he said to Shelby.

The XO shrugged and shook his head. "Maybe...maybe we got the only one of them with passive sonar...?"

The CO ordered a course that would circle around the cruiser at Ahead Standard.

They waited that way for half an hour. The North Korean pinged away on Active the entire time. At one point, the cruiser dropped a depth charge that exploded at 435 feet, some fifteen hundred yards away from *Omaha*. Probably blew up a school of fish.

"They're blind," Parnette pronounced to the Control watchstanders. "Chief of the Watch, in five minutes, secure from Battlestations. Diving Officer, come left, course zero-one-zero, Ahead Full."

"We're leaving," the XO said.

"Right. We haven't received any orders to maximize tonnage on the ocean floor. At least, not that I've heard. They broke a pipe in our Aux Steam system. I sent a few hundred of their guys to the bottom. I'd say we're about even."

Parnette's face is different, Mark thought. *The color is gone. He looks like a man who had just evicted his own grand-mother.*

"XO, you have the Con. Get on the 1MC and update the crew. Pat them on the back. Talk to the Eng about where he thinks we ought to take a Scoping Array snapshot, then get us there. I'll be in my stateroom. Minimize disturbances."

The CO left, his head hanging. His stateroom door closed behind him.

Chapter Sixteen

The XO did as he was told. He got on the 1MC and briefly explained to the crew what had happened. He thanked them for their professionalism and secured Battlestations.

Mark was glad to leave Control. When he got down to Crew's Mess, the men were elated, filled with adrenaline, no doubt. They laughed boisterously and clapped each other on the back. A few guys (Mark had yet to memorize their names, and had no time to read their suits) grabbed him and shook his hand violently. Somebody hugged him.

He realized that he was going to vomit. He didn't know why. He left the party, bolting down another level to the head outside First Class Berthing.

Pork chops and potatoes, he thought, as he flushed the toilet. Someone came in wearing only a towel and hopped into the single shower. Mark almost laughed. The guy was going to shower and simply move on with his life, like nothing had happened.

Not a bad idea.

Mark went to his rack and stripped down. He would give the guy several minutes to shower, then it would be his turn. He stood there, holding his soap and shampoo in one hand, a plain white towel in the other. He thought about Joe Garcia briefly, crossing himself, then grabbing at his ruined knees. That only served to upset his stomach again.

He forced himself to think about something else. His

mind drifted to Liegert, then to J.L., then back to Liegert. He also thought about Paul Lawrence. He tried to come up with an idea for salvaging his career now that the spill incident would be permanently attached to his name. It was no use. He'd have to work on that one some more later.

Liegert came to mind yet again. He suddenly admitted to himself that he was considering the possibility that Liegert had been murdered. Apparently, he and Lawrence had some bad blood between them, which was a little hard to imagine, granted. Could Paul be serious enough for a sustained period of time to hate someone, much less kill him?

Maybe it was a Cain and Abel thing. They came on the ship together, worked side by side. Maybe Lawrence was even a better ELT. But Liegert got promoted and became the boss. Maybe jealousy and resentment got the best of Paul, just like it did Cain.

Wait a second. Who is this? He had to shake his head. Oh, it was him all right. Part of it he could believe. He could believe he was beginning to suspect Liegert had been murdered, and maybe Paul Lawrence had done the deed. What he couldn't believe is that he, Mark Reed, was couching those thoughts in the context of a Bible story!

Still, with something resembling disbelief at his own actions, he fished out Liegert's journal again. He flipped it open and read.

Today I was struck by the words of Jesus, when he said, 'What will it profit a man, if he gains the whole world, but loses his own soul?'

I'm starting to see that he did a lot of that. He asks the question. You answer it.

I realize there are a lot of things in this world I could be tempted to lose my soul over. Forget the 'whole world', like he said--I'd sell myself for a lot less than that, most days. But, let's say I got it all. I meet a genie and get three wishes, only I lose my soul. What could possibly be worth it? Of course, I'd never take that deal. But, then, it seems to me that I do take that deal, in little ways, every day. I pursue things I know I shouldn't. I seek after goals that have nothing to do with eternity. I say things I instantly regret, knowing before I say them that they are wrong.

I wonder, when I pursue those things that are eventually devastating to me, is there someone, somewhere, watching me and just laughing it up when I take my eyes off the eternal goal God has in mind for me?

Mark closed the notebook and slowly shook his head. He didn't understand much of what Liegert said, but he was struck by the amount of introspection the journal evinced. He had no idea people would spend so much effort analyzing and re-analyzing the way they lived their lives. From what he could see, Liegert was not easy on himself in the process, either. *Heck of a way to deal with yourself.*

On a hunch, he flipped the notebook to the last page. Maybe he would find a statement like, "I think so-and-so may try to kill me." No such luck. The last twenty pages seemed to be notes on various Psalms.

He put the notebook away, turned off his rack light, and went into the head across the hall. Whoever had been showering had left, and the little space was all his. It had a single toilet, two sink basins, one (tiny!) shower stall. He put his plastic soap dish and his shampoo on the metal shelf in the metal shower, hung his towel on the peg on the bulkhead, and stepped inside.

He had been briefed early on by the Cob on submarine shower etiquette. The goal was to use as little water as possible. Fresh water had to be made by the engineers back aft with a temperamental contraption they called a 10K plant. Additionally, all the water drained to a gray-water holding tank of limited capacity; and, it wasn't always convenient to pump that water overboard. The more conservative you could be with the water, the greater the likelihood there would always be water when you wanted some.

The Cob had related a story from his days, decades ago, on a diesel boat. It was routine for them to go two weeks without washing their clothes, without taking showers, except in raw seawater. Their pure water was reserved absolutely for cooking and drinking. There was no laundry.

The diesel boat bubbleheads were inventive, though. They could get eight solid days out of one pair of underwear. (Wear 'em normally for two, then turn them around, for two more. Then turn them inside-out for a couple and then rotate them around again for a total of eight.) As Mark had listened to the Cob's sea-story, he had also begun to smell it.

So he followed the Cob's steps, feeling a little silly. Step one, turn on the shower and get yourself real wet. Step two, turn off the shower. Step three, get out your soap and shampoo and get all lathered up. Step four, turn on the water just long enough to rinse off.

He was in the middle of step four when the lights went off. He hadn't heard anyone come in, but someone must have. His stomach tightened. All he could imagine was that he was about to fall victim to some juvenile submarine initiation ritual. Was he the only one who realized how close they had all just come to dying? The whole crew was hyped-up about being alive and now ready to play. He really wasn't in the mood.

He'd crossed the Equator, and gone through the disgusting ritual to become a Shellback. He had played along with being made to crawl through a tunnel filled with day-old garbage from the galley, with having to drink some of the Royal Baby's "Milk", made of God-knows-what, and all the other foolishness that came with that ancient Naval Tradition, but he was not in the mood right now.

"All right," he said, deepening his voice. "Quit messing with the lights."

He listened. There was no sound.

"Hey," he said, "what's going--"

The door of the shower stall was constructed like a phone booth's, with a second hinge down the middle which allowed it to fold in half. It burst in on him, hitting his right "funny bone" ("Ain't much funny about that, is there?" was his grandma's standard comment).

Then an arm grabbed at him in the pitch of the new

blackness.

The hand seized his hair and yanked, hard.

Startled, Mark was suddenly off-balance and falling in the dark, out of the shower. He knew he was headed for the sinks and their countertop, so he put out his hands to stop his fall.

He misjudged the whole thing, badly, and fell against the upraised metal lip with his chest, just below the neck. Now he was mad. He could take a joke as well as the next guy, but a couple inches this way and he could have a crushed larynx and be thirty seconds from death right now--

The first blow landed below his shoulder blades.

He couldn't believe it. Had it not been for the instant, numbing pain, he would have simply refused. But the pain was real.

He crumpled all the way to the floor, on his right hip.

He was hit again, this time across his left shoulder. His whole arm tingled.

At the impact, he heard a definite "clink" of metal on metal, aside from the "smack" of metal on wet flesh, and he caught a whiff of heavy grease. He realized someone was hitting him with a large pipe wrench.

He raised his arms to cover his head, and the wrench came down there.

He heard a snap as it landed on his left wrist.

It also crashed into the back of his head. Colors exploded and swam in front of his eyes.

Somehow, his right hand closed tight around the wrench.

He knew if he let it go, he would die.

He had one chance to hold onto it. There would be no surviving another shot to the head like that.

He heard someone grunting and breathing heavy now and felt him trying to jerk the wrench away.

Mark could not move his mangled left arm and so it stayed there, coiled on top of his head like an impotent snake.

Suddenly, amazingly, his right hand was supporting the entire weight of the wrench and he heard the man stumble backwards. Mark drew the wrench in to his chest and rolled over on it the best he could.

A volcanic eruption of pain went through his left arm, as two hands were now reaching for him, brushing the useless limb aside.

The hands searched for a second and found Mark's throat.

The man was straddling him. Mark tried to throw him off but could not.

Then he realized he didn't want to try anymore.

In the dark, he saw J.L., like he had seen her in his dream. Dressed for summer, hair blazing, new baby cooing and chortling, saying good-bye.

And he saw himself, strangely enough, laid out in a casket, about to receive a full military burial. He was there in the uniform of a Chief Petty Officer. *At least I got what I wanted*, he thought.

Then, even those images went dark.

****

An American man with shaggy, unwashed hair and a bad goatee stepped up to the counter and said, "I want to be on that plane you have going to Los Angeles, California." He was animated with nervous energy. He rubbed his chin a lot and kept looking behind him, over his shoulders.

The blonde woman was tall, dressed intelligently, with a dark vest, white long-sleeve shirt and a red bow around her collar. She spoke with a heavy British accent.

"I'm terribly sorry, sir. That flight is booked and boarding in ten minutes."

He laughed and said, "No, see, I don't think you understand. I need to be on that flight. What about first class?"

She raised her eyebrows and punched keys at her computer terminal. She said, "First class is full, sir, as is the rest of the--"

"How much does a first class ticket cost?"

"Eight thousand, Hong Kong, but I told you--"

"I'll give you thirty thousand right now to get me one of those seats." He reached into his denim jeans, cut off at the knees, and came out with a five-inch bundle of multi-colored Hong Kong currency.

She looked amused and said, "If you'll wait one moment I'll talk to my supervisor."

Of course, the supervisor came to the astounding conclusion that they would be able to find a seat for him in first class. They printed out a ticket in the name of Reginald Nelson and he walked away smiling. All he carried was a leather briefcase. His laptop was shot so he had left it in the room at the Empress. But he brought the money.

He walked through the immense crowd of mostly black hair and round, Asian faces bustling through Hong Kong International.

He needed to use the restroom. He hated going in those airplane versions. He had a few minutes, so he ducked into the men's room.

It was a large room, with sky blue tile on the floor and halfway up the wall. On one side were six stalls. Opposite them, on the wall, was a single porcelain trough, about knee high. At intervals of three feet, spigots doused the trough with a continuous stream of water.

He set down his briefcase. The restroom door quietly opened behind him.

He unzipped his shorts. The wall immediately in front of him became splashed with red liquid, which ran down the tile to the trough. *That's strange,* he thought.

He looked down and saw that his pea-green shirt now had a bloody hole in the center of the chest.

Three more bullets entered his torso in rapid succession. His body jerked for a moment, like a marionette animated by someone with sudden spasms.

He hit the wall with a thud and slid down, into the trough. He turned the water to blood.

The North Korean assassin unscrewed the silencer from his pistol and replaced the gun in the shoulder holster, under his blue suit jacket. He almost forgot to grab Mr. Lee's briefcase full of cash before he left.

****

Agent Kim woke from his two hours of sleep in a bad mood.

When he got to Honolulu, P.D. headquarters, he was no better. He had commandeered an office. He didn't know whose. He didn't care.

There were three messages on his desk. Someone had called at about 1:30 in the morning. They were sure they had seen the lady on television dancing the night away at the Sandpiper. He smirked and shook his head.

One lady called in at 4:36, absolutely certain that the woman on T.V. was her son's new girlfriend. (She had realized it in a dream.)

Minutes before sunrise, a Filipino transvestite, most likely on PCP, burst into a precinct building in Waipahu, wearing a long, blonde wig. He was there to confess. He was the notorious blonde bomber.

Kim crumpled them all up and threw them away.

He turned on his computer and logged onto the National Crime Information Computer. At the first site, he entered a numerical code where most officers entered their precinct location. Seconds later, the screen shifted into a blue background with the FBI logo in gold and a list of several menu choices.

He made his choice. A blurb came up on the screen.

Attention and Alert, Agent Daniel Kim. You have requested access to information that requires the signed order of a Federal Judge prior to release. Unauthorized access into this area is a third degree felony under Federal Privacy Act legislation.

Do you wish to Proceed, or Cancel?

Kim pushed the "P" button.

Please be aware that your personal code has been recorded as having requested this access and may be used as evidence against you in the future.

Proceed, or Cancel?

He pushed "P" again, and the screen changed once more.

Please establish search parameters.

He entered the words, "Financial Institutions, Oahu, Hawaii." On the next line he wrote "Rita Kelly."

Search in process.

After some narrowing-down, Kim was able to get the numbers for Rita Kelly's three accounts at the Bank of Hawaii. One savings, one checking, one money-market CD/Retirement. He got the computer to list all her checks written during the last three months.

At that point, what he was looking for jumped out. Within the first seven days of each of the months, she had written checks for $300 apiece to something called "King of The Islands Bible Fellowship".

That was all he needed. He shut down the computer and picked up a phone book. He found a yellow-page ad for King of The Islands. The ad said, in small print at the bottom, Brother Robbie McClain, Pastor. He found an entry for Robert and JoAnna McClain in the white pages. He wrote down the address and phone number.

When he left his office, he was feeling much better.

Chapter Seventeen

J.L. woke up a little after sunrise. Her stomach churned.

She started to put her own clothes back on, but noticed a floral print dress, light red with subdued colors, hanging over the back of a chair in a corner of the room. It had not been there when she went to sleep. There was a pair of open-toed, cream-colored shoes next to the dress, as well as a tasteful, tan straw hat with a large brim.

J.L. smiled and tried it all on. With the exception of the shoes, which were a little snug, the fit was fine. She folded her own clothes and set them in the chair. She left the room dressed in the borrowed clothes, holding the straw hat and her bag containing her wallet. She was smiling.

As soon as she opened the bedroom door, she smelled bacon frying and coffee brewing. And she heard a woman singing, softly. She made her way to the kitchen where JoAnna McClain was stirring the eggs with a metal whisk. JoAnna looked up and saw her, then smiled. She looks so tired, J.L. thought.

"That stuff fits you pretty good, huh?"

J.L. said, "Yes, it does."

"It belongs to my youngest. She went to the Mainland for college. I'm sure she won't mind you using them. I thought you two were about the same size."

"Thanks."

"Now, listen, child," she said, turning back around and dumping the scrambled eggs on a plate next to two slices of toast, "Robert has arranged some things for you. One of the sisters from the ladies' circle works at the Turtle Bay Hilton on the North Shore--you know how to get to the North Shore?"

"No, ma'am."

"Well, that's okay, I'll draw you a map. Anyhow, this sister is working at the front desk right now. We checked you into a room facing the beach, room 109. The key is on the counter, there."

J.L. looked and saw the hotel key. She was stunned.

"So you can just walk around to it when you get there and don't have to go through no lobby, okay? Then, brother Ray loaned Robert his little pickup truck. I drove it home from the hospital about an hour ago. You'll take that."

JoAnna scurried to the table, where a single place was set. She set down the plate and a steaming cup of coffee. J.L. said, "I--I probably shouldn't have caffeine--"

JoAnna froze and smiled at her. "Good. It's decaf. Now, anyway, the room is registered in Robert's name, so you better just be Mrs. McClain if anyone asks!"

J.L. didn't know what to say.

JoAnna said, "Now you sit down and eat. Keep your strength up, child."

J.L. did as she was told. JoAnna, looking like a whirlwind that had blown itself out, sat across from her with her own cup.

J.L. asked, "Where is Robert?"

"The hospital. Rita's still in intensive care. She's come in and out of consciousness."

J.L. looked down. She said, "Is she going to be all right?"

"Every minute she stays alive, it starts looking better for her. Let me tell you, that woman is in the hand of God. The doctors took seven bullets out of her. They say her heart stopped beating twice on the table. The fact she's alive is a miracle."

"I wish I could see her."

"You will. After this is all over, you will."

J.L. ate some more, and the food seemed to calm her stomach. *Will wonders never cease?*

JoAnna asked her, "Did you sleep well?"

J.L. smiled and said, "Yes, thank you. Better than I have in weeks, actually."

JoAnna got up and rushed past her. J.L. turned around to watch her. The woman dashed into the living room. She picked up the television remote from the end table beside Robbie's chair, and turned up the volume. J.L. noticed the picture was the composite drawing of her face.

"...remains at large, although police believe she is still on the island. Remember, if you should see this woman, please call the number on the bottom of your screen, or dial 9-1-1."

The picture shifted to an Asian woman in a blue jacket. She said, "Military base commanders issued a joint statement to the press this morning, saying they would remain at an increased level of readiness until this suspect is apprehended as a precaution, but that they do expect their operations to return to normal very shortly. Additionally, the Admiral in charge of all Pacific submarine operations, Admiral Crabb, was asked if the annual Submarine Ball would be canceled. The Ball was to be held tonight and would welcome several VIP's including Admiral Westergard of the Joint Chiefs of Staff and new Secretary of the Navy, Josephine J. Riddle. His answer was a strong no. He said to cancel the Ball would be to capitulate to the desires of those who seek to gain from inspiring fear."

The report then ended and JoAnna muted the television's volume. When she turned around, J.L. was on her feet, wearing the straw hat, her hair tucked up under it.

"I don't know how to thank you and your husband, Mrs. McClain. There is not a doubt in my mind that you have saved my life. But I need to be leaving now."

JoAnna drew a small map to get her to the Turtle Bay Hilton. J.L. took it, the keys to the pickup and the room, and the computer disc, and left.

****

"Officer of the Deck!" The near-shout came from the young man who was serving as the Control Phonetalker. He wore a sound-powered phone headset, consisting of black "earmuffs" and a round, black mouthpiece, mounted to a metal chestplate on a flexible arm. His face was overrun with acne, and he looked horrified.

"Yes," said the XO, rolling his eyes.

"D...Diesel reports Medical Emergency in the Lower Level Head!"

"Where's the Doc?" asked the XO, his voice calm and slow in contrast.

The Phonetalker held up a finger and listened for several seconds. He said, "The Doc is on scene. The injured man is Petty Officer Reed. He is unconscious but breathing...he is bleeding from a head wound..."

The XO walked over to the shaking young man. "What happened?"

The Phonetalker listened some more. "Not much word yet, sir. The Diesel Operator went to use the head and found him...the lights had been turned off and the door was shut."

The XO's face screwed up. "What--"

The Phonetalker held up a hand and pressed an earpiece to his head with the other. "Sir, the Doc reports that Reed has a broken left arm, a dislocated shoulder, possible broken ribs, probable concussion and ...and...deep bruising around the neck...someone's strangled him, Sir."

The young man's face had gone white. The XO put a hand on his shoulder and spoke slowly. "Listen, Phonetalker. To all stations, there has been a Security Violation. Begin Security Violation protocol."

The Phonetalker stumbled through a repeat-back of

the order, and then sent it out over the phone. The XO turned away from him and cursed a single time under his breath.

He turned back and said, "Phonetalker, to all stations. Locate the Captain and ensure he is informed of the Security Violation; then ask him to come to Control at his convenience."

The Phonetalker repeated it back.

"And make sure someone is manning the phones with the Doc at all times. Tell them I want continuous reports on Reed's condition."

"Aye, sir."

The XO shook his head and cursed, like a golfer nipping the cup on a three foot put for par. A suicide less than forty-eight hours ago, and now an attempted murder. This would be a rotten time to say, "I told you so," he thought. So he would not. But, for the record, he had been right. *Omaha* was not ready. There's a reason why the Navy calls an "All Stop" after suicides. Shelby had argued with Captain Parnette about it two hours after Liegert had been found.

The XO had been in favor of halting everything. Shut down all maintenance, shut down training, definitely don't plunge out to sea on Spec-Op! Take it slow and follow the numbers on this thing. Even wait until the Naval Investigative Service was able to get someone out to them.

Parnette had gotten mad at the whole line of thinking. Absolutely not, he'd said. WestPac was the only peace-time opportunity a boat had to show how good it was, and a successful Spec-Op was the crowning jewel of the six-month cruise. "Some idiot wants to kill himself, that's his own problem," Parnette had yelled. "But don't expect me to let one man's idiocy destroy my career! What about you, Adam? You're in line for a boat of your own. You ready to endanger that?"

"Is it about careers, Jim? A guy who worked for us, for you, is dead. How's your career going to be helped by taking a shell-shocked crew on Spec-Op?"

The CO had said, "Adam, I appreciate your advice

on this matter, but I have made my decision and I've gotten Squadron to agree with me. If that isn't good enough for you, then make a note in the Ship's Log. Is that what you want?"

Of course, it wasn't — at least, not at the time. Now, with a crewman freaking out under the stress of a real battle and attempting murder, it was looking like that might have been a pretty decent idea.

****

Mark woke up all at once. There was no grogginess, no blurry vision that slowly came into focus, no garbled voices becoming clear. Just, bang! He was out one second, fully conscious the next. He decided right away that being out was better. He hurt all over, but worst of all in his left wrist and forearm. He thought for an instant he had awakened in Hell.

But, he knew where he was. It was the Doc's office. Well, "office" was probably too generous. It was the Doc's cubby-hole adjacent to Crew's Mess, a literal hole in the wall with just enough space for a small desk and one bed.

Doc was hovering over him. Mark suddenly had Doc's hair-color pegged: orange peel. "Hey...hey, Reed! Can you hear me, buddy?"

Doc was holding a clear, plastic mask over Mark's mouth and nose.

"Yeah...yeah, I can."

Mark hadn't tried to whisper, but that's all that came out. Doc smiled and said, "Good, that's good."

He took the mask away. He said, "Where does it hurt?"

"Everywhere."

"Really? Can you feel everything? 'Cause that's a good sign if you feel everything."

"Believe me, I feel everything."

"Do you know who you are?"

Mark laughed, and it hurt so he stopped, "Sure, Tonto. Did Silver get away?"

For a moment, a puzzled look came over Doc's face, then he grinned. He turned back over his shoulder and spoke to someone Mark couldn't see. "Reed has regained consciousness. No apparent brain damage due to oxygen deprivation."

Something was said that Mark couldn't hear. The Doc spoke slower. "Ox-y-gen De-pri-vation....yeah, that's right...deprivation..."

The Doc was shaking his head in disgust when he turned back to look at Mark.

"Can you tell me specifically what hurts on you?"

Mark thought about it. "My head, my throat, my left arm, my back, my chest is sore. I may be getting an ingrown toenail..."

"All right, Mr. Comedy Guy. It's your left forearm, right?"

"Right. Left."

"Thought so. The bone wasn't quite sticking through the skin, but it was close. I can work on setting that, now that you look like you're going to live."

"Oh, wonderful. You couldn't do that while I was sleeping...?"

"You weren't sleeping, you nimrod! You were dying!"

The Engineer, Mr. Bushler, stuck his head in the space and said, "Petty Officer Reed. You still with us?"

"Think so, sir."

"Good. And don't think a stunt like this will exempt you from standing midwatch like the remainder of the crew."

Bushler grinned, maybe.

Then he said, "Are you aware of the identity of your attacker, Petty Officer Reed?"

Mark closed his eyes and almost laughed. Why couldn't he just blurt out, "Holy cow! Who did this to you?" like a normal person?

Mark shook his head "No. No, sir. Too dark."

The Engineer shook his head and headed up to Control after wishing Reed a speedy recovery.

****

Brother Robbie sat in a chair at Community General Hospital, in a waiting room in the Intensive Care ward. Beside him was another, younger black man who had fallen asleep.

Robbie was reading his Bible, in the Psalms. Normally, they comforted him. Now, they seemed to serve only to reinforce everything Charles Hodge had been saying...*that darn book.* He checked his watch. It wouldn't be long before JoAnna would be coming back. She would try to sleep, as they had agreed. But she wouldn't actually go to sleep, he knew. She would come marching in at any moment, looking and smelling fresh, full of energy. He had seen her go on like that for ten days at a time before.

By contrast, the only reason Robbie had not drifted off like the man next to him was that none of the waiting room chairs was half as comfortable as his Chair back home. Ah, his Chair. Now there was real comforting power for you. He hoped God would let him have a Chair like that, if not that one exactly, in his mansion in Glory.

He smiled at the thought and softly hummed "Great Is Thy Faithfulness," returning to the Psalms.

In the 32nd Psalm, he came to this phrase: "Thou shalt preserve me from trouble." Suddenly, he knew that his wife needed prayer. She needed to be preserved from trouble. He'd walked with Jesus long enough to know not to question that conviction. So he prayed for his wife. As he did, the old story of Rahab entered his mind and fell off of his lips.

"Rahab showed her faith by lying to the agents of Satan when they came huntin' Your people, Lord. Give Jo that faith, O God, and watch over her."

****

Being at the Turtle Bay Hilton on Oahu's famous North Shore was like being on a whole new continent. The continent she'd left, down around Waikiki, was all about doing things fast. It was about surviving in the crowds. It was a continent where native Hawaiians made up a quietly resentful minority, or so it seemed, and where the entire place was overrun with people like J.L. Light-skinned, blonde people with accents betraying their origins in places like Texas and the deep South, or New York; military people and their families.

But the Turtle Bay Continent was the postcard Hawaii. Nobody hurried here to do anything, except maybe paddle back out to meet the next wave or retrieve an umbrella-adorned frozen drink from the poolside bar. Native Hawaiians were all over the place here; and, unlike their oppressed brethren near Waikiki, they all seemed to be smiling.

J.L. was glad to find that the Gideons had ventured this far, leaving their signature blue hardback Bible in the top drawer of one of the wicker dressers in her hotel room. She opened it. On the flyleaf just inside the front cover, someone had written in blue ink, "Any one who belives this stuff is a idiot". She had to smile. "Belives."

"Hmmm," she said to herself, exaggerating her drawl, "I'm a 'beliver'. Guess that means I'm a idiot. Next thing ya know I won't be able to spell real good, neither."

It was crazy, really, but even that mocking sort of confession did her soul good. She was a believer. And she would live. She was a beliver.

She flipped forward and came to the book of Joshua. She was still too agitated to sit and read slowly, even though she tried. The verses of Joshua, chapter one seemed to come at her in pieces, all at once.

"Every place that the sole of your foot shall tread upon, that have I given unto you..."

"There shall not any man be able to stand before thee..."

"...I will not fail thee, nor forsake thee..."

"...be not afraid, neither be thou dismayed: for the LORD thy God is with thee whithersoever thou goest..."

The verses made her want to sit straighter, pull her shoulders back. After all, if God was for her, who could be against her?

That reminded her of a song they sang at King of the Islands church the first time she had visited. It was a surprisingly raucous, happy, hand-clapping song that made her a bit nervous. The choir was swaying back and forth, clapping their hands at shoulder level to the beat, their yellow gowns all waving like flags. The congregation mirrored them, and Rita's exuberance in belting out the chorus made J.L. wonder what sort of woman she'd met here.

Brother Robbie sat in a high-backed chair, between two empty ones, just behind the pulpit and in front of the choir. He looked out of place in all the motion and the noise. He sat in his black robe with his eyes closed and brows furrowed. J.L. was beginning to wonder about that as well, when another chorus began, with the organist shifting keys upward a bit and the tempo jumping.

Brother Robbie hopped out of his chair. His eyes were big and round, and his smile was impossibly toothy. He threw his hands in the air, and danced. Something about it all struck J.L. as funny, without being comical; and her nervousness left as she laughed and clapped and sang.

The song was, "Who Can Be Against Us?" and the answer that was obvious on everyone's face was, "No one." There had been a heady sense of confidence that J.L. remembered. It was a feeling that nearly brought embarrassment along with it because it seemed to border on arrogance. She was feeling that again.

She smiled, closed the Bible, and reached into her pack containing her stuff. From the pocket on the outside of her wallet, she retrieved the ticket that Rita had given her to the annual Submarine Ball. She rubbed it gently between her thumb and forefinger. She made plans.

Chapter Eighteen

"Deploy the Scoping Array," ordered Mr. Bushler, now standing OOD.

"Deploy the Scoping Array, aye" answered the Chief of the Watch.

They were holding at one hundred fifty feet, making turns for five knots. A minute later, the Chief of the Watch said, "Officer of the Deck, the Scoping Array is deployed to one-nine-nine feet."

"Very well."

The Engineer grabbed the mike to Sonar and said, "Sonar, Con, configure the Scoping Array for long-range forward."

After a couple of minutes Sonar reported they were ready.

Mr. Bushler picked up the 1MC and announced, "Commencing Scoping Array snapshots. Maintain silence about the decks."

Then, back to Sonar, "Sonar, Con, perform one dozen snapshots, sixty degree arc."

No one spoke until Sonar reported the snapshots completed.

On the 1MC, the Engineer said, "Scoping Array operations complete."

He ordered Sonar to print out the snapshot results and told the Chief of the Watch to retract the Array. He raised the radio mast and received message traffic.

****

The snapshots took five minutes to develop, after the radio messages had been received. Captain Parnette and Commander Shelby spent the time in the CO's Stateroom. Neither man sat down.

"So what are you saying, Adam?" Parnette said, not quite yelling, yet.

"I'm saying we ought to consider aborting this thing and turning back for Guam."

"Back to Guam!"

"Yes, Jim. We have to--"

"We are on station, Mr. Shelby."

The use of his last name was not lost on the XO. He held several sheets of white paper in his hand, which he now lifted up to chest-level. "Excuse me, Captain, sir. This is no longer a normal Spec-Op. This...this isn't even an extraordinary Spec-Op...! This has become an international incident, or it will when word gets out."

"I had just cause to launch weapons, XO—"

"I'm not saying you didn't. I'm just stating a fact. When word of this gets out, it's gonna be way beyond hitting the fan, here."

The Captain sighed and rolled his eyes. "You don't know that, XO. We did the right thing, and those snapshots are going to prove it."

"And if they don't?"

"They will."

The XO looked down at his shoes and shook his head. He ran his free hand through his hair. He held up the papers again. "Sir, even if we were right, there is still this stuff."

"What about it?"

"Didn't you read the traffic?"

"I did."

Shelby almost laughed. He pointed at the page on

top of the stack and said, "Respectfully, sir, I don't think you did. If you did, you would've read this: 'Be advised, routine autopsy on MM1 Liegert reveals blunt force trauma to back of head and neck, probably non-lethal, sometime prior to death. Possibility of murder should not be discounted'..."

"I read the messages, XO. You'll note we haven't been recalled--"

"You know they'll yank us back when they find out about Reed nearly getting killed--"

"I know no such thing."

"You're crazy."

The Captain thrust a finger under Shelby's nose, very nearly touching his mustache. Neither one of them moved. The Captain whispered, "Then I'm a crazy man whose oak leaves outrank your own. If you want to resign, then resign. Want to relieve yourself from duty, then do it."

They glared at each other.

Parnette lowered his finger and snatched the papers out of the XO's hand. He shuffled them and read out loud. "Satellite recon confirms continued buildup of North Korean troops and armored vehicles along the Demilitarized Zone."

Parnette raised his eyes and looked at Shelby over the paper, then went on. "North Korean airbases also show increased activity. Parallel buildup and movement of military forces taking place in Iraq and Syria."

Parnette lowered the papers and took a deep breath. "Look, Adam, you and I have been friends for a long, long time, and I know you're not disagreeing with me just to make trouble. This really is your best counsel, right?"

Shelby nodded.

"Right," he said. "And that's what I need from you. I'm not asking you to shut up, here. But here's what we know. North Korea's just blown almost a year's worth of intel work in order to get us to take the *Quiet Tiger* bait. Those cruisers were prepared to kill or be killed to keep us from seeing what these snapshots are about to show us. We're not talking about the Cold War Evil Empire here. They played the same game we did, with even more bureaucracy and controls between themselves and a nuke launch code than we have.

"This is serious, Adam. For all we know, the only control North Korea's got on whatever nukes it may have is one big red button labeled, 'Push this to destroy all your enemies.'"

"Something is going on. Something huge, and we're a couple of minutes away from seeing what it is."

The XO had to agree.

"And, yes, there is a high probability that Liegert was murdered by a member of the crew. And I'm guessing you might remind me that even if Liegert was a suicide, someone has tried to kill Liegert's replacement. Am I right?"

"Yes, sir."

"So, what then? Do we break off saving the free world because someone on my ship is a whacko?"

Shelby smirked and shook his head in resignation.

"Look, Adam. You put the crew on security alert. Everybody's got an escort. Everybody's accounted for. No one's going to do anything now. And if they do, it's easy to spot who it is--the only guy whose escort is missing. Not the best way to handle a murderer, but we still have a job to perform. We are still a warship. Okay?"

The XO reached out his hand and the Captain shook it.

They both heard a muffled, yet still unnerving male scream. They burst out of the stateroom and into Control.

"What in the world was that?" the XO asked.

The Phonetalker raised one finger. He looked unsettled. He said, "Crew's Mess reports that was the sound of the Doc resetting Reed's broken arm."

The officers looked at each other. They both tried to conceal a shudder.

****

The CO, XO and Engineer gathered over the snapshots

at the brightly-lit Quartermaster's table. They were twelve pictures, six inches high by nine inches wide. They looked like common photograph negatives. The backgrounds were solid black, with an occasional less-dark haze, indicating biologics of some sort. On ten of them, there was nothing more.

The other two contained a white, oblong blob, about a quarter of an inch long. On one shot, it was in the lower right corner. It was in the lower left on the other.

The Sonar Supervisor had taken the liberty of printing out magnifications of the grids containing the blob.

The three officers furrowed their brows in unison. These pictures showed the white blob as a three-inch long cigar shape. Attached to the top of it was an oval shape, one inch long on the picture.

"What's this?" said the XO, pointing at the smaller oval.

The Engineer shook his head.

"Diving bell," said the Captain.

Understanding lit up the Engineer's face. "Like the *Sam Houston!*"

The Captain nodded.

"I don't understand," Shelby said.

Parnette grinned. "You've spent too much of your career on boomers. We genuine sailors of the fast-attack fleet get exposure to more stuff like this."

Shelby rolled his eyes.

"If I may, Captain...," the Eng said.

Parnette nodded. The Eng continued. "For all intents and purposes, it's simply a decompression chamber mounted to the hull, with access to the boat via the forward escape trunk hatch--"

"All right, all right," Shelby said. "An attachment for sending out and receiving divers. I get it."

"Not just divers. Commandos," Parnette said.

"That's what it was on *Sam Houston*. We have no way of ascertaining its purpose on this particular boat," said Mr. Bushler.

The XO pointed to the string of numeric and alphabetic codes at the bottom of the print they were studying. "Whatever it is, they're about to leave international waters with it and enter Japanese space."

The CO shook his head. "When do you suppose Japan was going to decide to let us know about it?"

The other two shrugged.

The CO stood straight and said, over his shoulder, "Chief of the Watch, get the Radio Officer in here, please."

He looked at the others and said, "If they're not going to tell us, I guess we ought to let them know how honest and forthcoming we are."

****

Civil Defense in Yokosuka was thrown into an uproar when word reached the Watch Supervisor that a North Korean submarine had made it to the edge of Japanese waters. In fact, the Watch Sup took it personally.

Worthy Wife was working. Her self-diagnostics checked out. The whole staff had watched *Omaha's* battle with the cruisers in breathless disbelief. They'd seen *Quiet Tiger* turn and head for home long before that. Diagnostics negative, virus checker negative...it was maddening.

In a flash of insight, he decided to try something he had not done even a single time since going to college for his degree in advanced computer design. He turned it off.

His staff of four, two men and two women, stared at him open-mouthed. He counted to ten under his breath and turned Line 87 back on. The re-booting process took seven minutes. When it was done, an alarm flashed.

There it was, on the screen. A Soviet Victor-class. With a diving bell. It was a mere thirteen miles off the coast of Tokyo.

But that wasn't all.

Three years ago, Japanese scientists working in research and development for a communications company did something quite by accident, something previously thought beyond reach. They invented a neutrino detector.

Neutrinos are sub-atomic particles that accompany every nuclear reactive process. They are without electrical charge, without mass, and had existed until that day only as a theoretical necessity, needed to clear up some rough edges in the mathematical analysis of nuclear interaction.

But these guys built a detector. Later, they built a whole bunch of them, and retired as extremely wealthy technicians who had happened to bumble into something useful.

Line 87 had incorporated this technology. Not only could Worthy Wife detect, on a good day, the difference between a bilge pump and a brine pump, but she could analyze the configuration of radioactive material well enough to know the difference between a fission reactor and a multiple megaton warhead.

The Japanese government fully intended to reveal this information to the United States, some time in the near future.

Green computer crosshairs converged on the diving bell. It was unmistakable. There was a nuclear weapon inside it.

The Civil Defense Watch Supervisor fumbled with a phone and dialed a number with fingers overcome by tremors.

****

JoAnna had tried. Really, she had. She had lain in bed, lain across the bed, lain on the couch. But, she was not going to sleep.

So, she got up and took a shower. When she finished, she called her best friend, a sixty-year old Samoan woman named Kayla. She asked if she would mind picking her up and giving her a ride to the hospital.

Kayla never called her Sister JoAnna. That was one of the reasons JoAnna liked her. She had to put up with everyone in the world calling her that. If her husband was

"Brother", she must be "Sister." She grinned and put up with it.

She understood people liked to talk like that. Maybe they felt better that way, thinking of themselves as members of one big family. And, she understood where that came from. The Bible refers to the Church as a family. Still, it irritated her.

Kayla confessed to her that she thought it sounded insane for people to walk around saying, "Hey, brother! Hey, brother! Hey, brother!" The fact that she pronounced it "brudda" just amplified her point. JoAnna knew then that they would become good friends.

A knock on the front door interrupted their phone conversation.

"Kayla, I've got company at the door. Gotta go, okay? Okay. See you in a few minutes. Bye," she said.

There was a man dressed in a black suit at the door. He was Asian, and had a sunken, almost spooky face. Robert always told her not to judge people by the way they looked. And, of course, she didn't need her husband, the Pastor, to preach to her about that. But this time she felt like it was warranted. She couldn't smell him, but the thought crossed her mind, he reeks of no good. She regretted opening the door.

"May I help you, Mister?" she said.

The man smiled, and she thought it looked like roadkill trying to disguise itself as birthday cake. "I hope so, ma'am. My name is Special Agent Kim with the FBI."

He flashed his badge for a few seconds. She nodded.

His smile sunk away. "Is Pastor Robert McClain handy?"

"He asleep."

Kim's eyebrows went up. "Sleeping? Oh, well, wouldn't want to wake him up at this hour...what is it now...going on noon?"

"I ain't gonna wake him up."

Kim nodded. "Well, maybe you can help me."

"Maybe."

"Yes...well. I'm investigating a bombing incident at Pearl Harbor yesterday. I don't guess you've heard about it..."

"I heard. Saw it on the T.V.."

Kim produced a sheet of paper from a pocket and unfolded it. It was a copy of the drawing of J.L.'s face. "I'm looking for this girl. She's about five-five, a hundred and twenty pounds or so..."

"Did she run this way?"

Kim blinked his eyes a couple of times. "You don't recognize her at all? She's attended your husband's church recently...I assume you're JoAnna McClain."

She wondered how he knew her name, but thought it best not to highlight the issue. "No, we get lots of visitors on Sunday."

Kim nodded. "Let's go back a little bit. You know Rita Kelly."

"I know the name."

"But she wasn't a friend?"

"More like an acquaintance."

"Ah. I see. Rita attends your husband's church on a regular basis?"

"Never gave it much thought."

"She was there the last several Sundays."

"Maybe. Can't say as I recall right now."

"You don't remember her sitting with a young, white girl?"

"Nah. Don't believe I do."

She could see the muscles in his temples working, like his jaws were grinding. He said, "I think I'm going to have to ask you to wake your husband for me, ma'am. Not that you haven't been helpful--"

"I said I ain't wakin' him up."

He took a half-step forward and said, in something barely above a whisper, "Then let me in and I'll wake him up."

Ninety-nine percent of her was screaming, *Slam the door*

and run! But she followed the one percent which told her to stand her ground and stare him in the eye.

They stayed that way for several seconds. Several long seconds, she would say later. ("Last time the clock ticked that slow, Joshua had the sun standing still!")

A beeping noise came from Agent Kim. Without breaking the stare, he reached into his front pants pocket and brought out a black pager. He looked away from her, at the pager number. He put it back in his pocket.

He stood there for a while, then said, "Do me a favor Mrs. McClain. If you see that woman, please call the police. I suspect she may come here seeking help."

She nodded, more with her eyes than with the rest of her head.

He walked off, got into his car, and sped away.

JoAnna closed the door and put a hand on her chest. Her heart was pounding. She could hear it in her ears. She closed her eyes and raised her other hand in the air. She whispered, "Thank you, Jesus."

****

Kim was furious. As he drove, he dialed the number from his pager on his car phone.

"Kim, here," he said.

"Yeah, Mr. Kim, this is Officer Lujan with Honolulu, P.D.--"

"That must have something to do with why you answered the phone at police headquarters, then?"

"Uh, yeah. Um, we just got a tip on your mystery girl."

"And?"

"Cindy, a hairdresser at Aloha Hair on the North Shore...She calls in and says the girl just got a perm in her shop!"

Kim clicked his tongue off the roof of his mouth and closed his eyes. These guys were unbelievable. Mrs. Reed would not be getting a perm.

"Hey! So maybe it really was her dancing at the Sand-piper last night? What do you think?" Kim said.

The officer was silent for a while. "Um, I wouldn't know about that, sir. But this girl was pretty talkative, sounds like."

"How so?"

"Well, she didn't give up a name, but she said her ini-tials were J.L.. None of the girls in the shop snapped about who she was until half an hour after she left."

Kim had stopped his car. "Give me the address to that hair place."

Chapter
Nineteen

J.L. sat on the edge of the bed in her hotel room and pulled on hose. She was watching the television. Watching in some amazement, actually, because she was no longer the headline story on the 24 hour news channels. Now, the big news was about Japan.

Japan's entire navy was being mobilized at panic speed, apparently. The screen showed images of helicopters dragging something by cable in the water of the Sea of Japan. The weather looked horrible, all gray and stormy.

The rumor was that a North Korean submarine had been spotted off the coast. Of course, at that point, the story shifted to a quick recap of the Cold War incident in which a Soviet submarine was spotted off the coast of Norway and eventually was evacuated because of a reactor casualty.

The scene shifted again, this time to a press briefing room at the Pentagon, where the Secretary of State spoke from behind a podium. J.L. put on some earrings as he droned on and on.

When he was finished, the scene shifted back to the network's news desk, where the female anchor was joined by a middle-aged man with no hair. Whenever the camera was on him, beneath his name was written the title, "Defense Analyst."

At one point, he said, "The Secretary's words were very pointed, especially for a Clinton Administration official. They obviously reject the North Korean assertion that the submarine somehow got off-course and has wandered so close to the coast by accident."

The woman asked, "What do you make of the fact that North Korea is apparently launching several ships in that direction as well?"

He shook his head. "That's a tough one. Normally, it would be seen as a routine show of strength. The North Koreans have got one lone sub out there, and the whole Japanese navy coming down on its head. They have to do something to try and protect their boat, or at least make like they can."

The woman said, "You said that would be the case normally."

He nodded. "The wildcard factor in all this is North Korea's new government. I'm just not sure how stable it is, either in its own hold on power, or in its decision making, for that matter. If they actually believe the vicious anti-Japanese rhetoric they've been spouting since they seized power, well then, who knows? Do they really blame Japan for all their economic problems?"

"So you think this could be a real showdown?"

"I suppose anything's possible," he said. "But I find it hard to believe that North Korea has the stomach for that, despite what they've said." As J.L. turned away and began to slip on the dress she had bought that afternoon, she wondered vaguely where Mark's submarine was in all of that mess. Probably nowhere near, she thought. She said a prayer for his safety anyway.

****

Okay, okay, he thought. *It's not something you want to do more than once, but maybe the grandkids will get a kick out of it one day. Having a broken arm set and splinted with no painkiller stronger than aspirin, that is.*

Mark remembered reading an article by a guy named P.J. O'Rourke, who said, "Whenever I hear someone moaning for the Good Old Days, I think about one word: Dentistry."

As Mark was being helped down some stairs to his rack, he was ready to add 'anesthesia' to that thought.

The man helping him along was one of the two African-Americans on Omaha. He introduced himself as IC3 (SS) Cardman. He was muscular, which was good. The last thing Mark could use was some wimp to fall down the stairs with him.

"No offense," Cardman said, straining to keep them both upright, "but you are the most messed-up looking guy I've ever seen."

"That's good," Mark whispered, "I'd hate to feel this rotten and only come in second place."

Cardman laughed, but kept a firm grip on Mark's right arm and shoulder.

"You haven't seen yourself, have you?" he asked.

"Should I?"

"Wouldn't you hate to feel this rotten and not see how bad you look?"

Mark smiled weakly as they came down off the stairs onto Lower Level. First Class Berthing was on his left, the head where he'd been attacked on his right. Mark nodded toward the head.

The mess in the head was all cleaned up. He wondered which poor E-1 or E-2 had gotten that job.

"Doc says there was a huge wrench in here, all bloody, when they found you."

"Oh, yeah?"

"Yeah. He said it was three feet long and weighed about fifteen pounds."

Mark nodded. "Sounds right."

"I think they put it in a trash bag. Maybe they can get some prints off it later..."

Mark didn't recognize himself in the mirror over the sink. Someone had fished some of his underwear out of his rack for him, and now that's all he wore. His hair was a mess.

His eyes disturbed him most. There was no longer any

white area in his left eye. It was solid red, the result of a simultaneous bursting of a large amount of blood vessels.

A giant purple discoloration started above his left ear and came around to circle his left eye. The bruise extended halfway down his cheek, across the bridge of his nose and almost around his right eye.

He raised his chin. His neck looked like a horizon at sunset, crowded with red, blue and purple blotches.

There was a horizontal red line across his chest at collarbone level, surrounded by more bruising. His left shoulder was red, as if he'd been sunburned there, and it was swollen from the dislocation.

Doc had fashioned a sling using a tan athletic ankle wrap. His forearm was mummified in white bandages.

"I know you can't see it," said Cardman, from behind him, "but you've got a nasty bruise about the size of a football right below your shoulder-blades."

Mark stood there and looked at himself. A day ago, he had felt confident and darn near indestructible. He could not look away from his own eyes.

"Oh, yeah," Cardman said, jingling something around in his own front pocket. "These were found on the deck in here. Are they yours?"

Cardman extended his hand and Mark looked. It was his set of keys. Mark nodded and took them. Something about them was different. He looked more closely. The carousel horse had been broken. Its head was gone.

And suddenly Mark Reed was four years old again. It was a hot summer night and his nostrils were flared, taking in the heavy scent of fresh popcorn and cotton candy. The world around him was a kaleidoscope of colored lights and not-too-distant screams of teenage girls, the roar of a roller coaster speeding downhill.

He was walking between his mom and dad. By this time in his life, he already knew his dad was not going to stay with them. It was a matter of time. But mom overlooked that fact. In this atmosphere, he found that he could, too. They each held one of his hands, and he was able to look up and see them smiling, sometimes at him, sometimes at each other.

Midway barkers called out to them, and his dad would wave them off politely as they passed. The colors, the sounds, the costumes, the metallic, happy music…it was magical. Mom and dad were smiling together, with him. Magic.

They kept walking and then it was as if Mark laid eyes on the source of the magic of the place. It was the carousel, on its perpetual, circular journey. The magic of the whole setting was spinning out of there, he knew. His little eyes had widened as he watched the fantastic parade go by, over and over. The carousel was like the center of the galaxy, around which everything else orbited.

He watched the horses, some with riders, some without. Different colors, different poses, all shining and brilliant. Some prancing, some galloping full out. Some festooned for escorting royalty, some armored for war. Some snarling, some almost grinning.

All going. All leaving. All headed for…someplace mystical and fantastic. Someplace he knew he wanted to find. Someplace where reality was a little bit different. A place where, perchance, people who got married and had children would stay that way, in love, forever.

The ride had stopped. His mom and dad, laughing, had placed him on a giant, gleaming, green steed. He had clutched the pole with a mixture of childish joy and utter terror. His feet could not reach the stirrups. And then they were off, and the tinny, plinckety-plinckety music of celebration filled his ears.

Each time he went around, there were his parents. His father had his arm around her now and they both were laughing, waving at him. They waved and looked excited each time he came by. He never released his clutch on the pole to wave back. He never relaxed enough to smile. That might break the spell.

It had remained an important night in his life for years. It had remained idyllic. Even when his dad had built up the nerve to go, that night remained, the magic of it beyond his reach, but only by a little. He had clung to it in his memories like a lifeline.

When he got his driver's license more than a decade later, his grandmother, who had no money for any real gift, had given him a key chain. It was the carousel horse. He had never spoken of that night to anyone. He looked in her eyes. Had she known? Surely not.

Five years later, he had asked J.L. Isaacs to marry him. He hadn't known anything about love, really. He'd have admitted that. Did he really love her? He couldn't say. But, he had to marry her, because she was the only person, the only thing, in the world that ever came close to that night on the carousel. Something about the shining green of her eyes …it was like the sparkle of that green stallion so long ago.

Something about her, he had thought. The carousel's magic was about her, like an imperceptible perfume. She could take him. He could go with her to that fantastic place he had dreamed of all his life.

But now he looked down at the keys in his hand. The head was gone. The magic was broken. It had never been there at all, except in the imagination of a very small boy. The shapeless lump of pewter he held was the proof of that. It was powerless. It would not take him anywhere.

This was his reality. Mark looked up again into the mirror of the Lower Level Head, at his eyes. At a man with no career left, and very nearly no life. No marriage, either, he thought. J.L. was not magic. She was as ordinary as the lump of cheap metal in his hand.

There were no more happy, plunky tunes. The ride had come to a stop. Time to get off.

"Um…I think I'd like to go lay down, now…" Mark said to his escort, feeling some nausea.

Cardman hurried to his side and regained his steadying grip. "Yeah, yeah. No doubt. If I were you I'd stay there for about six months."

After a lot of slow progress, they made it to his rack.

He was about to crawl in, but stopped and looked at Card-man in the dark. "Um, do you think you could lift up my bedlid for me?"

"Sure, man. Whatever you need." Cardman lifted Mark's rack.

Mark bent over, painfully, and reached inside. "Be careful," Cardman whispered.

"Just don't let that thing drop on me," Mark said.

At last, he straightened up. "Okay, thanks. I think I'll be all right from here."

"You sure?"

"Yeah, thanks."

Cardman closed the rack lid. "Okay. I'll be right outside, here. My instructions were to latch the door open so I can see or hear you from there, all right?"

Mark nodded. Cardman did as he was told. Mark watched him assume his position at the door, facing out.

Climbing into his rack in his condition was nearly as painful as getting his arm set. But, he didn't cry out this time. He lay on his back and rested there, breathing hard for some time.

He was sick to his stomach. He was amazed at how weak he was, and realized, matter-of-factly, that he had never been so scared in his entire life.

He reached across his face with his right hand and turned on the reading light above him. He was holding the book he had hunted for. In silver letters on its burgundy cover, it said, simply, Holy Bible.

With his one good hand, he flipped it open and began to read.

Much later, there was a knocking outside his rack. It woke him up. Normally, that might have made him angry, but Mark didn't mind it this time. He had read the Bible and portions of Liegert's journal until his eyes stung, then he'd drifted to sleep without turning off his rack light.

"Yeah," he said, in answer to the knocking. His voice

was still raspy, but a little stronger than before. He pulled back the curtain. The first thing he saw was Cardman's back. He was still there. But now Paul Lawrence was here, too, escorted by a small, blonde kid Mark hadn't met.

"Hey!" Paul whispered. "Hope I didn't wake you up or nothing."

"No, that's all right."

"Well, I was on my way to go on watch. Just thought I'd stop and see how you were doing."

"I'll live."

"Yeah," he said. "That's good. I've just been talking to the XO. He says I have to be the Leading ELT until you get back on your feet."

Mark nodded.

Paul said, "I told him I didn't want to do it."

"What'd he say?"

"He said, 'How come?'"

"And?"

"I said, 'I'm the SNOB. Lead ELT is way too much responsibility for a guy with just eighty-one days left in this man's Navy.'"

"Eighty."

"Huh?"

"Last time we spoke, you said it was eighty days."

"Oh...oh, yeah, you're right. Added a day somewhere in there."

Mark smiled. It was hard to keep his eyes open.

Paul said, "Anyway, I was thinkin' what I should've told the XO was that Leading ELT on *Omaha* is a job that ought to qualify for hazard pay these days."

Paul laughed at his own joke. He went on for several more minutes. Mark drifted in and out, while Paul talked and laughed.

At last, Paul wished Mark well, from the whole department, and left, dragging his escort behind him.

****

The man sat on a round, metal trashcan in Engineroom Upper Level, aft of the Main Engine. His escort had to be back here to perform some off-watch maintenance that had been delayed by the time in Ultra Quiet. So he sat and drank some coffee, while the electrician walked back and forth past him, alternately carrying a Megger, screwdrivers and pliers.

The man looked at the white cup, held in one hand. Perfectly steady. No shaking.

Although his heart was beating fast in his chest, he was able to control his outward appearance. He smiled to himself.

Reed still lived, and that was the cause of his elevated heart rate. It baffled him. How long was he supposed to keep choking the guy after he passed out to make sure he was dead?

But, here he was. He had not been seen or caught, or they'd have come to get him by now. He smiled again.

His nightmares would prove false. He would make sure of that. Mark Reed was in no position to administer anyone's wrath, God's least of all.

He would prove that he was the true Chosen One.

The Almighty had not abandoned him for another.

And yet. And yet, Reed lived. He had taken his shot, but Reed lived. *Proof of Divine Protection? No. Just luck. Plain, dumb luck.*

Or was it a sign? That's always a good thought. *A sign. Of what? A sign that he was going about his business all wrong, maybe?*

Was he thinking too small? Could be. Maybe the Holy One was chastising him for lack of imagination in his ministry.

He pondered the question, intrigued. He sipped his coffee and waited for his escort to finish his work.

****

It wasn't long before *Omaha* acquired the submerged North Korean on passive sonar. The new contact was designated Whiskey One and the computer pegged her as an old Soviet Victor Class.

Omaha went back to Battlestations, with the CO at the Con again. He had not re-stowed the four torpedoes that had been loaded into their tubes during the cruiser confrontation. In fact, he ordered the two empty tubes filled.

The boat was at periscope depth, and the Sea of Japan was living up to its reputation for nastiness. *Omaha* rose and fell, leaning port and starboard with sickening irregularity. The Captain was on the phone with Squadron, via satellite link.

It was Admiral Crabb who spoke. "Jim, what in heaven's name is going on out there?"

"I don't have any details for you other than what we sent by radio. *Whiskey One* is turning circles. She's got to know that there is some pretty severe tonnage on her head right now."

"You got that right. Japan hasn't mustered that kind of naval power since Midway."

"I just hope they can tell the difference between us and them," Parnette said, half-joking.

"Well, they better! Word is that Clinton's been on the phone with the Prime Minister. Turns out Worthy Wife can detect nukes!"

"No kidding?"

"Yeah, and *Whiskey* One's got one in that bell of hers."

Parnette was silent. He had no idea what to say.

Finally Crabb said, "Jim, you're going to have more company pretty soon. North Korea's sending six ships. None very big. It'll be a long time before they get there. But, they're also scrambling fighters from three air-bases."

Parnette dropped his head and, with his free hand, rubbed his eyes. "So what's the word?"

There was a pause on the other end. "The word is stalemate, I guess. Japan wants to send *Whiskey One* to the bottom. North Korea says it will absolutely declare war if any Japanese weapons are fired at their submarine."

"Great. And what about our Commander-in-Chief."

There was a string of colorful, Texas-accented obscenity. "What do you think, Jim? He sure doesn't want to have a war going on right before the mid-term elections. But he knows enough history to understand why Japan would be extra sensitive about nuclear weapons off their coast. And he's in favor of doing whatever it takes to eliminate or reduce North Korea's nuclear arsenal."

"And so?"

Crabb was silent for a while. Then, he said, "Captain Parnette, your orders are to down *Whiskey One.*"

Chapter Twenty

Parnette pulled aside the blue curtain leading from Control into the Sonar Space. He leaned in. Gulledge was on watch for Battlestations.

"What do you think?" Parnette asked.

Gulledge pursed his lips and shook his head as if to say, "No problem." He said, "They've got sounds shorts up the whazoo, Cap'n. We can track them all day. Easy."

Parnette nodded and went back to the command dais, where the XO and the Engineer both stood. It was almost 0400, but they all looked alert.

"Still going in circles," the XO said.

Parnette nodded. Bushler said, "Can they not know about the navy on the surface?"

Parnette said, "Oh, they know. Japan's been blasting them with active sonar continuously."

"So why doesn't she leave?" asked the XO.

Parnette shrugged. "Maybe they can't for some reason."

A loud series of whistling high-pitched tones surrounded them. The bulkheads vibrated. That noise stopped, and then started again, almost immediately.

The CO hurried to the mike to speak to Sonar. "Sonar, Con. Who is that pinging us?"

"Con, Sonar. Wait one."

Parnette turned and looked at his senior officers with

an irritated frown. "Better not be Japan."

Gulledge's voice came back. "Con, Sonar. Active bursts are coming from *Whiskey One*. She's got us."

The Captain didn't acknowledge the information but turned directly to the Diving Officer. "Thirty degree down angle. Ahead full. Avoid cavitation."

The boat took on the steep angle rapidly. Commander Bushler asked, "What do you think they're going to do?"

The Captain shrugged again but did not look worried. "I don't know. But I've spent most of this day completely baffled, and I'm not going to get caught like that again."

Gulledge's voice again: "Con, Sonar. I've got a torpedo tube filling on *Whiskey One*."

Parnette said, "Chief of the Watch, flood tubes three and four."

"Passing 900 feet, Captain," announced the Diving Officer.

"Con, Sonar. *Whiskey One* is opening a tube door!"

The Captain seemed to ignore it. He said, "Diving Officer, mark your depth."

"Passing nine five zero, sir."

"Very well, come left to course, two-six-five." Parnette turned back to Fire Control and said, "Plot a solution to Whiskey One."

Seconds later: "Con, Sonar. Torpedo in the water! Torpedo in the water!"

The XO sounded the wailing Collision Alarm and announced on the 1MC, "Torpedo in the water."

Simultaneous with that announcement, the CO ordered, "Emergency Flank."

There was nervousness in the Diving Officer's voice when he said, "Passing Test Depth, sir. Approaching Crush Depth."

Still businesslike, the CO said, "Very well, Dive. Zero bubble. Chief of the Watch, trim the boat at 1700 feet."

The Engineer cleared his throat. Parnette looked over at him.

Gulledge announced, "Con, Sonar. Torpedo range 1000 yards and closing."

Bushler said, "Begging your pardon, Captain. But isn't 1700 feet significantly below our Crush Depth?"

Parnette grinned. He nodded. "And the whole world knows it. No one thinks we'll go this deep on purpose."

Seconds later, Gulledge announced, "Con, Sonar. I've got an implosion. Looks like the torpedo crushed at about 1575 feet, sir."

The XO smiled and clapped the Eng on the back. He whispered to him, "I may have spent too much time on boomers, my friend, but you oughta get some time in the Atlantic fleet, where we dealt with the Ruskies every day. You're right, Eng. As far as nuke subs go, the 688's got a shallow Crush Depth. But it's deeper than anything the Soviets ever made to be fired from a Victor."

The Engineer's face turned red as the XO announced to the crew that the torpedo was no longer a threat.

"How's that solution coming, Fire Control?" the CO asked.

"I've got it, sir," answered the enlisted man who sat with earphones in front of the computer screen. "We're green, Captain."

Parnette stood tall and straightened his shoulders. After a deep breath he said, "Fire Control, shoot tube three."

Fire Control repeated back the command and carried it out. *Omaha* shuddered as 3000 pounds-per-square-inch air was used to slam home a giant plunger assembly, forcing one Mark 48 torpedo ahead of *Omaha* at over 50 knots.

Gulledge called out the successive events of the torpedo's run, as the Captain stood with hands behind his back, staring at the deck. There was the start of the torpedo's own screw propulsion, the snap as it outran the length of its wire guidance, and finally its sonar system going active on the hull of *Whiskey One*. That lasted several seconds.

Then there came an explosion. Sonar was able to track *Whiskey One* for several hundred feet on her way down. After the Mark 48's payload detonated, there were two smaller secondary explosions. Very quickly after that, there came the implosion, as *Whiskey One* folded up like an empty beer can in the hands of an experienced viewer of televised sports.

The CO never looked up. He said to the XO softly, "You've got the Con. Squadron wants us to hang around and be able to tell the Japanese where she went down so they can send some Deep Submergence unit down after the nuke. I'll be in my stateroom. Secure the men from Battlestations."

The CO walked away alone, lacking completely the bravado that had come to be the trademark of the fast-attack sub sailor.

At the moment that *Omaha* began turning circles over the secret, de facto burial site of a North Korean submarine designated *Whiskey One* by the Americans, J.L. Reed walked past the men and women who manned the front desk of the Hale Koa Hotel in Waikiki.

Her hair was full of brand new curls, and was a shade more auburn. She walked with her shoulders back. She wore a black evening gown. Its neckline followed the advise of a syndicated columnist: low enough to show she was a woman, high enough to show she was a lady. She carried a black handbag and wore tasteful, medium-heeled shoes.

It was a long time before the men at the desk looked away from her, but a woman there noticed, with some shock, that the photocopy of the Blonde Bomber, as the T.V. had started calling her, resembled her. It resembled her a lot. Almost unable to speak, she pointed it out to them after J.L. entered an elevator going up.

They agreed to call the number written at the bottom of the picture.

****

Kim answered his car phone. It was the Hale Koa. What luck, he thought, to be right down town when the call came. He'd be there in moments.

****

J.L. got off the elevator on the second floor and immediately saw a placard standing against the wall which read, "Submarine Ball - Kamehameha Room", and had an arrow pointing left. She followed it.

She rounded a corner and approached two sets of double doors, about one hundred feet apart. A small table had been set up between them, where a gray-haired lady sat. A sign said, "Registration".

J.L. went there. The woman smiled and said, "My, but you look lovely this evening!"

"Thank you!" J.L. returned the smile.

"I need your ticket, please, and if you'll sign the guest book."

J.L. opened her handbag and produced the yellow ticket Rita had given her yesterday at lunch. The woman looked at it and said, "Okay, you've got a Subase ticket. Those seats are all on the first two rows next to the stage, dear. Just go on in and have a wonderful evening."

After she went through one of the sets of doors, the woman read the name she had signed: "Jael Leah Reed".

J.L. was overwhelmed. Her nerves were shot, but she was determined to hold her head up and smile. The giant ballroom was paneled all around in dark wood grain. The carpet was dark as well. In the middle of the room was the largest dance floor she had ever seen, made of squares of wood tile, each one with the grain running perpendicular to the one beside it.

A dozen chandeliers, five feet across, hung from the high ceiling in rows of three. Their lights were on, but dimmed way down. Large, white tables, seating up to twelve in a circle, filled the rest of the floor.

Hundreds of people were there; and, thankfully, none of them seemed to noticed her. All of the women were dressed as if they were attending a function at the Prince's Magic Castle in some fairy tale. Their dresses flowed in slow motion as they danced with their men.

The men were divided into two categories, as always: Officer and Enlisted. The enlisted wore their dress whites, a long-sleeved white version of the famous "Cracker Jack" outfit. They sported their medals and ribbons. The Chief Petty Officers and the Officers wore much different uniforms: white, formal dinner jackets, with cummerbunds. The Officers wore white gloves.

Through this crowd, J.L. slipped unnoticed. Several of the men were already very drunk, and pockets of them around the room would randomly start howling, or chanting, or singing. Each time they did, the rest of the room seemed to answer with laughter. A uniformed Navy band played subdued jazz from a low stage at the front of the room.

J.L. scanned the place for Admiral Crabb. She had never seen so many military men in one place, and she wasn't even sure she'd recognize an Admiral if she bumped into one. She figured an Admiral would be old. She studied the faces of all the old men. After several minutes, her whole idea was starting to look crazy.

"Excuse me, ma'am."

Startled, she turned to the voice. It was an older man in an officer's uniform. But she knew enough to know that Navy Captains wore eagles. That's what he had. Silver Eagles. He was smiling and she tried to smile back.

He extended a hand and said, "May I have the pleasure of a dance?"

She almost laughed. Dancing wasn't even visible on her list of things she wanted to do. But, she said, "Yes, thank you very much."

She took his hand, and he led her to the floor, where he

assumed a very formal, ballroom style embrace with her. She kept a grip on her purse, resting her hand on his shoulder as they turned graceful circles.

"Do you know Admiral Crabb?" she asked.

He was taken aback with her blunt question, but he laughed and said, "Yes. I guess I better. I work down the hall from the old coot."

"Is he here?" she asked.

"Why, yes. It's his party. He better be here."

When J.L. did not laugh, he cleared his throat and said, "He's right over there, by the stage, the bald guy, the one who looks like a fat Captain Stubing. You know, from the Love Boat?"

She still didn't laugh. She was staring at Admiral Crabb. She glanced back up at the Captain and smiled. "Thank you. I've had a wonderful time. You're a lovely dancer."

She left him stammering by himself on the dance floor. She focused on Admiral Crabb until she could see nothing else. She wove and dodged to avoid dancers on her way across the room to him.

Suddenly, there was a very sharp pain in her lower abdomen. Agent Kim was pressed up against her. She looked down. He held a wide, short-bladed knife and had pressed it against her, several inches below her navel. She looked back up at him.

"Hello again, Mrs. Reed," he said, with a toothy grin. His breath was terrible.

She started to back away, but his other arm tightened around her waist, holding her in place.

He whispered, "I wouldn't try that if I were you. I wouldn't try anything...unless you're ready for a very premature C-section."

He jammed the blade harder. She winced. He said, "Now, we are going to walk over here and find someplace quiet to talk."

He guided them away from the crowd, all too busy

dancing and enjoying their drunkenness to notice them, to one wall behind the stage. He opened a service door with one hand, pressing the blade against her with the other.

As they started going through the door, she realized that this was her last chance to scream. But, if she did, she had no doubt he would stab her as deeply as he could before he took off running. And she thought about Megan, thought about watching the nurse carry her little, dead form out of the room in a bloody cloth...she let the door close behind them.

He took them to another door. He opened it. It was dark, and he felt around on the inside wall with his hand until he found a light switch. Florescent lights flickered on haltingly. It was an empty meeting room with one long table and several chairs. He closed the door behind them. It had no lock. He lowered the knife and smiled.

"Now, I believe you have something I want," he said.

She said nothing. He said, "Give it to me. If you do not, I will order my men to attack Rita Kelly in the hospital and make sure that she dies this time."

He had no men, of course. Ironically, it was Ms. Kelly who could take credit for that, but what the girl didn't know...

He saw it. She flinched — not much, but it was there. He took a gamble. "And, we will kill the McClains as well."

Bingo! Eyes are like open books to those who know the language, as he did. *I knew it,* he thought, *I knew that old, black woman was lying. I may have to go skin her alive when this is over just for the heck of it.*

He saw tears form in her eyes as she opened her handbag. He tore it from her trembling hands and dumped it on the table. A small wallet, lipstick tube, keys...and a computer disc!

He grabbed it.

The door seemed to explode in on them. It slammed against the wall with a loud bang. J.L. screamed and dove away from Kim. Two men in suits, pistols drawn, lunged into the room yelling, "Freeze, FBI!"

Kim stood there and froze. His eyes went to the knife he held in one hand, and to the disc in the other, trying to decide whether he thought they'd be any match for the two pistols. He had his CP-1, of course, but didn't think he could empty his hands, then draw the 9mm, before the agents could pull the triggers.

He said, "I *am* FBI!"

One of the men said flatly, "Consider this your pink slip. Drop the knife."

Kim dropped it.

"Now," the man said, "hand over the disc."

Kim smiled and waved it around. "You're too late to use anything on here, anyway."

Kim raised his arm and threw the disc as hard as he could. It impacted on the wall, four feet away. It shattered. Black splinters of plastic spun in all directions.

The two men rushed him. They bent him over the table with his hands behind his back. They took his gun and cuffed him.

As they jerked him upright, a tall, overweight bald man in an officer's uniform walked in and said, "Are you Mrs. Reed?"

"Admiral Crabb?" She gulped. It was almost hard to believe he was standing there.

"Yes."

"I have something for you," she said.

She hitched up her dress around her right leg, to the middle of her thigh. Stuck in the hem of her stocking was a computer disc. It had a red label, with a brownish-red thumbprint. She handed it to him.

She said, "This is what Rita Kelly almost died for."

They pushed Kim past them both. His eyes were wide. "You're too late!" he spat, as they moved him out.

****

They hustled J.L. down with Admiral Crabb, to his car,

where a driver waited. It was a white car, with small, blue flags, each bearing two stars, at its front corners. They took off. The Admiral told the driver, "Don't spare the horses, son!"

J.L. sat between the large admiral and another, thankfully much smaller, officer. This man was reaching under the passenger's seat. "Mrs. Reed," the Admiral said, "this here is Commander Tom Gentry, with the Naval Investigative Service."

The man raised his lowered head and smiled briefly. He said, "How do you do?"

He went back to digging. He finally came up with a laptop computer, which he opened.

"Fire that thing up, Tom," the Admiral said, handing him the disc.

"Admiral, sir," J.L. said, "What...? How...?"

"How do I know you?"

She nodded.

"Your face has been on T.V. for goin' on thirty-six hours! And, if I may say so, that drawing did a poor job of capturing your charm."

She didn't know what to say.

"Listen," he said. "I was watching like everyone else when that walking piece of trash, that Kim guy, went on television and claimed that Kenneth Sung had conspired with Rita Kelly to blow up my base! Well, I *know* them, but I didn't know who in the world *he* was, or who you were."

She nodded.

"So, a few hours after your picture goes up, I get a call from an Officer Segura with the Honolulu P.D.. Drunk out of his head. He's mad because this Kim guy has put him and his partner on administrative leave and threatened them with their jobs if they said anything to anyone. Well, he got drunk enough and mad enough to call me. He's an old submariner, you know...He knew who you were."

She nodded some more. Gentry typed in commands.

"I got mad, too, and called my spook buddy, Tom,

here. And I say, Tom, this Kim guy is stuck in my craw like a chicken bone sideways, and I want to find out just who in the world he is. Tom says okay and hacks into the FBI's personnel file. Kim spent thirteen years in North Korea as an undercover agent, then came home and got put in charge of all Asian terrorist investigation. Our guess is that, somewhere during those thirteen years, he turned."

"You mean, he started working for them?" she asked.

"That's right," Gentry said. "We were able to get a hold of some FBI agents in California, and we told them what we thought and they went to work on it."

"I'm just glad you showed up here, tonight," Crabb said. "I've been telling the media every chance I had, yes, we are still having Suball, and I will be there."

"Here we go," Gentry said. "Looks like e-mail from Sung to Miss Kelly."

"Read it," Crabb said.

"**Quiet Tiger** *info was all food. Only a decoy for* **Omaha**. *N.K. has old Soviet Victor and a way to get it into Japan undetected. May have hacked Japan's Line 87. Victor carrying N.K. nuc wep. Plan to transport from Akiwa over land into government region Tokyo. Tokyo blows up, economy in chaos, Japan investors liquidate everything, including bonds financing the American Government's debt. Wall Street collapse. America grinds to a halt. No one left to defend South Korea. N.K. crosses DMZ and annexes South under current hard-line communists. IMPORTANT: Victor's nuc wep does not have any detonation or disarm codes. They figure they can't trust own sailors to do job. The nuc wep is on a timer device and WILL detonate at noon, Sunday, Tokyo time.*"

"What is that, like only half an hour from now?" asked Crabb.

"That sounds about right, sir," Gentry said, looking at his watch and counting hours on his fingers.

The Admiral said, "Driver! Give me that cell phone...and go faster!"

Chapter Twenty One

Captain Parnette sat at his stateroom desk with his feet up on his rack. He was leaned back against the door. His left elbow was on the desk and his left hand covered his eyes. His black hair was a mess. He tried to think of easier days. Being CO of a boat on a normal WestPac, a "normal" SpecOp.

He thought about days, not too long ago, when all he had to worry about was how his Engineering Department would perform on their Operational Reactor Safeguards Exam. That was the life.

Today, his personal orders had taken the lives of right around four hundred men. He knew that most of them were men pressed into military service by a government that cared not a whit for them. Men with wives and children and parents.

He tried to think about swinging in the hammock he had strung between the two mango trees in his back yard on Oahu. But it didn't work.

He thought about his actions again and again. He was sure he had followed rules of engagement and protocol. He would not be reprimanded. He would be commended. He would get a medal and a promotion, ahead of schedule, to full Captain.

He knew that he could, and would, keep the medal in a shoe box in his closet. But what about the birds? Would it ever feel good to wear them?

He rubbed his eyes. He needed to sleep. Things would be clearer after some shut-eye.

"Cap'n, Sir. This is the Engineer. A priority one message has arrived," squawked the speaker next to his head. "I think you'll want to see this ASAP, Sir."

He punched the white button. "I'll be right there."

James Parnette stood up and blinked to clear his eyes. He walked out as Commanding Officer of the *USS Omaha*, ready for all contingencies.

Bushler was at the door waiting for him. He handed him the message.

It took Parnette twenty seconds to read it. He threw it back at the Eng and passed him on his way into Control.

"Captain on the Bridge!" the Diving Officer announced.

"I've got the Con," Parnette said. "Diving Officer, Ahead Flank, Cavitate. Make your depth seven hundred feet. Come left to course one-nine-five."

****

The Captain's voice came over the 1MC. "Gentlemen, may I have your attention."

It wasn't a question, but a command.

"I want to echo and emphasize the words of the XO earlier. I have never been more proud of the performance of any group of sailors I have worked with. This crew is the finest I have known. You have performed under pressure as well as any have before you and have emerged as survivors and winners. I am not merely proud, but count myself privileged to work with men of such high caliber and professionalism.

"That is why I feel I must let you know what our situation is at this moment. The North Korean submarine that we downed was carrying a nuclear warhead, designed to detonate at a pre-set time. That predetermined time is twenty-two minutes from now, which is why we are at Ahead Flank.

"I must be honest with you. On the one hand, we know that the Victor imploded and was crushed. It is possible that the warhead has been destroyed.

"However, it may be intact. We do not know how large it is. Our best guess is that it is very small. But, that's like saying you have a small brain tumor. It's still not good.

"I have authorized the Engineer to remove reactor safeguards and get us all the speed we can have. We should easily be outside any conceivable blast range when the clock reaches zero. The Doc will also be making rounds to all stations, distributing neutron dosimeters to the crew."

Mark could hardly digest what he was hearing. The CO paused and then said, "My best guess is that we will come out of this all right. However, if any of you men are praying people, this might not be a bad time...That is all."

Mark found himself praying. It seemed natural.

****

The Control space was silent. No one spoke, or even looked at each other any more than they had to. The Quartermaster's table became a popular place, as people happened to stroll by and take a glance at what sort of distances they were opening.

"Captain!" the Chief of the Watch said, "Maneuvering reports that EM3 Reynolds has been found unconscious in Engineroom Middle Level!"

Parnette turned his head to the Chief. "Who was he escorting?"

The Chief shook his head. "They don't know, Sir. The Engineer is in Maneuvering and has ordered a head-count."

The CO turned back around. He lowered his head and closed his eyes. He ordered word passed to all stations to be on the lookout for an unescorted individual.

****

Mark re-read the passage in Liegert's journal. He read it again. His mouth went dry. He held his breath and struggled out of his rack. He was getting better at it. Using the restroom like a normal human had demanded that much.

Everything ached as he began putting on a poopie-suit for the first time since his first submarine shower. Cardman turned and asked him, "Everything okay?"

Mark nodded, and gritted his teeth against the pain that coursed through his body.

While Mark continued to dress, Cardman grew increasingly agitated, mumbling something about a nuclear bomb, over and over. Sweat was visible all over his skin. He eventually broke down and said, "Hey, Reed. You gonna be okay? Cuz I think I need to go to the head."

Mark grinned and nodded at him. Cardman disappeared. Mark headed up the ladder to Crew's Mess. Two men sat at the tables there. One of them said, "Hey, what are you doing up?"

Mark ignored them. The other said, "Yeah. And where's your escort, Reed! You ought to know you need an escort."

Mark looked at them and said, "My escort's in the head, puking his guts out, probably. I didn't feel like joining him. I just need to go talk to someone back aft."

"Well, you still ought to have an escort..."

Mark smiled. "Yeah. You got me. I'm the bad guy. Beat myself to a pulp to throw everyone off my scent."

He continued on, through the watertight door to the Engineroom. He carried a blue, spiral notebook.

Though each step seemed to jostle his left eye, and send spikes of pain shooting from his arm and ribs, Mark made it all the way aft. Using only his right arm, he climbed the starboard ladder down to Shaft Alley. The hum of all four heavy air conditioning units running to capacity drowned out all other sound.

The Main Shaft provides a partial separation through the space, dividing port from starboard. Add in the four large A/C units and big lockers stacked like building blocks in every possible place, and Mark knew that a man could escape detection in here for a long time, even with pairs of men coming through to "search", as they surely had. He figured even a big man could hide in here, so he didn't bother looking.

He went to the Steering and Diving Hydraulic plant, as far aft as one could go. And he yelled, "Jason!" It hurt his throat badly.

No one answered. He yelled again, "MM2 Lorde! I know you're in here! Don't make me call again!"

Jason Lorde lowered himself to the deck from on top of some lockers. He turned and faced Mark. He held one arm behind his back. His eyes were bloodshot and he was drenched in his own sweat.

"No one knows," he growled.

Mark held up the notebook in his right hand. "You'd be right except for me...and God, I suppose."

Jason brought his arm forward. His meaty fist was wrapped around a foot-long screwdriver.

Mark said, "So, what's the deal? Gonna finish the job this time, Jason?"

Lorde nodded, smiling. "Oh, yes. But not with this."

"What then? Marlin line and a light fixture?"

Jason raised his empty left hand and pointed at him. "You...you're a mocker. That's what you are."

"Like Liegert?"

Jason grinned and shook his head. "No, no. Liegert's crime was worse. His was the ultimate sin...he was a blasphemer."

Mark nodded, opening the notebook to the place where his thumb was inserted, and then read, "Jason said something that unnerved me today. Did I think that people hear from God anymore. I said, sure. He speaks through his Word, through the created world around us, through his Spirit. The first thing we see God doing is speaking. Jason told me that he had heard God's voice. I said, really? What did he say?"

Mark paused and looked at Jason. The big mechanic's eyes were wide, and he chewed on his lower lip. Mark went on. "He said God told him that he was his only begotten Son. I laughed. Jason didn't. He said, God has given all judgment into my hand and has made Shaft Alley my judgment seat. I laughed again. I didn't know what else to do. Why Shaft Alley? He said that Shaft Alley is the place where power becomes real. We can't see the fissions taking place in the reactor vessel, but you can reach out and touch the Shaft as it spins."

Jason took a step forward, but Mark didn't notice, as he kept reading. "I figure he had to be kidding me. Some people stop cussing around Christians; other people cuss worse, just to get a reaction from them. That's what this had to be. Trying to get me to freak out."

Jason yelled in rage and rushed forward. It happened too fast for Mark to stop him, especially in his condition. Jason tackled him and they went down, Mark on the bottom. He landed on his left side. The pain flared so intensely that his consciousness flickered like lights during a thunderstorm, threatening to go out for good.

Jason grabbed the collar of his poopie-suit and lifted him up. Mark grimaced at the pain. Jason propped him against a hydraulic oil tank. He rammed the screwdriver up into the flesh under Mark's jaw, forcing his head back.

Lorde giggled and said, "Now. This is time I have appointed. Liegert was judged for his doubting, and now I will judge the rest of the idiots on this boat!"

Jason used his other hand to open the "book" of laminated procedures that hung beside Mark's head. He took out one page. He spun Mark around and placed his massive left arm around his neck from behind. Squeezing. Mark could hardly breathe.

Soon, Jason had turned all the orange valve handles that he had simulated turning during the last drill set. Mark noted that he had *not* forgotten the one beneath the deck this time. *The value of training*, he thought crazily.

Control no longer *had* control of the ship, although they would not recognize that fact until they tried to change course or depth.

Desperate to stall the man, Mark said, "You're the one who cut the bag on the MINSY rig."

Jason spun him back around and replaced the screwdriver in his throat. "A warning you disregarded. When I judged Liegert, I cursed him, even his memory. You disobeyed my judgment. You came to replace him. You slept where he slept, you dared to question me about him. You have been judged."

Without really thinking about it, Mark spoke. "You're right. I'm guilty. I deserve punishment."

Jason nodded deeply.

"But, the *true* God took my death sentence on himself at the cross—"

Jason screamed, a wild, insane animal noise, and punched Mark in the face. He fell to the floor in a heap.

Almost slipping into unconsciousness, Mark heard the noise of steel-toed shoes coming down the metal ladder from Upper Level. Then, Jason's hands were on him again, rolling him onto his back.

Jason placed his foot across Mark's neck. Immediately, Mark started coughing and gagging, struggling to move the man, but Jason was too large. Senior Chief Markiss came down, cussing.

"Stop there, Markiss! Don't move or I crush this one!"

"What the--?" Markiss said.

Jason reached into the overhead and grabbed the shiny metal handle there. He yelled, "The hour of judgment has come!"

He jammed the handle all the way forward. The nose of the ship lurched down immediately. Markiss fell toward the front of the ship, bouncing roughly off lockers as he went. Mark started to slide, but reached out with his left arm and hooked it over a pipe near the deck. His shoulder screamed at him.

The 1MC blared, "Jam Dive! Loss of planes in Control! Answer back emergency!"

The Main Shaft started to slow down. Jason was having a hard time keeping himself upright. "In three days, I will rise again in glory! You idiots are too late!"

The hull popped and creaked around them. The 1MC said, "Passing Crush Depth! Expedite Back Emergency!"

Jason roared in laughter.

A deck plate flew open next to Mark due to the angle. He saw the orange handle of a hydraulic valve. He glanced up. Jason was shouting into the overhead.

Mark reached over with his right hand and turned the valve. Three turns, four, five. *Lord God! Help me!* The valve hit against its closed seat.

The nose of the boat began to rise.

Jason looked down. His eyes went big and round when he realized what had happened. "Planes control has been restored!" someone yelled over the 1MC.

"Nooo!!" Jason bellowed and dove for the valve. Mark flung himself on top of it, wrenching his shoulder back out of socket in the process.

Jason stomped on him, over and over and over; but he held on.

Senior Chief Markiss, himself a large man, ran up and tackled Jason. They both flew back into the hydraulic pumps and equipment. Seconds later, more men rushed into the space. One by one they hurdled Mark on the deck and went to aid the Senior Chief.

Jason kept shouting, "No! No!"

Chapter Twenty Two

Paul Lawrence and Senior Chief Markiss carried Mark back to his rack. The Senior Chief had a big gash above his left eye but was clearly proud of it.

Mark, on the other hand, was bad off. His broken arm was killing him and he was bleeding from somewhere inside his mouth. He wondered if his jaw was broken.

His two helpers eased him into his rack.

"We should probably strap him in, huh, Senior?" Lawrence asked, turning to Markiss.

The Senior Chief nodded. They dug out the little-used straps the crew called "seatbelts" and used them to block the open side of Mark's rack, to keep him from rolling out.

Paul looked down at Mark and asked, "You gonna be all right, there, boss?"

Mark tried to grin and nodded. The two men left after telling him to "hang on".

****

Captain Parnette and the XO stood in the former's stateroom. Each one glanced at his wristwatch at intervals of about thirty seconds.

"It's time to get ready," the CO said, finally.

Adam Shelby nodded, his face set and determined. But before they walked out, the XO said, almost meekly, "Jim, if it means anything to you...I think it's obvious you did the right thing. If you had made some other decision, we wouldn't be running from a nuke right now, but only because it would be ticking down someplace in the middle of Tokyo."

Parnette looked at the deck for a few seconds then nodded. "Yeah. Yeah, I think so. Still, my orders within the last several hours sent a few hundred men to their graves. It's hard to realize that and still say what I did was right. I don't know if it was right, so much as it was my only option."

Shelby clasped him on the shoulder and nodded.

Parnette said, "Pray when you get your own boat that you never have to do that sort of 'right thing'."

The two men nodded gravely and straightened their shoulders. Both knew that it was going to be important, for a few minutes anyway, to show the crew that the command was unified and confident, fearless even. They took large strides into Control.

"Go ahead, XO," Parnette said, folding his arms across his chest and positioning himself between the periscope wells, facing forward.

Shelby looked at the current Officer of the Deck and said, quietly, "I have the con."

"Aye, sir," came the response. The relieved OOD announced, "The XO has the con."

Shelby spoke confidently and quickly. "Ahead one-third. Diving Officer, make your depth one-zero-zero feet and bring us around one hundred and eighty degrees."

The Control crew was silent, except for the regular communications protocols, as they obviously sought to be quick about obeying their orders.

The XO grabbed the 1MC mike and said, "Rig ship for reduced electrical power."

Going to 100 feet put as much water as possible between them and the bomb on the ocean floor, while hopefully not going so shallow as to be destroyed by the immense waves the explosion would create. Turning the boat around pointed *Omaha's* nose at the blast, rather than allow the shaft seals at the aft end to take the brunt of whatever shockwave. The seals were especially vulnerable and would most likely blow out and cause unstoppable flooding. Rigging for reduced electrical power prepared the ship for the next order.

When the Diving Officer reported the ordered actions taken, the XO said, "Chief of the Watch, to Maneuvering, scram the reactor."

Better to drop the control rods now, as a monitored evolution, than to wait for it to happen during the blast.

Seaman Elgin now manned the sound-powered phones in Control. The ship was at Battlestations, its most ready condition from which to combat not only other vessels, but any other sort of internal casualties, like fire and flooding. The XO turned to Elgin and said, "Phonetalker, perform one last phone check. Make sure everyone's on line."

The XO was thinking especially of the extra watch-standers he had stationed at all the manual flood-control valves and bilge-pumping stations. As these preparations were being completed, the XO joined the CO at the Quarter-master's table and checked the map.

The XO looked at his captain. His eyes said, "Well, whaddaya think?"

The CO shrugged his shoulders. The episode with Petty Officer Lorde and the jam dive had robbed them of some precious minutes, and miles.

****

"I've heard a lot about foxhole conversions, God," Mark Reed whispered in the darkness of berthing. Then he almost laughed and said, "The thing is, I think I would be doing this even if I was healthy, and there was no nuclear weapon...I hope I would, anyway,

"You know how new I am to praying. I'm probably not doing it right. But I remember Grandma and how she prayed; like she was just talking on the phone to her best friend....

"All I know is that I have lived my life convinced that only weaklings and fools believe in You. And now...and now it's like You've shown me that I fit that description!"

He did actually laugh at that one, and felt crazy for it, noticing that there were tears on his cheeks.

"I guess...I guess, bottom line, I know that I have been wrong. I know that Liegert was right. I know that what I've read so far in the Bible is right. I know that I need You to forgive me. I think, I know that's why You sent Jesus, and that's why He did what He did and suffered what He suffered.

"I feel like I'm content to hope for Your mercy concerning whatever judgment about me You want to make. But I do pray that whatever happens, You would find some way to let J.L. know that I love her, and that I love the baby, and that I've come to know You, like she has. Thank you, Lord. Amen."

Mark Reed shut his eyes in the darkness and waited.

****

For several minutes, *Omaha* hovered at one hundred feet, moving backward as fast as possible, first on residual steam after the reactor shutdown, then on the Emergency Propulsion Motor, powered by the battery.

The Captain had made up his mind not to keep checking his watch. So he stood there, holding on to the polished railing around the periscope dais.

The XO, on the other hand, kept checking his watch. The appointed time came. Then passed. He watched the digital seconds keep ticking up, and as they did, his breathing was less strained.

Control went completely dark and the boat lurched with the sudden stop of the EPM. The glowing lights which normally illuminated all the gauge faces in Control were gone, as were the ever-present images of the sonar and fire control computer screens.

Elgin yelled something about Maneuvering and a loss of all electrical power. But it was the CO's voice that Shelby heard.

"Electromagnetic Pulse! Here we go!"

The watchstanders in Control managed to turn on several yellow, box-shaped Battle Lanterns. Shelby yelled, "Phonetalker, to all stations: Brace for impact!" Then, to the Chief of the Watch, "Get your hands on those chicken-switches, Chief!"

The Chief stood and got a firm grip on a silver pipe positioned just inches from the emergency main ballast tank blow valves.

There was a low sound that built quickly, beginning like the purr of a cat and ending like one sustained peel of thunder, and it surrounded them, coming from all directions at once. The deck shifted, as it had under the assault of the North Korean depth charges, except that it continued.

Omaha shook, and the violence of her convulsions was joined suddenly by a deafening hiss in Control. Men screamed and tried to move away from the fire control station as a dark cloud descended from the overhead. Shelby smelled oil instantly and yelled, wondering how he'd ever be heard, "Hydraulic leak! Kresge, isolate that line!"

He heard no reply, but the hissing began to subside, slowly. The shaking and rumbling went on, and it became apparent that they were not exactly facing the blast head-on, as they had hoped. *Omaha* was listing to port, and it was getting worse.

Men started to fall across Control in the darkness to the port bulkhead when Elgin screamed, "Flooding in the Engineroom...fire in the Torpedo Room--now flooding in AMR...Oh, God!"

There was nothing to be said, no order to be given, yet. Either the crew was trained enough, or...not. Shelby held his breath. What was normally the horizontal line of the deck was now, to his estimation, close to forty-five degrees, and heading toward sixty more rapidly than he ever would have liked. If it got to vertical, so that *Omaha* was really on her side, it would be all over. Submarines aren't like bathtub toys that automatically right themselves. So he gripped the railing that he was holding and waited, watching in the scarce light and the chorus of screams and crashing noises that were all around.

Lord God, have mercy! he thought.

****

Jason Lorde was tied up, his hands behind his back, with several thick, plastic tie-wraps. They made good cuffs. The more one struggled, the tighter they became, until the plastic edges began to bite into flesh. They encouraged complacency.

After he had been subdued in Shaft Alley, he was dragged forward, cussing and spitting, and at the command of Captain Parnette, was locked in the Reefer, the boat's storage area for frozen food stuffs.

He had started laughing when the boat took on its heavy list in the blast. Then, stuff started falling out of the shelves: whole chickens, hams, roasts, boxes, and boxes of frozen vegetables.

By the time *Omaha* finally eased off her list, then went through a slightly smaller replay of the entire ordeal when the secondary shockwave hit, Lorde had been pummeled unconscious.

Someone did eventually think to check on him when it was all over, and it was apparent that *Omaha* was going to survive, however badly damaged. Lorde had to be excavated from under a respectable mountain of groceries, where he had come close to freezing to death.

****

Omaha floated motionless on the surface for some time. The electricians were able, after several attempts, to get the main battery breaker to close, and so they regained power. All of her control system computers had supposedly been hardened against the affects of an Electromagnetic Pulse, or EMP.

Supposedly. Only the radio worked. That turned out to be enough.

Ships from the Japanese Civil Defense Ministry arrived in a few hours. The worst of *Omaha's* injuries were helo'd off. Mark Reed was one of them. He was conscious, and silently thanking his Lord for the life he still lived.

Epilog

The transport plane from Guam landed on Oahu in the relative cool of mid-morning, and the injured were transported to Trippler Army Medical Center, a World War II era salmon-colored complex that looked like some sort of pagan temple village, set high on a hill, surrounded by jungle green. Admiral Crabb made arrangements for J.L. Reed to be picked up and brought to meet them.

She made her way through the huge site, a spotless place bustling with men and women in green Army and white Navy uniforms. She found Room 118 as she had been instructed. Inside were two beds, one empty. Mark lay in the other, although it took a few seconds for her to recognize him. Admiral Crabb stood at his bedside, as did a stocky man with silver oak leaves on his collar. The man's black nametag said simply, USS OMAHA (SSN-692). Below that, written in much smaller letters, "Commander Parnette".

The Admiral smiled very big. Everything he did was very big, she'd learned. More so, it seemed, since learning that J.L. was a fellow Texan. "Mrs. Reed," he said, with a welcoming flourish, "I've just been debriefing your wounded man here on your escapade as an impromptu NIS agent."

J.L. smiled and walked to the other side of Mark's bed. He looked so tired. Or maybe that was just the redness and swelling around both eyes. She'd been told Mark was injured, but given no details. He was the last scene of a Rocky movie.

"Hi," he said. His voice was just a whisper, scratchy.

"What happened to you?"

Mark's mouth began to open and the man she had not met cleared his throat. She looked up and the man was extending a hand to her. She shook it.

"Ma'am, my name is James Parnette. I'm your husband's commanding officer on the *Omaha*."

She nodded and smiled at him.

Parnette said, "There was a very deranged individual onboard my boat when your husband arrived, only no one knew about it. This man murdered the man your husband came to replace. He tried to kill your husband as well."

J.L. felt her jaw drop as she looked from Parnette to Mark, back to Parnette, back to Mark.

"That's not all," Parnette said. "This man attempted to commit suicide by destroying the whole boat. It was Petty Officer Reed here who stopped him, even though he was badly injured at the time."

J.L.'s eyes filled with tears, and they overflowed. It was too much to digest. Mark reached up with his right arm and grabbed her hand. Gently squeezed it. It felt large to her, and strong, much more powerful than he looked at the moment.

Admiral Crabb nudged Parnette, and they both began walking to the door. Parnette said, "Ma'am, you can be very proud of your husband. I am, and I'm darn glad he's working for me."

She nodded and tried to smile at him.

"Good day, Mr. and Mrs. Reed," the Admiral said. Then, to Mark, "Heal up fast, son."

"Yessir," Mark mumbled.

The door closed behind the two officers.

The two Reeds looked at each other. She put her head gently on his chest and wept.

"Y'know?" Mark said, finally, "I've been doing some reading, pretty interesting stuff."

"Really? What?"

Mark told her about reading the Gospel of John. How he'd been shocked by how blatantly the Bible just came right out and said that Jesus Christ is God. He'd thought all along that was just the invention of His more fanatical followers. But he saw Jesus claiming deity for Himself. More than that, he saw Jesus challenging him — him, Mark Reed, personally. The challenge was to have the courage to trust Jesus.

And he told her about how he had decided to accept that challenge.

****

Major Rita Kelly required two more surgeries after the one that saved her life. Finally, her left lung and kidney were removed. One slug had nicked a bone in her lower spine. The prognosis was that she would not have the use of her legs again.

She was commended and awarded by both the Marine Corps and the Navy.

One of the surgeons assisting in her initial operation was a man named Jonathan Cornelius Ray. His oft-repeated story was that there was something about holding Rita's heart in his hands that made him fall in love with her right then and there. Most people laughed and acted disgusted, but his feelings for her were obvious.

As soon as she could speak, Rita was telling everyone that she would walk again. But it was more than merely "telling". She was instructing. However much work it took, she would do it, and God would bless her efforts.

****

MM2(SS) Jason Lorde was committed to a maximum security psychiatric ward on Oahu and Court Martialed in absentia for the first degree murder of MM1(SS) Liegert, the attempted murder of MM1(SW) Reed, and the attempted destruction of USS Omaha (SSN-692).

****

Former FBI Agent Kim was convicted in Federal Court in California of murder in the death of Kenneth Sung, conspiracy to commit murder in regards to Major Rita Kelly, espionage and conspiracy to commit espionage against the United States of America, and terrorism against the Federal Government. He began serving three consecutive life sentences at the Federal Penitentiary at Leavenworth before J.L. Reed entered her second trimester.

****

A high-ranking official named Lee underwent the Communist version of a trial in the concrete basement of a government building somewhere in North Korea. In less than five minutes he was found guilty, after no testimony or evidence whatsoever, of botching an operation code-named Blind Widow. He was sentenced to one large-caliber bullet in the base of the skull, and so it went. He fell on his face, what remained of it, on the cold floor beneath the harsh light of a single white bulb, which somehow failed to really illuminate the room.

The fallout from the nuclear explosion on Japan's coast was not nearly so deadly as the economic chokehold a fully enraged Japan and the United States enforced on North Korea, and threatened upon every country that might consider aiding her at all.

At China's insistence, North Korea opened itself up to large teams of U.N. inspectors looking for evidence of production or storage of nuclear materials.

****

After the normal passage of time, J.L. Reed gave birth to a son. Granted, that sort of thing happens every day all over the world. But this was a miracle. None of the things that had conspired inside her body to result in her previous miscarriage harmed this pregnancy at all. The baby emerged wrinkled and red, covered with some stuff that Mark could only speculate about.

The Navy allowed J.L. two "coaches" in the delivery room with her. Mark was one and Rita was the other. (By then, Rita had slight movement in all her lower joints and was just as determined as ever to get out of that chair someday soon.)

The nurse placed the boy in a towel on J.L.'s still-heaving chest. For a moment, she wondered what the boy meant. Then she knew that God had given her a son. Not only that, but He had given her His Son as well. And both gifts meant the same thing. She was loved.

And, maybe, Megan's untimely death meant exactly the same thing, in a way she would spend her lifetime trying to understand.

****

There were a lot of people in church many Sundays later at King Of The Islands. Mark had been reading enough in the Bible to know that Christian baptism was the next step he should take. As was the predominantly black church's home-grown custom, there came a point when Brother Robbie asked Mark to step up to the podium and say just a few words.

He went up and looked out over the sea of smiling, friendly faces. The same faces had wept and clapped and shouted months ago when Brother Robbie related the whole story of Mark and J.L. a few weeks back. Mark's voice was embarrassingly weak, and he tried several times to clear his throat, but there was a lump there that was not going away.

"I,...I never got to really know my own dad, my father. All I remember is this image of a really big, emotionless man. I think--I think I have struggled my whole life trying to work through the feeling that he rejected me. I was going to show him I didn't need him. That functioned as a major motivation for the rest of my life. Until now, I think."

Mark looked behind him, where J.L. stood, holding his son.

"What is tough to...admit...is...is that," he stammered, and had to stop for several seconds. "It's tough to admit that I was becoming just like him."

He felt his own eyes begin to tear. He saw that several old ladies in the crowd were already dabbing at their eyes with tissues.

"When God finally got a hold of me, I was...I was ready...to leave my wife. I was ready to let her have the baby on her own and just...just deal with it all. I figured, she loves Jesus so much, let him help her."

He looked back at J.L. again. Tears had gone down both cheeks, but she was still smiling. She nodded to him.

He said, "But then I knew that was wrong. I asked the Lord to make me the man he wants me to be."

He felt some strength return. He stood a little straighter and went on.

"My son is going to know his father."

The crying women were nodding now. From somewhere out there, some people said, "Amen!"

"And not only that. He will know his Father in heaven."

Many more amens came from the congregation.

"I'm saying that I want to be a godly parent."

The amens got a little stronger. He looked back at his wife again, who was laughing now at how the crowd was responding to him. He smiled at her and said, without turning away,

"And I'm saying that I want to fulfill the vows I made to my wife. I want to love, honor and cherish her."

By now, people were clapping and saying, "Thank you, Jesus!" and, "Come on, brother!"

Mark walked over to J.L. and took his son into his arms. In the midst of the roar of rejoicing, J.L. said, "You mean that, Mark Reed?"

And he said, "I do."

****

"Dad, what's this?"

Mark Reed was pushing forty years old, and his sandy blonde hair was highlighted throughout with silver streaks. He straightened from the mess of extension cords he'd been trying to untangle for the last fifteen minutes. He turned and looked back at his oldest boy, now fifteen. The guy was a darn fine looking young man, if Mark had to say so himself. He was staring at his dad, and holding a cardboard box in his arms.

Mark said, across the garage to him, "What's it say?"

The young man looked at the box and said, "Grandma Wilson's."

Mark had to step high over the junk in the garage on his way there. It was a box of personal items that had belonged to his grandmother. For years, it was nothing more than a box that took up space, and they'd have probably thrown it out except that it had been hers.

"That'd be your great-grandmother," Mark said, taking the box from his son.

"What's in it?"

"Y'know? Your mom boxed this up right after we got married, and no one's looked in it since. I'll be darned if I remember."

They found a clear space on the garage floor and Mark peeled off the packing tape. It was brittle by now and came off easily. Mark was expecting a musty smell, but instead, amazingly, it was the smell of Grandma, soft and a little powdery. They picked out the little items. Most of them were trinkets he hadn't thought about for decades, but as he held them, he remembered seeing them all as a child, where they had sat on bookshelves and dressers in Grandma's old house. In spite of himself, he felt his eyes begin to fill with tears.

One of the last things they picked out was a black, leather Bible, and it too made a sudden reappearance in Mark's memory. His grandmother always had it in her hands.

Now, it felt ancient in his. The pages were dog-eared and some were about to fall out.

As he gently flipped through it, looking through tears at all the highlighted passages and words circled and underlined in different inks, he came across a thicker piece of paper folded in half. He opened it, and it took some time for him to figure out what he was reading. It was a certificate, complete with gold filigree around the border. In large, archaic font, the title read, "Certificate of Baptism". And it was his name that had been filled in the blank space. He checked the date. He had been fifteen months old. How Grandma had talked his mom and dad into baptizing him at her church, he could only wonder.

He let out a short, sort of amazed laugh and turned the page over. There in his grandmother's handwriting was a message addressed to him, dated on the same day.

"Mark,

"How old will you be when you read this? I don't know. I can't know the sorts of things that have happened to you up until now. But I want you to know today that you are loved very much. I want you to know that this day I have claimed the promise of Exodus 20:5. The Lord will bless the generations of the righteous. I want you to be able all your life to look back on this event and see Jesus Christ saying to you what he said to Jeremiah.

" 'Before I formed thee in the belly I knew thee; and before thou camest forth out of the womb I sanctified thee'."

He sat there on the garage floor for a long time, and spent the rest of the day on the verge of weeping. He lived out his life as a man of faith, thankful for the godly heritage he had, and for the grace of his Lord, Who had held Mark Reed in the palm of His hand from the beginning.

THE END

DEO VOLENTE

PUBLISHING

P.O. BOX 4847
LOS ALAMOS, NM   87544

Visit our Website at:
www.deovolente.net

What others have said about *Prowl*.

"Whether it's to the edge of tears and laughter or to the edge of one's seat, Gordan Runyan brings the reader to the edge of something extraordinary. A master of delightful, tounge-in-cheek absurdities, Runyan also communicates a very real and profound search for meaning, providing a banquet for both mind and heart. In the vein of George MacDonald, this writer draws one in and stays with the reader long after the book is put down."

Laurie Petresin
Author of Government 101

"Danger...intrigue...suspense...romance--played out in the context of God's triumphal grace and enduring love. Gordan Runyan's new novel, Prowl, is a spiritual thriller you won't want to put down. Buy more than one copy and give them to your friends. They'll be glad you did!"

Carol Ruvolo,
Author of Faith at Work

"PROWL pulled me right in. Very realistic. The characters are genuine people, blue & gold all the way! I feel like I worked along side of these men for years. Runyan gives us a mystery, but also a whole other deeper dimension that encircles us as the story progresses, he knows his business:

PROWL is great!"

Commander E. Peter Denlea, USN Retired